Forever Willow Walk

Book Three in the Kahill Family Saga

by

S. K. Hamilton

Forever Willow Walk is wholly and completely a work of fiction.
No similarity to individuals living or dead is intended.
Any such resemblance that may occur is coincidental.

Cover Art by Sylvia K. Hamilton

Printed in the United States of America

ISBN: 978-0-9769989-6-9

Pen & Sword Publishers Ltd.
www.penandswordpublishing.com

Acknowledgements

Linda Lane of Pen and Swords Publishers, Ltd.

You are truly a credit to your profession. I thank you for all the suggestions, advice, and help you have given me. Your editing is first class, and I am truly blessed to have found you. Thank you, my friend, editor, and publisher.

Lin Bayhi

I want to thank you for all the brainstorming we did and for the suggestions you gave me. This was a great help throughout the book, and I appreciate the time and effort you put into it. Thank you, Lin. You are a sweetheart.

Douglas Glassford

Doogie, you've been wonderful to help me with ideas, suggestions, and corrections. I want to thank you for working with me on the family trees and the historical parts of this novel. Thank you, dear Doogie, my good buddy. You are a *Wiz*.

Dedication

To my husband, Ralph G. Hamilton

You kept me going when the going got rough. You kept me focused during the time it took to write this book. You've been steadfast, supportive, encouraging, and even sympathetic on the days nothing went right. You've been firm when I needed it and understanding always. You are forever my ideal reader. And once more, you are the man I adore.

I'll Remember Always

Willow Walk and country meadows
Morning sun and evening shadows
Quiet nights and lazy days
Our secret paths and hideaways

What is...is only now, you see
What was...will always be.

I'll remember always.

S. K. Hamilton

Chapter One

The cemetery was still now. Not quiet...just still.

The man leaned against the rough trunk of an ancient oak tree, apart from the mourners, yet close enough to see and hear them. His gaze locked on the dark-haired woman next to the grave site. *It's been a long time, Katarina. Too long.* He wiped at his eyes with the back of his hand.

The mammoth oak spread its roots under his feet and stretched its nearly-naked limbs over the meadow as though laying claim to all lying within the reach of its broad shadow. In the late afternoon sun, that shadow embraced those who stood around the fresh grave.

He sighed and dropped his head into his hands. His eyes blurred. He wept.

Perilous black storm clouds drifted low overhead. The wind wound its way through the branches of the oak, whispering like the rustling of silk, until his entire mind filled with doubt, fear, and sadness. He turned the collar of his coat up around his neck and listened. If he hadn't known better, he would've thought the gruff echo in his mind was the voice of his longtime comrade, Jedediah Joseph Kahill.

His tears gave way to a silent chuckle. Ole Jed would still be giving him orders if he could, and the man knew exactly what he'd say in the commanding tone that only Jed could muster.

"Listen close now. It's high time you disclosed the family secret before it's too late. And don't tell me you can't. With the exception of stayin' out of trouble, Cannon Fox, you can do just about anything. Now you be takin' good care of Maggie—she's a dear, that one. You know, it's been a coon's age since we've seen each other. This is not exactly the way I wanted our last meetin' to be."

For a moment the wind died down, and the voice disappeared. Another gust brought it back. "Have a brandy for me, you ole coot. I know you'll be soaking it up anyway, so you might as well tie one on for me. Well, I best be goin'. So long, my friend. And don't you dare do anything I wouldn't do, you hear me now?"

Cannon nodded without even thinking about it. The persistent tapping of the branches against one another, so like the sound of his old comrade's cane, faded. The wind weakened, and the voice was gone.

He dabbed salty tears from his eyes and tightened his scarf around his neck. Winter would be here much too soon.

Dawson Kahill fastened his arm a little tighter around Kat. The finality of this goodbye had sucked the color out of everything, leaving in its place lifeless gray land and sky. He focused on his wife and son standing with him. Katarina wept in silence. Little Joey stiffened. Huge tears welled in his eyes. Dawson shared the only words of comfort he could think of. "Try not to cry, son, unless you have to. Then go ahead—it's alright."

Joey looked up at him, a tiny hint of a smile on his lips. "That's what Granddaddy used to tell me."

"That's what he told me, too, Joey, when I was a little boy just like you."

A dark corner of the sky cracked open, torn by a jagged bolt of lightning. Thunder roared in the distance, then grew closer. Large drops of rain began to fall. In the valley below the cemetery, gray smoke plumed upward from chimneys. Soon snow would shroud the land in a clean white cover. Granddad would want it that way. *A fresh start for the new season*, that's what he would say.

Days of his childhood skipped through Dawson's mind. Granddad pulling him around Willow Walk on his first sled while he shouted with glee. The two of them rushing into the kitchen for steaming cups of hot chocolate with plenty of marshmallows when they were cold and wet, and Grandma Emma chasing them back onto the porch to take off their wet coats and boots because she'd just mopped and waxed her floor. The time when he—

"Amen." The minister raised his eyes to the family and reached for the picture that sat atop the closed casket. "Joey, your grandfather would want you to have this. He loved you very much, you know."

Joey looked up at his mother. She nodded. He gazed at the photo for a long moment before he wrapped both arms around it, held it to his heart, and bowed his head. *"I love you, too, Granddaddy."*

Kat nudged him. "We need to go soon. We're going to get wet."

The memories faded. He stood straight and tall and fine looking despite his sorrow as he reached out to shake the hands of the many neighbors and town folk who had gathered to pay last respects to their old friend. Most had worn the traditional black apparel, but Dawson couldn't bring himself to do that. Like his beloved granddad would have done, he had dressed in jeans, Western boots, and a plain dark shirt under his corduroy jacket. He turned his gaze toward Kat. After all their years together, her beauty continued to captivate him. Her dark hair cascaded down around her ears onto her shoulders. It was hard to tell where it stopped and her black dress started.

Little Joey whimpered and burrowed the toe of his new shoe into the dirt. He jabbed and twisted it into the ground with such force that Kat nudged him and shook her head. He stopped and covered his face with his hands. He had vented his anger and all that was left was the sadness. He didn't understand. He didn't make a sound. He just stood there with his eyes covered and let the tears roll down his cheeks, now and then catching them with his tongue. He had been proud of his new shoes last week, but they didn't matter anymore. Nothing mattered anymore. Great-granddaddy was gone.

The stranger looked on. His hat dropped low on his forehead, leaving only slits for eyes. The collar of his too-large coat hid the most part of him. *How dare you go first, Jedediah Kahill. You've taken our secret with you. What am I supposed to do now, my dear friend?*

Dawson glanced out beyond the parting mourners. Large maples and elms with almost leafless branches sprawled above gray concrete tombstones and brown grass, but the yellows and pinks of fresh flowers surrounding his grandfather's grave provided some small measure of comfort.

Dawson looked at his son and blessed the day he came into the world. They'd almost lost their baby boy. Now he was a healthy, strong little fellow. No wonder Granddad's chest puffed out with the mention of his great grandson. A haunting echo of Jedediah's tapping his cane and boasting about Joey, transported him to those many times when Jedediah would say, *Strong and upright that boy is. Takes after his ole Great-grandaddy.* Dawson broke the sober moment and smiled.

Joey sniffed and wiped his nose with the back of his hand. "Domit, I ain't no little kid no more." His eyes grew wide with alarm, and his hand flew to his open mouth. "Oh, Great-grandaddy, I'm sorry. I didn't meant to say that bad word, and I didn't meant to say ain't. But...but...Great-grandaddy, I didn't want you to go and die. I won't have no one like you to play with." Standing pigeon-toed as he often did, he lowered his chin to his chest, and mumbled under his breath.

"Daddy said you—you was old and tired and it was time for you to git a lot of rest. Well, heck, Great-grandaddy, how come you can't git a lot of rest right here at Willow Walk? I'd be quiet and not make no noise so you could sleep! Well, I guess that don't matter now. I don't git to say much 'bout nothin' 'round here till I get growed up. Wonder when that's 'posed to be. Probably next year or maybe the year after that." He shook his head. "You know what Great-grandaddy? We won't never git to play 'when the cows come home' no more... and who's gonna remind me not to say domit and ain't? Oh Great-grandaddy, I miss you too much."

Still holding his wife's hand, Dawson frowned. The loss of his granddad had reminded him how precious life and loved ones were. Twice he had almost lost Kat. The time in childbirth wasn't his fault, but the other time—after the accident that nearly cost him his leg...and his marriage—that was his own foolishness. He had been a knucklehead. The accident left him with a steel rod in his leg and a head full of self-pity. He'd blamed everyone for his disability, even God. Gluing himself to a wheelchair, he rolled around at Willow Walk in his own private fog. The exercises ordered by his therapist were never done. He ignored his family and their needs. They had their world—he had his wheelchair. Thank goodness, he had come to his senses before it was too late.

He glanced out over the top of Kat's head. "See that man leaning on the oak out there? Have you ever seen him before?"

"Hmmm...No, I don't think so. Actually I can't see much more than a coat and hat."

"You know Granddad made an occasional enemy along the way with his rather severe presence. But I suppose the guy could be an old friend or...oh, I don't know."

The mourners continued to file past, each sharing a word of sympathy or a fond memory. Dawson nodded. His grandfather had meant so much to so many. He had saved Mr. and Mrs. Murphy from bankruptcy and the Evans family from losing their farm. When little Mary Carter's parents couldn't afford a wheel chair for her, Jedediah stepped in and bought her one. The list went on and on, and many of them never knew who their benefactor had been.

Other than the muffled voices of people, no sound could be heard—not even a cricket or tree frog. The thunder had ceased, and the air was still as death. Dawson looked down at the tombstone on his right; the epitaph was barely readable.

HERE LIES
Silas J. Kahill
Born 1830 — Died 1866
Son of Tobias and Sarah J. Kahill
"NOT ONE LOUSY HAT"

The story Jedediah had told one dark night by the fireplace in the drawing room at Willow Walk rose up in his mind. Flashes of red, yellow, and orange flames had danced on the walls and ceiling; Joey and Molly Anna sat spellbound on the rug in front of the hearth. Side-by-side, cross-legged and wide-eyed, they listened to Jedediah's grizzly tale of his great-grandfather, Silas Kahill. Jedediah's cane came alive, tapping on the hardwood floors as he paced back and forth. Their eyes followed his every move.

"It seemed there wasn't a hat left among the infantry back in the Civil War days." Jedediah had stopped pacing and looked straight at them. "Yeah, by golly, at least that's what Silas said in his journal. Because, while a man's head could stand the sleet-filled winds, a man's feet left bloody tracks across the mud that turned the ice black unless he wrapped them in something—and a felt hat made a fine warm covering for one foot." Jedediah leaned on his cane, lifted one foot, and sighed. "That musta been awful because, for every man who had *both* feet wrapped in felt, you could be sure two comrades had fallen and his hat confiscated. But poor Silas didn't have even one felt hat, for he had lost his own and someone always beat him to the corpses to snatch them." Jed began pacing again. "You know now that Silas Kahill cherished Willow Walk. After all, he had made it into what it is today, every stone, every plank of wood, every inch of the great house." His eyebrows jumped up and down. "Poor Silas lived to tell the story of how the lack of two lousy hats caused his feet to freeze. He didn't live long after both feet were amputated because, I guess—"

"What's amputated mean, Granddaddy?" Joey had interrupted.

"It means—cut off. Gone! His feet were gone."

"Oh, Great-grandaddy, that's awful." Joey's mouth flew open. His cheeks turned pink from the slap he gave himself.

"Yep. His last words were—Not one lousy hat."

Dawson suppressed a grin as he reminded each passing mourner to retreat to Willow Walk for the reception he knew Granddad would have expected. He imagined some broadminded folks were thinking a little brandy punch on a day like this would hit the spot. They wouldn't be disappointed— Carla would see to that.

"Come on." Kat shivered in the cold steady drizzle. "You're getting wet."

He lagged behind. "You and Joey go back to the house in the limo, Kat. I'll be there shortly. Maybe I can catch up with that stranger. He shifted his body and grimaced. "With this leg of mine acting up again, I probably couldn't catch a turtle. The way it lets me know when snow is on the way...maybe I should become a weather man." He tried to laugh, but it came out more like a groan.

"Don't be long, sweetheart. The sky looks like we'll have a downpour any moment. You know what Granddad would say. I can just see him shaking his cane at you. "Sonny, let that stranger go his own way." Kat made her voice gruff.

"He sure liked waving that cane around, didn't he? But I think he'd rather I catch up with whoever is invading Willow Walk's privacy. I don't think that stranger belongs here."

"But...you don't really know for sure, Daw. Maybe he's someone Granddad knew. Anyway, be careful. I don't like the looks of him, and I don't understand why he kept his distance, standing off from the rest of us like that. Maybe he's trying to hide something."

"Probably the boogie man from your childhood." Dawson raised an eyebrow.

"Oh, you're insufferable."

He winked at his wife, but his mouth didn't turn up. As he watched her walk away, the wind picking up and whipping her coat tight around her body, a great weight settled on his shoulders. *Can I fill Granddad's shoes?* No options. *I have to.* He watched the limo pull away behind the line of cars streaming out of the cemetery.

The thunder rolling in the valley seemed to echo Jedediah's words that he had repeated so often these last years. *You're a good boy, Sonny. I taught you well. Willow Walk has been saved to show the glory of the past. That's why we must stand by her. I know you'll do that for me. That's what we Kahills are all about.*

"I will Granddad. I promise." The sound of his words floated away on a powerful gust. "And I'll take care of the ski lodge, too. You know the blood, sweat, and tears that went into that venture. You helped it flourish, and I'm counting on an even better season this winter." Dawson bit his lip. "Oh, how I wish you were here to share it with me."

He stared at the ground. Fallen leaves that would have skittered about like children playing tag lay soggy and still, held down by the rain that came with even greater insistence. *Another winter. Another season of guests at Willow Walk Ski Lodge. Gotta remember to hire a new desk clerk before we get too busy.*

Looking up toward the stranger by the oak tree, he saw the man move toward the path along the fence. Like a marathon runner in slow motion, he wove between and around oaks and willow trees. Dawson followed, but his leg wouldn't let him run. He had seen only half a face; a hat covered the other half. Hard as he tried, he couldn't place him. *This guy seems to know his way around. Bet he's been here before.*

"Stop! Stop, sir. Please! I mean you no harm."

The man ran faster.

Dawson gulped fresh air. The main highway meandered into town through gentle rolling hills now covered with haystacks. The stranger followed the fence line separating Willow Walk's main cemetery from the slave burial grounds. He followed the split-rail fence to the dirt road, where an old jalopy sat on the shoulder.

He stopped short. Pain shot through his leg. He grabbed the fence to keep from going down. With no hope of catching the man, he turned back the way he had come and limped toward his truck. His foot hit something solid, and he kicked away the wet leaves. On the ground lay a small black book. He picked it up and glanced at the first page. The rain had already distorted the writing. Closing it up, he shoved it inside his coat pocket and looked over his shoulder just in time to see the dilapidated vehicle pull away.

What does that man have to do with Granddad, with Willow Walk, with anything regarding the Kahills? Something's not right here. He took a long deep breath and glanced one last time at the disappearing truck before checking his watch. It was after five. He'd been gone too long.

Go ahead... run stranger...you with your ragged coat and bent back. For whatever reason you ran away, I have a gut feeling you'll be back.

Chapter Two

*L*eaves covered the ground, stacked high where the wind had blown them against tree trunks and bushes before the rain grounded them in place. Lifeless reminders that winter's chill had come too soon, they left barren the freshly turned ground that covered the new grave.

Moving as fast as his pain allowed, Dawson retraced his steps. Tears filled his eyes as he limped past his grandfather's final resting place, stopping just long enough to say good-bye one last time. Then he turned toward the road that curved around the cemetery, where his truck was parked, and didn't look back. Hard times were not foreign to him, but never had he faced the kind of heartbreak that wracked his whole body. He dropped the notebook beside him on the seat and started down the road. After he and Kat had tucked Joey into bed, they would search the book for any clues that might lead to the identity of the stranger. Later would be soon enough.

He inched along the private road to Willow Walk that wound between symmetrically placed weeping willows planted sometime in the mid 1800s, so Granddad had told him. Their massive trunks, bigger around than the width of three large men standing abreast, stood like sentinels on either side of the drive. Approaching the clearing where the homestead sprawled in its immensity, he felt his heart swell. This was his home, the home of his children, the Kahill legacy from generations past to those in the future. For the first time, he fully understood Granddad's attachment to Willow Walk.

The main house stood large and daunting in the shadows of the early night. Deprived of the waning light of the sunset that normally drenched the hillsides surrounding it, the structure cast eerie images onto the ground. Snow clouds rolled low, willful, and threatening across the horizon.

Dawson climbed the steps on the porch, and the voices of the mourners who had come to the reception floated out to meet him. Willow Walk's round wooden columns rose high above him to frame the plantation style home. A veranda wrapped around the entire house. Ivy climbed the white clapboard siding on the south side, a striking contrast of green against white in the sunlight but almost ominous twist of ebony vines and leaves in the darkness. Black shutters framed the windows. White wicker rockers, placed side-by-side on the porch, invited friends and family to sit a spell. Tonight their emptiness acknowledged the passing of the old patriarch and the arrival of the new one.

He reached out to open the door, then hesitated as the big house seemed to call out to him. The monolithic structure, an enormous undertaking at the time of its construction, had seen many Kahills come and go. He stood at attention, as though being inspected, visions of the mansion's grandeur bounding through his mind. Its builder, his great-great grandfather, had been a humble man in most matters, at least according to family tradition. Yet he had boasted in his journal that Willow Walk was the grandest house in all the territory.

Past and present collided, gripping Dawson with a sense of pride that reached out to soothe his pain and fill the gaping hole in his heart. The Kahills who had come before—strong men like Silas and Granddad Jedediah—had set the example. He squared his shoulders. His turn had come to live up to the name. What was it Granddad used to say? *A man needs a dream to hold onto. Willow Walk is that dream.*

"Where's my daddy?"

Joey's shout on the other side of the large double door startled him. He shook his head to dislodge his digression into the past and, with quiet steps, left the porch and entered the mud room on the west side of the house. He removed his wet coat and boots, but he hesitated before joining the guests who had come to pay their respects. Longing for comfort from generations past to ground him— for the time when peals of laughter and strains of string music must have filled the rooms and hallways—he imagined the soft, rich glow of furniture polished by loving hands. Dark green velvet drapes with gold fringed trim hung in perfect folds. Cypress and Longwood pine paneling and bookshelves embellished the rooms. Warmth radiated from the many glowing hearths. Most of that past splendor remained intact and functional, but it felt so cold now, so remote. No laughter rang out in Willow Walk this night as he forced himself to walk through the kitchen into the main part of the house. Mourners moved around the drawing room, parlor, and library, their low voices sounding much like the hum of a reed organ. He eyed the busy dining room across the grand hall, where the non-roamers had congregated.

A blackberry brandy decanter stared at him from a large buffet. He'd shared many drinks and discussions over the years with his grandfather at the long oak table that dominated the center of the room, but tonight, as he poured his glass half full, he felt it was, instead, half empty. Many friends and acquaintances filled Willow Walk's lower floor, but he had never felt so alone.

Go for it, Sonny. Jedediah's voice seemed to whisper from the dark corners of the room. *And while you're at it, pour me three fingers of that toothsome stuff. A little brandy is good for the soul, ya know.*

His eyes welled as he downed the throat-stinging brandy. The corners of his mouth turned up for a moment in a slight smile. He could always tell when Granddad had swallowed a sip because his nose twitched, his eyebrows bobbed up and down, and his cane tapped to the tune of *Ole Jed Kahill Was a Fine Old Man*, a little ditty his precious Emma had written for him. Then Dawson would clamp his jaw tight to squelch his laughter and pretend not to be amused.

He sniffed, poured three fingers for the grand old man, and downed it in one gulp. Visions of Grandma Emma chasing him and Granddad out of her just-mopped kitchen with her broom flashed through his mind. *I can't believe they're both gone now. Willow Walk will never be the same.*

His thoughts turned to the notebook on the seat of his truck. *Who was he? What did he have to do with Granddad? If he was a friend, why didn't he join us at the grave site?* Envisioning the stranger heightened the mystery, but now was not the time to dwell on the matter. Paying respect to Jedediah Joseph Kahill—the only real father he'd ever known and loved—took precedence this evening.

Still hesitant to join the flock of mourners, he leaned against the door frame of the study, gazing into the gathering of family and friends. Their faces wore a mixture of expressions from somber and teary-eyed to smiles at recalling some fond memory. A buzz of voices made its way full circle around the room.

"Last time I saw Jedediah, he..."

"He could be a cantankerous old fool, but never was there a kinder hearted..."

"I already miss the visits we had and so will...."

He turned to the parlor. Kat, her friends, Debbie and Bonny, and Bonny's big Irish husband, Clancy, stared into the night from one of the windows in the parlor. The four of them sipped Sangria punch that Carla, the longtime housekeeper, had provided as a tribute to Jedediah. A willow's delicate branch reached out to touch the pane, almost as though it wept for the fallen patriarch along with the mourners inside.

The old man had tried in vain to talk Carla out of her secret recipe. "Not on your life, Jedediah Kahill. I would rather die first than tell you." Then Jed would slap his leg and laugh so hard you could hear him all the way to the barn.

Carla brought in a fresh punch bowl and took the nearly empty one back to the kitchen. She had become much more than just a housekeeper. After her years of putting up with Jedediah—and adoring him—the whole family considered her one of them. Dawson's gaze followed her as she moseyed from one group to another, playing the role of hostess, just as Granddad would have wanted her to do. He stifled a grin. Carla had been hired against Jedediah's will. At first he shunned the stern redheaded, roly-poly woman whose temperament matched his own. But as years went by, he had obviously grown to care for her. More than once he had watched her sneak a touch of brandy in his coffee, tea, or fruit juice. No wonder he had begun to see her in a different way. They were two peas in a pod, he used to say. Dawson wrinkled his brow. *I wonder if Granddad ever considered asking her to marry him. I thought a few times they had fallen in love, but he never mentioned anything to me about special feelings for her.*

He took a deep breath and headed toward Kat and the others.

"Kat, don't worry about a thing at the boutiques," Bonny was saying as he walked up. "Deb and I can handle both of them. With me here in town and Deb in our New York shop, you should be able to take some time off. We won't take no for an answer, girlfriend."

"C'mon, Kat. We've been friends since college. You know we won't let you down." Deb raised an eyebrow and gave her a straight look.

"Thanks, you two, but I can't do that. Well...maybe I'll take a couple days, but that's all. You know I have to get some designs off to Paris for Lil and Silka to work with. Wolf International's fashion show is in January. Plus we've got our own March show. That's the biggie. We have to create all the designs, have them made, and do everything. Got to make a whopping impression. Show the Big Apple who's boss when it comes to fashion design."

"Well, at least you won't be going to Paris this year." Bonny eyed Kat. "Well...will you?"

"Of course not. Whatever made you think of that?"

"Because I'm always the last to know everything around here." Bonny shrugged her shoulders.

Debbie shook her head. "Not true, my dear. Your hubby says your perceptiveness is amazing."

Clancy grinned, flexed a well-developed muscle, and winked at his wife. Good-natured, good-hearted Clancy was the apple of her eye. No one who spent any time with them could miss that. Nor could they miss the fact that he adored her. They'd been married just a short time. It was Bonny's first, but Clancy provided her with a ready-made family. His wife had died shortly after his daughter, Molly Anna, was born on the same day Kat had given an early and difficult birth to Joey. Jedediah met Clancy and his brood of young sons in the hospital waiting room, and their friendship had blossomed when Jed learned that Clancy had fallen on hard times.

"Oh, he did, did he?" Bonny waggled a finger at Clancy.

"Okay, me favorite li'l lassie. Ye know ye always figure things out ten Blarney stones ahead of anyone else." Clancy's mouth formed a wry curve.

Dawson raised an eyebrow. *I'd envy their great relationship if I didn't have Kat.* Her back was to him, and the heavy coils of her dark hair fell in spirals on top of her shoulders and across the neck of her black linen sheath. She must have felt the intensity of his gaze because she turned to face him. Her flirty grin lightened his mood. He bent to kiss her cheek and drank in her perfume. Its sweet, woodsy scent always made him want to touch her. Right now, he needed her at his side. She turned to him. The faraway look in her eyes caught him off guard.

"What are you thinking about, Kat?"

"Oh...I don't know. Mostly Granddad. Just remembering how he loved autumn." She smiled that unwavering star-bright smile, but then it faltered. "Uh... I guess that's about it."

"That's about it? What does that mean? Something you're not telling me?" He paused and laid his hand on her shoulder. With the forefinger of his other hand beneath her chin, he tilted her head until their eyes met. "So out with it, Kat. Is it Granddad's death or something more?"

"It's...nothing, Dawson." She turned her head away from him, but not before he saw the worry in her eyes.

"Whoa there, girl. Your irritability is showing. And this isn't the first time I've noticed it over the last few weeks. What's up? Oh pardon me, I forgot. You said nothing's up."

"I'm sorry, Daw. Just got a lot of things on my mind."

"When did you say you were leaving for New York?"

"Within the next week. So many things to do. So little time to get them all done. We have to plan our lines for the bi-annual collections, and that means designing and producing fashions based on what we think customers will want to wear a year from now. Then there's the show for Wolf International Fashions. I'm responsible for almost half the designs, the theme for the show, the prompts on stage, the..." She stopped to take a breath. "Of course, without Silka and Lillian facilitating the Paris show, I couldn't possibly get everything done. Between handling all that and the boutiques, I'd have no time to spend with you and Joey. You know I won't allow that to happen again." She looked over at her best friends. "I don't know what I'd do without those two managing the company for me. It's enough of a drain on my time with you when I have to go traipsing between the New York boutique and this one here in Wheeling. It saves time to fly, but you know how much I hate that."

He pulled her away from the group and into his arms. She rested her head on his broad chest. "No more talk about you being away from Joey and me. I don't want another Paris episode where you're gone for what seemed like forever."

"Nor do I." She smiled.

"Unlike last time, you don't have a valid reason to leave me."

"I had to get away then, Daw. You know that. You were breaking my heart, and I couldn't take it anymore."

"If you remember, I had good reason and...No, I *thought* I had good reason. I couldn't walk and... No, I take that back, too. I told myself I couldn't walk and...oh, never mind."

"Sorry, Daw. Let's close that painful chapter in our life, okay? What's past is past and what's done is done. We can't change it. Let it go, please."

Fresh tears filled her azure eyes. He pulled her closer. "I'm sorry, sweetheart." He wiped a tear from her cheek with his finger.

"Thank you, Dawson." She turned and looked back out the window. "Ski season's almost here. Have you hired anyone to help you at the lodge?"

"Not yet, but I'm considering a couple of applications." He reached for two cups of coffee from a tray offered by Carla, handed one to Kat, and took a sip of the other. He could almost see Granddad's scowl. *"That stuff will rust your pipes, boy."*

Kat's voice pulled him back to the present. "We both knew Clancy would be split two ways, helping Bonny at the boutique and also managing the front desk at the ski lodge." Kat puckered her mouth and then grinned. "What am I talking about? That Irishman can take the place of two heavyweight champions no matter what he needs to do. *However*, Bonny really does need him at the boutique. And our customers love him. He has a keen eye for what looks good, and the ladies thrive on having a male point of view. Of course, his wonderful Irish brogue doesn't hurt either."

"I'll look at those applications in the morning. And I've got an ad in the paper."

"Thanks, Daw. Deb's doing great in the New York boutique. It's so reassuring to have her there. Now that Bill's with CSI in New York, at least they're together even though he can't be a lot of help to her. I wish I could find someone reliable to help her handle New York. We're searching now for qualified personnel. I even suggested a couple people. Someone will come along to help you at the lodge, so don't worry too much."

"Are you always this understanding, or is this a trick to make me think you're terrific?"

Kat pressed her lips together and then burst out laughing. Dawson gave her a peck on the cheek before she had a chance to dodge him.

"I already know you're terrific.... just as terrific as I am."

She rolled her eyes upward.

Dawson flashed a devilish smile.

"Okay, Daw. No more bantering words." Kat winked at him, looked over her shoulder, and walked over to mingle with others. Among them were many family members who had drifted away over the years, but now gathered together in the Kahill ancestral home to mourn Granddad's passing.

The throng of people moved about, talking quietly, sipping punch, and nibbling on finger food. The Murphys, the Evans, and the Walkers, old family friends, stood together, reminiscing about how Jedediah had saved them from grave circumstances. Penelope Weatherbush, Jedediah's not-so-secret admirer, sat alone, her chubby cheeks and nose red from crying. She was almost as wide as she was tall, and her salt and pepper curls drooped down the sides of her face. Dawson smothered a smile. *Granddad almost tripped over his own feet backing away from her advances. With Grandma Emma as her rival, dead or alive, poor Penelope hadn't stood a chance.*

Tall tales, sad events, and good times danced in and out of conversations as he moseyed around the rooms, nodding to everyone. Memories were the magic of Willow Walk. He hoped it would stand for many generations to come.

The stranger at the cemetery crossed his mind again. *Who is he? Is he here?* He hadn't seen anyone so far that he didn't recognize. *Surely, he's someone Granddad knew. But if so, why didn't he join us and the other mourners? Why did he run? The dense, wooded area had no designated trail, yet he knew exactly which direction would take him to the main road. He'd obviously been there before.* Dawson closed his eyes and let out a sigh. His anxiety about the man was getting the better of him. He had to keep his mind focused on his family's well-being; he had to guard his own sanity. The weight of Willow Walk and all its entities now rested on his shoulders. With Granddad gone and the presence of the mysterious man gnawing at his gut, he felt powerless. Still, his mind would not allow him to release the burden of that enigma he could only address as... *the stranger.*

Chapter Three

The passing of the patriarchal torch to Dawson filled him with a sense of awe for Willow Walk. The home he had lived in and loved most of his life took on a new dimension as a family heirloom, a legacy to all Kahills, past, present, and future. He stood in the grand entrance hall, staring at the classic Georgian grandfather clock that stood like a sentinel in the right-hand corner. According to family history passed down from fathers to sons—or, in his case, from grandfathers to grandsons—Tobias Kahill had been so pleased with young Silas's outstanding construction of Willow Walk, with the help of neighbor Ezra Fox, that he brought the clock home from England in 1859 as a gift for his son. Kind but firm, Tobias Kahill had ruled his family with dignity and an iron hand. His extensive education, extremely rare at the time, and his dynamic personality made him a powerful patriarch and a force to be reckoned with. No one had ever dared to challenge his instructions concerning the clock; the magnificent timepiece was never to be moved from its designated location, lest the curse of misfortune upon the offender be executed. Dawson shook his head and suppressed a grin. *Sounds a lot like Granddad. Guess that apple didn't fall too far from the tree.* Although Jedediah had maintained that the threat was hogwash, he never moved the clock.

The stately clock chimed nine times before the last of the mourners prepared to leave. They had gestured and chattered from the drawing room through the parlor to the grand entrance hall before arriving at the double mahogany doors.

"Thank you for coming." Dawson extended his hand, opened the door, and stepped onto the porch.

"Yes, we do appreciate your being here." Kat placed Mrs. Osborne's jacket over the elderly woman's shoulders.

Dawson smiled. Poor, rotund Mrs. Osborne, white as a truce flag, believed that staying out of the sun was the only way to prevent wrinkles in old age. Kat had laughed when he told her not to try it because the woman presented living proof that it didn't work. The lady's eccentricities only endeared her to Granddad, who had thought the world of the Osbornes. Tonight, however, she might as well have been speaking in a foreign tongue because Dawson could not decipher a single word. A patient and tolerant man, Mr. Osborne had long ago accepted her as she was. Nonetheless, he frowned, gently took her arm, and guided her toward the car. "Darn, Harriet, it's freezing out here. You're making the Kahills stand outside. Let's go home and let these grieving folks get some rest."

"Oh, for heaven's sake, Will. I'm just expressing my sympathy. Now don't tell me what to do."

Out of the corner of his eye, Dawson watched the hint of a smile play at the corners of Kat's mouth as they waved goodbye. A brisk west wind trembled through the bare trees. Its swirling motion encircled them and sent them scurrying inside to Willow Walk's warmth.

Dawson pushed the solid doors closed behind them and shivered. "Let's go into the parlor by the fire. That cold went clear through to my bones. We're going to have snow by morning."

Kat snuggled up next to him on the love seat that sat in front of the hearth. "You sound like an old man, Daw. It's too early for snow. Up in the hills maybe, but I don't think we'll see it here." She stared into the waning embers. "Besides, we're not ready at the lodge."

"You wait and see. My bum leg has made me the world's most accurate weatherman. It's never been wrong yet. And that's more than you can say about those weather prognosticators on television."

"They cover their backsides with 'thirty percent chance of rain on Tuesday with possible afternoon clearing' or whatever. They're right in any case." She stood, stretched, and reached out her hand. "I'm heading for bed. It's been a long, sad day. Are you coming?"

"What about all those dirty dishes?"

"If I know Carla, they're already done. She brought in two extra people to help her in the kitchen today. I'd be willing to bet the dishes were washed, dried, and put away before the Osborne's walked out the door."

"Probably so. Don't know what we ever did without that woman. She's been a treasure since the first day she arrived, despite Granddad's determination to show her the door."

Kat laughed. "Who would've thought they'd become such fast friends? I think she took his passing as hard as we did. And I think she outdid herself today as a tribute to him. She wouldn't want us in her kitchen tonight." She looked up at him. "Now tell me what's happening at the lodge. I've been so busy getting ready for the upcoming shows that I feel completely out of the loop."

He nodded, took her hand, and limped up the stairs beside her. "I've done a lot more advertising for the ski resort this year. We're already booked for half of November, and new reservations are coming in every day. I think we'll have a great season despite the weak economy. People are stressed, and they need to get away. My early-bird pricing specials have tripled the inquiries I had by this time last year." He shut the bedroom door behind them and pulled her close. "You're right that it's been a long day. I'm not sure how we're going to get along without the old man to keep us in line."

She leaned back and ran her forefinger down his cheek. "We'll get along just fine. You know why?"

"Why?"

"Because he showed us how to do it, Daw. You just put yourself in his mind, and things will always work out. They did for Granddad. They will for you." She leaned her cheek against his shoulder.

He kissed the top of her head. "I love you, Katerina Kahill."

"And I love you, Dawson Kahill. Now I want you to stop all your worrying and know that you're going to find help for the lodge before the season gets busy. And you're going to know it's the perfect person because Granddad taught you how to judge people fairly and honestly."

"My heart knows you're right, but my head wants to argue with you."

"Listen to your heart, and take your head to bed. A good night's sleep will do wonders for all that self-doubt you're generating."

His head rested on the pillow, but his mind refused to shut down. The day had been difficult, a sad day, but life had a way of throwing curves and this one hit full force. *Focus, aim*, he told himself, *breathe deep, exhale slowly, and carry on*. Mental images of the graveside service rewound and replayed again and again as he waited for Kat to get out of the shower. Over and over, the reruns ended with the stranger outrunning him and the feeling that the man had some connection to the Kahills—a connection that Granddad knew but hadn't shared with the rest of them.

He shook his head to dislodge the images. They were instantly replaced with visions of Kat in the shower, the fragrance of her favorite body wash filling the room with its enticing aroma.

What's with her anyway? She hasn't been herself for weeks. Her sunny personality has an edgy overtone. I don't understand. Just like tonight...I asked her what's wrong, and she said it's nothing. She didn't seem concerned about the stranger while we were at the cemetery, but he must have made her uncomfortable. Why else would she have seemed so distracted at the reception?

She opened the bathroom door. The sweet scent of her shower gel floated into the bedroom. Suddenly, he wanted her more than anything else in the world. As quickly as the longing had come, it disappeared. Granddad's insistence that Joey needed a little sister popped into his mind. He tried to push it away, but it clung to his memory like contact cement. Making love on the night of Granddad's funeral seemed so...so disrespectful. Then Granddad's words echoed from a far corner of his memory. *Love your woman, boy, just like I loved my Emma. Kat's a lot like her, you know. And another thing you need to know—any night could be your last with her, so don't put off till tomorrow what you want to say or do today. Sometimes tomorrow never comes.* The wistful look of longing in Granddad's eyes when he'd said that sharpened until the old man's gaze seemed to penetrate every corner of Dawson's mind.

Haunting images replaced Granddad's face. An ambulance. Sirens. White coats. Emergency surgery. A tiny baby boy rushed off to intensive care. He tried to push them away, but they wouldn't go. Another baby? Now? Joey's birth had almost taken Kat's life.

She turned from the window after closing the drapes. Their gazes met. An unspoken force—as powerful as it had been the first time they came together—shot forth with such passion that he almost saw the lightning flash that passed between them. She sat down at the dressing table and began combing her hair. "It's chilly in here."

He sprang from the bed with more energy than he knew he had left and hurried over to the fireplace. Within moments a crackling fire blazed bright and warm in the grate. He adjusted the inner screen and closed the glass doors that kept the sparks safely within the confines of the firebox. As soon as the logs flamed, he turned on the fan that sent the heat into the room. Granddad had ordered the fans and glass doors installed in all the fireplaces to make them more efficient and reduce the risk of fire. The old man didn't want his family or Willow Walk in harm's way. *The old timber in this place would go up in a flash,* he'd said at the time. *Gotta keep everybody safe.*

The flames sent dancing images of light across the bed with its white lace canopy and the massive chests of drawers. Kat walked up beside him and slipped her hand into his. The warm flesh of her palm tingled against his and shot through him like sparks in a fireworks display.

"C'mon Kat. We need some quality time alone." The undercurrent vibrated in the air between them.

They reached the edge of the bed. She turned. That bewitching look she gave him, the way her mouth tilted to accept his kisses was sweeter than anything on earth. His fingers slid deep into her silky mane. He cupped her head and drew her closer. The glow of their unhurried kiss lingered with him long after their lips parted, soft and gentle in his mind.

She pulled away. "Sweetheart, why don't you pour us a brandy?"

"Now, Kat? How about afterwards?"

"Honey...I...I have something to tell you. I...well...it can wait till we've shared our drink." She touched his lips so lightly with two fingers that he couldn't be sure she had touched them at all.

"You know how I hate waiting. Tell me now while I pour the brandy." He opened the glass curio cabinet, a beautiful Victorian piece pampered for many years with love and care by Grandma Emma. Along with the antique clock in the grand hall, it had been among Jedediah's favorite pieces, not only because Emma showed it profound respect as a treasured family heirloom, but because it held his stash of corn liquor. He'd hide a bottle behind the clock and another one deep within the cabinet behind a Wedgwood plate, sure that Emma had no clue what he was doing. Everyone at Willow Walk knew, including the housekeeper who discovered them while dusting; but no one ever exposed the corn liquor secret on specific orders from Grandma Emma. She had beaten him at his own game...again. Dawson chuckled aloud and reached for the bottle.

"You want a peach brandy, Kat?"

She opened the drapes just enough to peer out at the windswept willows. "Just a little, sweetheart. My stomach's a bit touchy tonight. What are you snickering about?"

"Nothing important. Tell ya later."

"Oh...you're really a piece of work. In other words, I'll tell you my secret if you tell me yours?" With a teasing smile, she blew him a butterfly kiss and sashayed to her side of the bed.

He drew in a long labored breath, exhaled, and took a huge gulp of brandy. If this didn't relax him, nothing would. His uneasiness lingered. With Granddad gone, so many things would change. He glanced at Kat, who leaned against a pile of pillows, sipping her brandy and watching the flames in the hearth.

Turning back to the fire, he closed his eyes and set his mind free to dream. The images in his head came slowly at first, then grew so real that he could again smell the sweetness of her shampoo and the subtle fragrance of the perfume she always splashed on after her shower.

A hinge squeaked, and then a glow of yellow slid from under the door and across the floor. She posed in the doorway, her round face devoid of makeup. The blackest hair he'd ever seen cascaded in waves past her shoulders and down her back. Her lace nightdress played peek-a-boo with his mind. He squinted, not sure if it was Kat or a ribbon of white clouds floating closer to him.

Love mingled with desire rose until it burned like a torch within him. She came closer and closer, her eyes soft like those of a newborn fawn. His gaze locked on hers. He swallowed. His feet shifted. His heart smoldered. She was his purpose and his way. She was his.

Suddenly, he wanted her more than ever. *Why now...on the eve of Granddad's funeral? What kind of self-serving, detached, disrespectful man am I?* He had little control over his inclination. He was alive, he breathed, he functioned. He was human, and human desires can't tell time or feel pain. *At least she had the good grace to pull away from me. Was that her way of saying that making love isn't decent tonight? No one has ever been a more caring person than she is. She knows this isn't the time...* He opened his eyes.

Wait a minute! If anyone would understand how much I need her, Granddad would. He could almost hear the old man's stern, emphatic voice. *That's nothin' but stuff'n nonsense, Sonny. What's come to pass has come to pass, so move on with your life. I know you loved me, but I don't want you lollygaggin' around, feelin' mournful and pretendin' like you don't want to cuddle up when you know dang well you do. Besides, how ya gonna make that baby girl if ya don't cuddle good and proper?*

He glanced at her again. She stared at the fire, but she had that faraway look in her eyes that he'd noticed earlier. *What in the world could she have to tell me that makes her so hesitant? It's not like her to stammer over anything she needs to talk about.* Her preoccupation the last few weeks nagged at him, but he knew better than to push her. She would tell him when she was good and ready and not a moment before.

"Coming to bed, Daw?"

Her voice jolted him out of his reverie. He left the hypnotic trance of the fire and slipped beneath the covers.

She picked up his hand and rubbed it against her cheek. "I think it's time we listened to Granddad. You know—about a little sister for Joey." Her voice seemed to purr, much like that of a contented cat.

"Now? When you'll be going off to—"

"Yes, *now*." She dropped his hand.

"We need to think about it, Kat. Have you forgotten what a difficult time you had when Joey was born? I almost lost you. I don't want to go through that again, and I certainly don't want you to go through it."

"Nor do I, but Dr. Morgan said another pregnancy would not be dangerous if we took proper precautions, and he would see me on a weekly basis from the beginning until we're sure everything's okay. Surely you don't have a problem with his judgment after all his years of medical practice."

He did *not* want to have this conversation. "Keep in mind that it's *my* wife he's talking about, not his. He might think differently if he were speaking of Mrs. Morgan. As I see it, we shouldn't be putting your life at risk—or that of an unborn child. So, yes, there *is* a problem, Kat."

"But, Daw! I thought we wanted—"

He heard her sniff and knew she was crying. "Kat, sweetheart, we'll have the daughter we want, I promise you, even if we have to adopt her."

"Adopt? Don't even think about it! Granddad said—"

"Granddad would be the last person to want you to risk your life. We just can't take the chance now, Kat. Joey needs you. I need you. The girls at the boutiques need you. It *isn't* the right time. Maybe in a year or so we'll talk about it again…"

A year or so? Tears erupted from deep within her. Her throat tightened until the ache made her want to scream, but no sound would come out. Her hand drifted down to caress her belly. She thought her heart would stop. *What can I do? Oh, Daw, I need you, but I can't reach you. I don't think I can do this alone.*

If only you were here to help me, Granddad. I stopped taking the pill so I could give you a precious granddaughter. Remember when you said, "Yes, and her name shall be Willow. And Dawson—I wanted to give him the little girl he longed for, but now…nothing is right. You're gone, and he doesn't want a baby. It's my fault. I had no right to take it upon myself to make that decision. But—it's too late now.

For a moment Dawson said nothing. Then his voice came sweet and consoling. "By the way, sweetheart, what did you want to tell me?"

She stiffened. "It's not important, Daw."

"But you said—"

"I said it's not important. Now, please, I love you, and that's all I want to think about." She turned on her side. "Good night, Daw. I *really* do love you."

He patted her hip. "Rest well, sweetheart," he said in a sleepy voice.

She lay very still, as if she were dropping off to sleep, but her eyes were wide open. Burning tears rolled toward her pillow. *Why wipe them away? They'll just come back again. I'll be showing soon. What then?*

I can't tell Dawson I'm pregnant. Not now. Not until I'm sure he wants to hear it, if that time ever comes. Perhaps when I return home from New York will be a good time. That will be soon enough. Yes…that's when I'll tell him…when I come home from New York.

Chapter Four

*C*annon Fox shuddered. Time had demanded its due. His refuge in the timeless, womb of nowhere labored to expel him into a life that threatened to expose his past and send him naked into the present of someone who knew nothing of his part in her existence. He pulled his threadbare coat up around his ears to hide just a bit longer.

Rosy light tinted the western sky. Only the twittering of the birds in the treetops interrupted the quiet evening. Peace reigned all around him, but inside raged a war of questions with no answers. Without his friend and sounding board—his neighbor with whom he shared countless chats and tales of yore— and a snort or two of their favorite blackberry brandy—Willow Walk's cemetery had lost its importance in his life.

Sitting on autumn's dormant grass in front of Jedediah's headstone, he wrapped his arms around his bent knees and conversed with his old friend as though he could hear the frustrations of his dilemma.

He knew the answers he wanted would not reach his ears, but they would reach his heart, for they would come from the wisdom the man had imparted over many decades. The words on the stone still didn't seem real. He kept thinking he would wake up and Jed would be there, that it was all a bad dream.

Jedediah Joseph Kahill
Born 1890 • Died 1984
Ole Jed Kahill was a fine ole man.

The truthfulness of the last words on the headstone resounded in his mind. A willful, headstrong man, yes, but never a finer one.

"You might have died, Jedediah Joseph Kahill, but you'll never be dead to me. How many times did we meet right here in Willow Walk's cemetery to roister around? The secret has always been our common denominator, but it shouldn't be a secret anymore. Kat and Maggie need to know their connection now, and that's not all. But I guess one bombshell at a time is enough. Don't you think it's time to free the skeleton from its closet? I need to know what to do, Jed. You know I'm younger than you and not near as smart. Better looking, maybe, but not smarter." The hint of a grin touched his lips and faded.

He plucked pieces of grass from the sod next to him, threw them aside, and looked around at the huge century-old oaks and willows that graced the grounds. Their roots had long ago risen from the soil, as if searching for air after years of growing downward in West Virginia's red clay. "I wish you could rise up outta that ground, too, my friend." He pulled the collar of his torn coat up around his neck to fend off the evening chill.

Chipped and blackened tombstones dating back before the Civil War stood every few feet, but the side-by-side grave sites didn't make the Kahills one big happy family. Frowning, he looked down at Jed's grave once more. "Will there ever be peace between our kin? Not by a long shot, I'm afraid. Too many intermingled skeletons between the Kahills and the Foxes to allow every daughter and son of a Kahill to rest in peace." He lifted his gaze to the ornamental iron fence, green with corrosion. It seemed to whisper on the wind, commanding the dead to stay in and the living to keep out.

He shifted his position and let his shoulders droop.

"I know what you're thinking, Jed. What do I have to lose by telling? Hoards of money stashed in a Swiss bank? I don't think so. No, I've stripped, scourged, and wasted myself far too much of my lifetime. Sure, it's my own fault. But it's not just about me, is it? Others are involved. The truth would sting with all the fury of a woman scorned, you know that. It would be worse than the end of the world for the Kahills and the Foxes. It may be the end of *her* world. I don't want to do that."

He stretched out in the cool grass, arms folded behind his head, ankles crossed. "Remember that sleazy, old apartment next to the railroad track on North Market Street, the one they've been trying to condemn for years? It's still standing. The rats and I share that lovely place but not without fighting over the food and the blankets. Who would've thought back in the good ole days I'd be so down and out?" He looked off into the distance. "No fancy wallpaper or crystal chandeliers hanging over lace-covered tables. No gleaming silverware, no cloth napkins, no crystal wine glasses. No looking out the drawing room window to view the beautiful gardens surrounding Fox Run. But that's okay. With all that I've lost, I've still managed to keep my scavenging friends and me dry and fed. And the nearby shelter serves delicious bean soup—if you don't mind searching for a few beans floating in broth." He shook his head and turned his attention to the neatly carved tombstone.

"I see Maggie often. She's a fine daughter, Jed. She's all grown up now. But that doesn't matter anyway. I came to the funeral to say goodbye to you and to catch a glimpse of the pretty lady. Your grandson is handsome, too. He tried to catch me when the funeral ended, but these old legs of mine outran him. Don't you laugh now, but I sure am missing a good game of checkers. I don't suppose you're going to tap me on the shoulder and tell me this is all a nightmare?" He paused and listened. "I guess not. That young one, the little tot, how sweet he looked dressed in his suit and little bowtie. Even from a distance, I could see the way he squirmed. I bet you taught him to hate dress-up clothes. Ahhh, I'd love to stay and chat, but this one-sided conversation is getting me down. So I best be on my way before any of the family comes back and finds me here." The wind picked up, whistling through the nearly bare branches. "How's that? You're telling me to stop scratching my dirty beard and shave, comb my hair, and don't forget to take a bath before I do anything?" He laughed. "Yeah, we both know I clean up pretty good. I hate that it's been so long since we raised hell together. I bet you thought I'd fallen off the end of the earth. Wish I could have seen you just once more before…Oh well, that's just the way it is sometimes."

Pushing himself to his feet, he forced himself to quit listening for Jed's voice to bounce through the hallways of his mind. *How much longer can I go through life, knowing what I know, without blabbing it? How many years, months, or maybe days, are left of my life? How much longer will I wait before I find the courage to bring everything to light?*

He gazed down at the fresh grave for a long time. His mouth turned grim. *Why, Great-great grandfather Ezra, couldn't you have used the good sense God gave you? You forfeited it all in a brief season of sensual pleasure. Sheldon paid for it a hundred years ago or more, and I'm paying for it now—me, Maggie, and a whole bunch of other folks.*

He took a deep breath and stared off in the distance. If he could ever live down the misery that Ezra Fox had caused, he'd die a happy man. "I know what I've become, Jed, so you needn't think it. Outside, I'm a mountain of filth—inside, I'm still the man I used to be…and I'm a father." He turned to walk away, stopped, and turned back again. He raised one hand to wave and the other to wipe a tear from his tired eyes.

In the silence of his mind, he again shared the secret with his old friend, knowing that for now he'd have to live with it…but he dare not die with it.

Chapter Five

Dawson walked into the kitchen, scratching his head with one hand and holding the deteriorating notebook in the other. He pulled out a chair, sat down at the table, and opened the book to the first page.

"What's it say, Daw?" Kat poured coffee for them both. She placed a cup in front of Dawson and carried hers to the counter next to the sink.

"Best I can make out from all the blurred scribbling it reads...*They said, when trouble comes, close your eyes, and the white folks did.* Then the writing fades away. The next few pages are wrinkled and full of smeared ink."

"That's strange. Wonder who *they* are?" She sorted flowers at the kitchen sink. As beautiful as any of Willow Walk's prize blossoms raised in Grandma Emma's green house, the wild irises behind the barn had long been her favorite. Joey had beamed a few minutes before when he'd handed her the bouquet with a dusting of snow that glistened on the leaves and petals. She'd known what he was up to when he swallowed his orange juice in one gulp, left his toast on the plate, bundled up in his winter coat, and scurried out of the house with Molly Anna right behind him. A few minutes later he had strolled back into the kitchen.

"These are for you, Mama, 'cuz you're sad 'bout Great-granddaddy dyin'. But he wouldn't want you to be sad, and in my dream I heard him say that me an' Molly Anna should bring you some irises this morning 'cuz they're your fav'rite."

They had both stretched out hands full of the gorgeous purple flowers, and she had put them in the sink while the youngsters dashed back outside to make a snowman.

Retrieving Mama Suzanne's prized crystal vase from the top cabinet, she began trimming and arranging the lilies like her mama had taught her, a labor of love she'd never forget. She could almost feel her mama's soft hand guide hers as she placed the flowers one by one in the vase.

A sad smile pulled at the corners of her mouth. She paused, holding a flower in mid-air, and glanced out the window. Halfway up the side of the mountain, an eagle soared above the tops of the Douglas firs, its wings outstretched to catch the updrafts. *How proud and beautiful he is.* Unbidden thoughts of the father she had never known popped into her mind. For her whole life, he had proved himself to be the opposite of that magnificent bird. He didn't fly like an eagle...he slithered like a snake. If anyone was ever worthless... She placed the last flower in the vase and looked out the window again. The eagle disappeared and reappeared with something in its talons. *He's feeding his family. That's more than my dad ever did. Why...I don't even know who he is.* She hated him—whoever he was. *I know it's wrong to hate anyone, but I can't help it. He never even cared enough about me to find out who I am or even if I'm alive.* She shook her head and pushed her bitter thoughts away. *I'll not be the one to judge what he's done.* She filled the vase with water, carried it into the parlor, and set it on the credenza. Back in the kitchen, she grabbed her cup and walked to the table.

Dawson downed the last of his black coffee. "Kat, what do you think of this?" He waved his hand over the notebook and leaned back in his chair. "I first thought the stranger had dropped it at the funeral, but obviously it's been in bad weather for some time." He held out his cup for a refill.

She shot a quick glance at the book while filling his cup. "Good reasoning, Daw. You said you found it under the leaves, and it was closed. It didn't rain hard enough for long enough on the day of the funeral to cause that much damage."

"I know. This book looks like it's been through some hard times, and if not here at Willow Walk, then somewhere else. But where? And how did it end up in the family cemetery?"

Joey skipped into the kitchen from the back door, dripping fresh snow from his boots onto the floor. Molly Anna followed close behind.

"Daddy, Daddy, guess what we found."

Kat's eyes widened. "Where have you two been? Your coats are filthy."

"Yeah, but...but...but this is really 'portant." He turned to his father. "This looks like a letter, Daddy. We found it out in the barn in that old wood pile." Joey waved the paper in the air.

Molly Anna waggled her finger at Joey. "I told ya, Joey, we better not play in the wood pile."

"But I told ya it wouldn't hurt nothin', Molly. You ain't, I mean, *aren't* mad at us, are you, Daddy?"

"Don't talk sassy to Molly, Joey. It's not nice. No, I'm not mad, but I'll not tell you again. Both of you, stay out of that woodpile. Could be snakes or rats or even possums or other critters in there."

"Yes, sir," Joey said. "But I ain't...I mean, I aren't...'fraid of those things." He folded his arms across his chest and stuck his chin out.

"Yes, sir," Molly Anna said. "I aren't afraid either." She shook her head.

"Kat, I think we've got a couple of brave youngsters here. What kind of special job do you think such great courage deserves? I'm considering the old chicken house needs a good cleaning. I don't know if the fox is gone, but he won't bother Joey or Molly because they're not afraid. And the wolf with the big teeth hasn't been back this year. Of course, now that it's snowing, it could come any time."

Joey and Molly Anna's eyes grew wide. Kat suppressed a grin.

"I think that's a great idea, Daw. Let me fix them a little snack because that's hard work. Do you have some gloves that will fit them? Good thing they'll be wearing boots. That chicken house is pretty messy. Oh, get Joey's little work coat out of the back closet, will you? Do you have a work coat, Molly Anna?"

"I'll get his coat in just a minute, sweetheart...right after I finish my coffee."

Joey looked at Molly Anna. He gulped hard, turned to Kat, and gave her a big smile. "I love you, Mama. You'll 'member that won't you, if that big, bad wolf gets us?"

"I sure will, Joey. I promise. Thank you so much for telling me." She returned his smile and bent to kiss his forehead. "Now you two wash up and sit down at the table. I'll scramble you some eggs and fix you each a cup of hot chocolate. Can't have you working on an empty stomach."

A minute later, they rushed to the table and sat down on either side of Dawson.

"Daddy, me an' Molly was hopin' you'd take us with you to the ski lodge today."

Dawson scratched his head. "I'm not sure you'll have time. That chicken coop is a pretty big job."

"Molly an' me ain...aren't sure 'bout that wolf. Wolfs are pretty big, Daddy, and they got lotsa sharp teeth."

"I see." Dawson looked at Kat. "Do you think they can remember to stay away from the wood pile if we let them out of that job *this* time?"

Kat set cups of hot chocolate in front of them. "I don't know. They haven't remembered so far, and I think a stern reminder might be good for both of them." She sat down across from Dawson.

"We won't forget again, Mama. I promise."

"I promises, too. An' I'll make sure Joey 'members."

Their pleading expressions tugged at her heart. "Maybe we should give them one more chance, Daw."

He nodded. "I suppose we could, but not one more time after this." He looked at Joey, then at Molly Anna. "You hear that? This is your last chance."

With solemn expressions, they both nodded.

"Okay, son. Now what about that letter?"

Joey reached in his pocket, pulled out the crumpled paper, and handed it to his father. Dawson flattened it out on the table and read the words aloud.

"My dearest friend, Haven't heard hide nor hair from you in a coon's age. I'm worried. Granted, we both know there was never no love lost between our families. Like the Hatfields and the McCoys, feudin' and fussin' 'bout nothin'. Only difference—we got a few dollars here and there, and those characters didn't. But you and me, well—after tracin' your great-great granddaddy Ezra's shenanigans back to the Civil War, seems like it bound us together a mite. He musta been a rip-snortin' rounder back in them days. Yep! More came out of that durn Civil War than just a win for the North and a loss for the South. Much more. That sweet Maggie of yours is proof enough of that. I told ya then, Can, there'd be hell to pay... But don't matter none. Maggie's too sweet not to love. Who would have ever thought it? So many good times we had drinkin' our brandy and talkin' it up. I remember sittin' in the grass at the cemetery, sharin' the stuff. And the time that...oh, curses...too many memories to count 'em. Let me hear from you soon. Your ol' snortin' buddy, Jed"

"That's from Great-granddaddy, ain't it? Can I keep it Daddy, please?" Joey put down his fork and reached his hand out.

"Uh...maybe later, Joey, when you're older." He turned to Kat. "Who's Maggie?"

She shrugged. "That letter was never mailed, Daw. Who was Granddad writing to? It's odd that he mentioned money. Granddad almost never talked about the Kahill fortune. He just guarded it well."

"That is curious. Also, the only family I can think of that the Kahills avoided was the Fox family. The Foxes have been our next door neighbors forever...since Willow Walk was built. Of course, with the size of their place and the size of ours, it's not all that close. When you and I were kids, we sometimes walked up the dirt road toward Fox Run. Remember, how it ran adjacent to the meadow where we sat under that weeping willow? You know, where the tiny meadow butterflies flew all around us? Remember the Fox brothers? I can't recall their names."

"I don't remember them. I was too young." Kat's fingers pressed on her temples. "I wouldn't know them if they were standing in front of me."

"I doubt I would either. I can't figure why Granddad didn't mail the letter. I can't even figure out why he wrote it. I didn't know he had any dealings with the Foxes. This sounds like they were buddies." He frowned.

"I guess we'll never know, Daw."

Joey and Molly jumped up from the table, put their plates in the sink, and headed for the screen door. "We're goin' back to the barn, Daddy, and see if we can find some more stuff under that old wood pile. I bet that was Great-granddaddy's hidin' place. Maybe he left a letter for me, too!"

"Joey Kahill, you get right back here. What did I just tell you, young man? My word, boy, your ears must have..."

"No, Daddy. I been washing them good so they won't grow potatoes, like Grandaddy said." He wrinkled his forehead, stuck his fingers in both ears and twisted them around. "See? Please, just a little while. We'll be careful."

"Yeah, Uncle Dawson. We'll be careful." Molly Anna chimed in.

He looked at the two eager little faces. "Back to the barn is okay, but *not* to the wood pile. Is that understood? I mean it, Joey."

"Yes, Daddy."

"We understands, Uncle Dawson." Molly Anna peeked out from behind Joey.

Kat shook her finger at them. "I'll call you only once for lunch. And you come right away. Do you hear me?"

"Yes ma'am." Joey said.

"Yes ma'am." Molly Anna repeated. The door slammed behind them.

"Kids!" Dawson gazed into the distance, then laid his hand on top of Kat's. "Honey, I know you're going to New York in the next week or so, and there's something I have to discuss with you before you leave."

"Sounds serious. I want to tell you something, too, Daw. You go first."

"All right. It's what we talked about briefly last night."

Her heart leapt to her throat. Her hand automatically slid down to protect her belly.

"We still haven't found someone to help with the ski lodge when Clancy is working with Bonny at the boutique. Polly Dee and Darrell can take care of housekeeping and maintenance like always. Cable can do the daily reports, handle reservations, and help in the kitchen. Winter's almost here, and the guests will be rolling in soon. I've put an ad in the *Wheeling Times* as well as surrounding areas. Shouldn't be too hard to find someone willing to work for the winter. I'm offering room and board plus salary."

"Honesty is a quality you've got to think about, Daw. Make sure you get good references."

"Yep. Most important, Kat."

"I hate to leave you in this situation." Kat hesitated. "But if you don't find someone by the time I should go, I'll just stay a couple days and come right back. Debbie is doing a fantastic job, but...well, you know, the boutique needs new pep and some *wow* factors. New designs for the January show are a must and..."

"We'll both be fine, Kat. I've already had two applicants. Their desirability is debatable, but someone will come along. More important than anything else, I want you to promise me that you'll take care of yourself."

"I'll be careful, sweetheart, but you must promise me that you'll do the same."

He stood up and laid a hand on her shoulder. "It's a deal. I worry about you, you know?"

Kat nodded. "I know how hard it will be to find someone as suitable as Bonny and Clancy. They're a dynamic team. The ski lodge seemed to come second nature to them. But then so does the fashion designing business." Kat said. "But Clancy will be free to devote most of his time to the lodge."

"Let's not forget about Conchita." Dawson raised his eyebrows.

"Ah, Conchita, she sure was the apple of Granddad's eye. Sweet, and sassy, spunky and very Mexican. It's funny how she came from a different culture, but she reminded him so much of Grandma Emma."

"Every guest we've had just falls in love with her. I don't think she realizes what a huge asset she is to the lodge. She and my little brother are quite a pair. And those twins? Cable's one lucky son-of-a gun."

"Conchita has also turned into quite a model. She's just the right size to show off the fashions. But getting back to the matter at hand, I don't plan on staying in New York too long. Debbie's keeping up with things. She's been working on some designs that I can't wait to see."

Dawson poured himself the last of the coffee from the coffeemaker. "I love you, honey. Don't worry about things here. You've got enough to do with the boutiques and Wolf International."

Kat laughed. "Fortunately, Wolf International is managing quite well with Lillian and Silka in charge. They've hired some great models and seamstresses. Rebecca has decided to get involved again. She said she felt much better now that her second round of chemo was over. And who knows more about the business than she does? She owned and ran the company for some time before she turned it over to me."

"Looks like you have matters under control, my busy and adorable executive wife. Now it's your turn. Tell me, what—"

"But I had a very smart mother who taught me well before she died. Then came the twelve-year-old kid who tucked me under his wing when I was only six and guided me along the right path."

"Yeah, right, and he has loved you since then and will forever. If only Suzanne Helen would have told you that Cable was not your biological father. She should have."

"Yeah, but we can't change that. Granddad denied knowing who my real father was, but I think he knew. I just don't understand why he didn't tell me."

"Call the kids, will you, hon? I'm going to start making sandwiches for lunch."

Kat stepped to the refrigerator and pulled out the makings for ham sandwiches with mayo and mustard, lettuce and tomatoes, and homemade bread and butter pickles.

Dawson opened the back door to call the children. They came running as soon as they heard him call, just like they promised, and nearly knocked him over as they charged through the door.

"Hey, Daddy, you know what? Molly Anna and me are gettin' married when we grow up. But, dang it, Daddy, she said I had to stop tryin' to kiss her or she wouldn't marry me."

"I don't want you to kiss me now, Joey Kahill. We need to wait till we're all growed up." Molly Anna frowned and pouted, looking first at Kat and then Dawson.

"That's what she said yesterday when we were playing at the ski lodge. I told her, "Molly Anna," I said, "I told cha! If ya don't want me to kiss ya, I won't try. But if I can't kiss ya, I won't marry ya. I'll just marry someone else that I can kiss."

"Just like a man," Kat said under her breath.

"What did you say, honey?"

She raised an eyebrow. "Just talking to myself."

"What did you say to that, Molly Anna?" Dawson tried to look concerned.

"Nothin. I just stuck my tongue out at him."

"Now listen to me, Joey. You are both too young to be talking about kissing and getting married. It's good you like each other and want to take care of each other, but kissing is for adults," Dawson said.

For a moment Joey looked like he was going to cry. "Well...maybe next year. We'll be in kindy-garden then." Joey wrinkled up his nose and tried to wink at Molly Anna. She giggled.

"I think that will be much better." Dawson covered his mouth to keep from laughing out loud.

"Dawson!" Kat scolded. "Don't tell them that."

"Why not, Mama? That's a long time away. I'll be all growed up by then."

"That's enough, Joey. You have plenty of time to be kissing girls. You pay attention to Molly Anna."

"Okay, but I wish Great-grandaddy was here. He'd tell me I didn't have to pay attention to no girl."

Molly Anna placed both hands on her hips. "No, Joey. That's wrong. Great-granddady would say, 'Molly Anna, you don't got to pay no attention to a silly ol' boy.'"

Kat coughed and covered her mouth with her hand. "That's the end of that now. Go wash your hands for lunch."

"Yes, ma'am, but—"

"No buts about it. Do as your mama says, Joey." Dawson gave them both a kiss on the forehead and sent them racing to the bathroom to wash up for lunch.

What would I ever do without Joey? I've built my whole life around that little fellow and his Mama. And now Molly Anna is like a daughter to me. I don't need another child. I have to tell Kat there won't be any more babies. I can't handle the possibility of losing her...

Chapter Six

*K*at hated to fly. How she ever got from West Virginia to Paris for the International Fashion Show without having a heart attack, she couldn't imagine. And she'd had to do it twice. Her quick trip home when Dawson took ill just before the show had been the turning point in her marriage, the time when she committed her heart and soul to Dawson, no matter what difficulties they would endure.

So why not drive to New York instead of flying? A one-hour flight made a lot more sense that a seven-hour drive. That didn't make flying any more desirable, but the less time away from Daw and Joey, the better. She hated leaving them even more than she hated flying; still at times, the New York boutique demanded her attention. She couldn't expect Deb to shoulder the full responsibility for making it a success.

She didn't like Pittsburgh International Airport Terminal any better than she did the flights that came and went. She'd heard the Allegheny airport terminal was the least hectic. Maybe she would try it on the way home. People scurried around like ants hurrying in and out of their anthills. The required procedure of checking bags and going through security, even for a short flight, irritated her; and the horror stories of passengers who were violated and humiliated by security personnel did nothing to make it a more desirable way to travel. But she accepted the necessity of it and appreciated that it had been created to make flights safer.

Fashions by Kat on Madison Avenue sat in the heart of the Big Apple. The shop required constant attention to maintain the early success that Wolf International Fashions had created when her winning design catapulted her from obscurity into the limelight. Her follow-up win at the last Paris show rocked the world once again, and business had been brisk ever since. She couldn't have hired better management than Debbie, yet the boutique's original designs bore *her* name and were sought after for the distinctive flair that only she created. And she loved the challenge. Like a magnet, she was drawn to meet the demands of the rich and fashionable circle of her loyal patrons. As proficient as Deb was at handling matters, she herself wanted to be a part of it all—the designs, window dressings, presentations, public relations, and everything else that made her boutiques unique.

The insane clamor at the airport hampered her attempts at audible conversation. So much chatter, the 'hellos' and 'goodbyes, the clatter of rolling luggage, the blaring loudspeaker that announced the flights—they all made her head begin to pound. In an effort to be heard, she had to shout when she bent to kiss Joey.

"Mama, when are ya coming back? I wish I could go with you. Will you be back by Christmas?"

"Yeah, will ya be back by Christmas, Aunt Kat?" Molly Anna echoed.

"Yeah, will you be home by Christmas, sweetheart?"

Dawson, Joey, and Molly Anna with straight faces, eyed each other, and then burst out laughing.

Kat smiled. "I'll try."

What would those children do without each other? Molly Anna copied Joey's every move. Jedediah's world revolved around the two little 'whippersnappers,' as he'd called them. When he died, it left a big hole in their days and their hearts.

"Aunt Kat, I'll write you a letter if you write to me. Will you? Please?"

"Yes, sweetie, of course I will."

Molly Anna had called her Aunt Kat from the time Clancy moved into their lives, and they became one large extended family. Bound by the youngsters who had been born on the same day and the baby girl that was left motherless, they were closer than many blood relatives. Thinking about Clancy with his seven boys and one little girl still boggled her mind. Thank goodness Bonny liked children.

She passed out another round of hugs and kisses and clung to Dawson for a long moment. "I have to hurry. They'll be calling my flight soon, and I need to get through security. I'll be home soon, kids. Take care of Daddy." She glanced at Molly Anna. "And Uncle Dawson. And be sure to brush your teeth, Joey."

"Yes ma'am, I will. I'll help Molly Anna brush her teeth and comb her hair, too."

"No you won't, Joey! I can do that stuff myself. And I don't want you to watch me."

"Oh, phooey! It's fun helping you, Molly Anna."

"Well, then you can if you want to. Just don't try to kiss me."

"Children!" Kat picked up her carry-on case. "I have to go now. Promise you'll be good?"

"We promise," Joey said.

"We promise," Molly Anna repeated.

Kat shook her head. "Those two will be the death of me yet. They're inseparable and insufferable at the same time."

Dawson winked at her and laughed. "Yeah, I know. They're going to get married—remember? Can you believe that? Take care of yourself, sweetheart. Remember, I'll be keeping the sheets warm."

Kat raised an eyebrow. "I bet you will. Can't say I won't be happy about that." She grinned wide. "Now, Daw, let me know if you hire someone to work at the lodge. If you don't get someone soon, I'll just come home and—"

"Stop right there. You do what you have to do, and I'll do what I have to do. Now, it's your turn to promise you won't think anymore about it, okay? Not that I wouldn't rather have you here with me." He wrapped his arms around her and whispered in her ear, "I love you, Katerina Kahill."

"I promise. Love you, too, *all* of you." She headed for the gate along with the other passengers.

"Love you," Joey hollered back.

"Love you," Molly Anna echoed.

She forced herself to board the plane. Someday, she wouldn't have to do this anymore. Much as she loved her work, a part of her looked forward to that time.

Closing her eyes, she felt the airplane's surge at takeoff. Soon, she could see the valleys between the mountains and on to the rim of the horizon and beyond.

Someday, I really will retire, and then I'll never fly again.

Chapter Seven

*F*ox Run stood tall and regal in the brilliance of its bright white exterior. The grounds covered hundreds of acres of lush gardens shaded with oaks, willow, and magnolia trees. In early spring, hues of pink and fuchsia azaleas created an aura of peaceful tranquility. Cannon Fox surveyed its elegance with an objective eye; it was almost as elegant and beautiful as Willow Walk—but not quite.

Bitter, caustic words, acidic with scorn, began early that Friday morning, just minutes after Cannon walked into the parlor at Fox Run. He had held out little hope that his conversation with his brother, Nick, would be anything less than adversarial. *All I need now is a pair of combat boots and a camouflage suit.*

Nick's superior attitude peeved him. For decades, their meetings had been nothing less than verbal fencing matches. Events of the past, the weather, the time of day—all topics, no matter how trivial, turned into verbal warfare. He knew it. His brother knew it. He tried to mellow their confrontations, but his efforts rarely worked. Instead, they spurred Nick on to be more disagreeable. Today the hostile attitude came on like the common cold.

Nicholas sat beside the hearth in the chair that had been passed down from one generation of Foxes to the next. A chair of many moods, its black leather upholstery and thick, ornate legs gave it a strong masculine look. Nicholas sat deep within its well-worn cushion, his assumed lordship over Fox Run apparent for all to see. His eyes, cold as marble, yet calm and silent, neither screamed nor darted. They just stared until the glare grew hot with resentment.

"I'm not asking for the world, Nick, just a little respect." He kept his voice even. "You know...basic human dignity?"

"Respect? Dignity? For you, Cannon? Just where do you think *that* would come from? I haven't any. Not a miserable damned bit. You ought to know that by now." Nicholas locked his gaze on his brother and refused to release it.

Looking eye-to-eye with him, Cannon tried to understand Nick's animosity. "I don't expect you to consider for one minute that I didn't know it was going to happen—Maggie..." Cannon paused in mid sentence.

"Say it, Cannon. Say it." Nicholas scowled as though he'd like to hit him for just breathing.

Cannon's thoughts exploded. He shoved his hands in the pockets of his patched jeans, turned his back on his brother, and walked to the huge picture window that overlooked the gardens. *I must be a glutton for punishment to think that a visit to Nicholas would turn out to be anything more than another clash.*

He missed a lot of family members he'd lost contact with, but missing Nick would be like missing a headache. No, it wasn't his brother he missed—it was Fox Run, the splendid family homestead. Why should he expect anything different from Nicholas, now? Even when they were children playing games, they were never on the same side.

"Wouldn't it be nice if we could put an end to all the pretense? I didn't want the controversy. I didn't choose the trouble. Now, in spite of it all, I'd do it all over again. Maggie is the sweetest human being in this whole corrupt world. She's better than any Fox ever hoped to be. If she can understand and cope with it, then, I dare say, it's none of the family's business. All you're worried about is what people will think. This age old story has been a thorn in my side for years. Quite frankly, I'm sick of it." Cannon paused. "Sometimes the truth costs a great deal, Nicolas, but it's always less expensive than the price we pay for hiding behind false pride."

"You're explanation has always left doubt in my mind, Cannon. What proof do you have that Maggie's *difference* came from our side of the family? It could have come from Lucy's side. What happened to our great-great grandfather's records that are supposed to hold the answers to these questions?"

"Damn you, brother. May God forgive you." Heat rose from his chest to burn his face. The fury of a cornered animal blazed in his eyes.

"Don't you dare curse me and summon heaven to forgive *me*."

"And don't you dare be pompous with me. I told you time and again that Great-great-grandfather Ezra found greener pastures, and the rest is history. Ezra's father was so embarrassed when he found out what happened that he immediately sold the slave, Pearl, and her brother, Bo, to the Kahills. But you know all that. You read Ezra's journal—I know you did." He hesitated, waiting for his brother to answer. Nicholas lowered his head but said nothing. "The whole episode was kept quiet. The boy, Sheldon, was born dark skinned, but not dark enough for anyone to be certain of his heritage. He was our grandfather, Nicolas. His blood flows in us, including Maggie. Can't you get that through your thick skull? The African bloodline chooses no particular time to show up, and now it's chosen Maggie."

"No need for insolence, Cannon." Nick didn't raise his head, but he lifted his eyes and bored a hole through him. "You could have stood up to Dad when

Maggie was born. You could have told him that Maggie was a Fox, no matter what the color of her skin, and that her mother's side of the family did not have an interracial heritage. That heritage belongs solely to the Foxes."

Cannon shook his head. "I could have done a lot of things, like show him the book, but I didn't. We've gone over this time and again, Nicholas. Everything's recorded in Ezra's journal. For years, it was in the old trunk in the attic. I know you must have read it." An angry flush crept up his neck and burned his cheeks. "Nick, if you can't believe the man who admits his own indiscretions, you're doomed to wallow in stupidity." He stopped at the thunderous sound of his own voice. He'd intended his words to be as spiny as thorns, but the last thing he wanted from this visit was a shouting match. Raising his voice would do nothing to cure his brother's reasoning problem.

"I did read the journal, and it made absolutely no sense. I dare say it wouldn't make sense now either. Anyway...it's nowhere to be found, Cannon, so it's a moot point."

"Oh, no, don't come off with that excuse. It's been here at Fox Run forever, and if it's not here now, you know where it is. What did you so with it, Nick? Did you destroy it so no one would ever know that the Fox bloodline wasn't *pure*? Let me tell you something, brother. No matter what the skin color, the blood is red. Impurity isn't in the color of the skin—it's in the heart." He waited for some reaction. None came. "That journal contains the truth, the secret we've lived with...and hidden...for generations. But you—you don't want to admit to the wrongdoing of any of our ancestors. It's time we opened the closet doors and let the skeletons out. Don't you see that? You're too damned self- righteous. It's always been someone else who muddies the waters, never a Fox. But this is our family heritage, like it or not, Nick."

"How about putting the blame where it lies—in *your* court? You're the one who knew the big dark secret before any of us. You could have refrained from... you know exactly what I mean."

"Yeah, I know what you mean. You're insinuating it would be better to let the Fox line die out than to acknowledge that it's contaminated with black blood. And by the way, *contaminated* is the wrong word, brother. The Fox bloodline has been *enriched* with the likes of Maggie. It's your loss that you can't seem to grasp that." He threw his arms in the air. "The hell with you! I came here to tell you I'm going to expose it all. It's long past the time for getting things out in the open. I had hoped we could be civil with each other, come to an agreement about this, and present a united front, but that obviously isn't going to happen. I guess we'll never be in accord about anything."

"You're right that we'll never be in accord about anything that *blackens* the good Fox name."

Cannon laughed, but without mirth. "*Blackens*? That's a good one, brother. Remember what I said about impurities of the heart. We're long past the evils of slavery and segregation." He stifled the tirade that threatened to erupt. "I have an interview for a job at a ski lodge close to here."

Nick gave him a cold, hard look.

"Yeah, you know the place. Jedediah's grandson, Dawson, runs it."

"Cable's kid." Nicholas shook his head. "I sure hope he's a better man than his father was."

"Jed thought the sun rose and set in that boy, so you can be sure he's a good man. You know the old man had no use for his son, Cable. Funny thing, though, Jed found out just before his boy died that Cable had suffered for years with a brain tumor. That was apparently the reason for his surly personality and despicable character."

"I guess that's as good a way as any to pass off bad genes. Blame it on a brain tumor. Cable Kahill was a worthless piece of human trash. Tumor or no tumor, he was no credit to the *esteemed* Kahill family name."

"You're impossible, Nick. It's no wonder you're wasting away here alone. Nobody wants to be with someone who can't see the good folks all around— even those named Kahill." He took a deep breath and let it out. "I don't want them to know who I am. Not yet. I want to meet my daughter, and I want to redeem myself if possible. There's so much I need to tell her, and she needs to know she has a sister."

"Do what you want. But as far as Jedediah goes, he was no different than the rest of the Kahill clan."

"Hmmm...I really feel sorry for you, brother. You'll never have a friend like Jed because you don't care about anyone but yourself. I'm only telling you about my plans so you won't be blindsided when the truth comes out. Do what you like with all your wealth—the wealth you've horded. I don't need it, and I don't want it. I threw mine away—so be it." Cannon's shoulders slumped. He turned and started to leave.

"Wait." Nicholas rounded the corner of his desk and opened the top drawer. He pulled out his checkbook and began to write. "Cannon, I would like to share with you what is mine, especially Fox Run, and I will, but first you need to show some responsibility for your own life. You know what Dad would say. 'Manage your finances even though you have enough to waste. You can't borrow yourself out of debt. Spend only your money that makes money. Leave the rest alone.'"

"Why are you doing this, Nick?"

"I'm really not the jerk you think I am." He allowed his voice to become very gentle. "If and when you get back on your feet, you'll be welcome here at Fox Run." He offered Cannon a check. "A little advice, brother. Whether you choose to see me again or not, the first thing you better do is clean yourself up. You'll never get a job looking like a bum." His expression was somber as he extended the check in his left hand, and the right one to his brother.

His anger had run its course. *Give it up Cannon. Reasoning with Nicholas is like trying to describe the colors of a sunset to a blind man.* He reached for Nick's right hand first. The strong clasp that said more than any words could have. He maintained eye contact as long as he could, swallowed hard, and accepted the money. "Thanks, Nick. Someday I'll pay you back."

"Yeah, sure." Nick sat down at his desk and shuffled papers around.

Cannon opened the door and then turned slowly back toward his brother. "Even a blind squirrel finds an acorn every now and then. I've been blind too long. It's time to find a few acorns." He walked out, closing the door behind him. He'd come out of that battle scarred, but in one piece. *Like it or not, Nick, I'm going to claim my daughter. Correct that—my other daughter.*

The following Saturday, Cannon Fox emerged from the dark pit he'd crawled into so long ago. For the first time in a long time, life seemed worth living. His new clothes suited a man who was applying for a job in a posh ski resort. He had taken his brother's words to heart. Being in the same room with Nicolas had made him feel like a draft horse beside a racing thoroughbred. He'd purchased a new suit for the interview at the lodge, gotten a haircut, and shaved off the scraggly beard.

Cannon, old boy, you clean up pretty good. I'd forgotten how dashing you are when you're clean-shaven and dressed up a bit. He smiled, staring into the cracked floor length mirror.

He would have to assume a bogus identity when he applied for the job at Willow Walk Ski Lodge. Being recognized as a Fox would kill his entire plan, but it was a chance he had to take if he was going to get to know his daughter. Nothing would get in the way of that. He couldn't fail after all these years. He might never get another chance.

He took one more glance in the mirror and slicked his hair back. *Hmmm... mirrors are like journals. They don't lie. But I have to lie. It's for a good cause, isn't it?*

The money from Nicholas got him out of the abandoned building and into a decent little house. The place looked a little lopsided, but it was clean and he didn't have to share it with any furry critters. In a way, he'd grown used to his hermit-type existence—even liked it. His way of life had no time schedules, no commitments, no one to answer to. How strange that the very things that recommended it also condemned it as no life at all. He feared failure in his new venture, but he wouldn't fail, *couldn't* fail. He'd get used to wearing dress shirts and ties and remember how to act the gentleman with impeccable manners and dandyisms. He wiped a tear from the corner of his eye.

That's not the problem. What about my daughter? I've neglected her all her life. Will she accept me at this late date? Will she give me a chance?

Chapter Eight

*C*annon stood before the immense entry doors of the ski lodge. He turned to look again at the beautifully landscaped grounds. *Jed was right about you, Dawson Kahill, you do have class. My little girl has class, too. I just hope I can muster up enough of my own to make this work.* He took a deep breath, straightened his shoulders, and opened the doors.

Stopping short just inside, he stared at the expansive interior. Never had he imagined that rustic could also be so luxurious. Overcome with a sudden sense of not belonging, he searched for the men's room and hurried into its sanctuary. A large oval mirror with a handcrafted wooden frame reflected the insecurity that overwhelmed him inside. *Get yourself together or you'll never be able to pull this off. You may be dressed in Sears' best instead of hand-tailored Saks Fifth Avenue, but you cleaned up nice.* He straightened his tie. *I bet if Jed were here, he'd tell me I look like a used Chevy with a fresh coat of paint, trying to pass myself off as a Mercedes Benz.* A nervous ache anchored itself in the pit of his stomach. What had happened to his confidence? All he had now was a bad case of the jitters.

He shook his head to dispel something he couldn't quite describe, something that scared the hell out of him. Could he hold fast to this new life and the commitments he had made to his brother and himself? He had no choice if he expected to regain his right as part owner of Fox Run and the respect of his daughter. Suddenly, he understood why Nicholas had turned him away from the old homestead. He had failed miserably in his responsibilities for the care of the estate. He wasn't worthy of one plank of wood on the big house or one blade of grass from the massive grounds. Proving himself morally and ethically worthy of Fox Run would put him in a man's shoes again. He needed this job. He needed his daughter. He needed his dignity.

With renewed determination, he entered the lobby and looked around. *Wow! This is like being in a gigantic forest of cedar, pine, and spruce.* A low whistle escaped his lips. He marveled at the seamless blending of nostalgic Early American decor and modern architecture. *So this is the good life— the new life I hope to fit into.*

The height of the open beamed ceiling and the vastness of the outdoors blazing through the plate glass window nearly swallowed him up. The log walls soared up, up, up until they reached the cedar beams. The cathedral ceiling seemed to pierce the sky. The slight aroma of cedar wood and pine drifted past his nose. Orange-blue flames crackled and spiraled upward from the four-sided stone fireplace in the center of the room. The ambiance made it difficult for him to concentrate on the task that lay ahead.

Jed's words came rushing back to him. He could almost see his old friend's mustache wiggle and his heavy gray eyebrows spring up and down like they used to when he talked. He forced himself to focus on what Jed had told him about Dawson. *Yes, sir, Cannon. I'll have you know that grandson of mine is nothin' like his sorry father. College was a playhouse to Cable and a place to chase skirts. I pulled him out before the university beat me to it. I tell you, Cable isn't the first Kahill to ignore moral decency, but he's the first that I know of to never waver from it. At least some folks learn from their mistakes. And then there's Dawson. He studied, made good grades, and earned his master's degree with honors. Bad as I hate to say it, Cable isn't worth a nickel off a dead man's eyes. I gave him every chance in the world to own up to the Kahill name and make something of himself, but he was all take and no give. That's why Dawson's going to inherent Willow Walk when I die. With the ol' homestead in my grandson's hands, it will thrive and become home to many future Kahills. I won't leave it in the hands of someone who doesn't give a dang about it. Don't get me wrong, I love my son in spite of his faults—I just don't like him.*

The winter season had just begun. A few early arrivals sat around the fireplace, sipping drinks, but no one seemed to notice him. On the far side of the room, stairs led to an upper floor that was cantilevered over the lobby. A balustrade surrounded the walkway around the guest rooms. What a clever layout. The notion of working in this magnificent lodge spurred him on. Shoving aside the sadness over Jed's death, the nagging of his brother, and his own feelings of inadequacy, he threw back his shoulders and walked over to the large, red-haired man behind the registration desk.

Green eyes sparkled and lit up the clerk's face. With Irish enthusiasm and a greeting smile, he said, "Top o' the mornin' to ya, sir. How can I be of help?"

Cannon grinned. It must have taken five storks to deliver this fellow to his parents. "Uh...yes, sir. I'm answering your ad in the paper for employment." He tried to interject a professional, businesslike quality into his voice, but he sounded more like a bullfrog croaking at the moon.

The man, still smiling, seemed not to notice. "Have ye ever done desk clerk work before?"

"No, but I learn fast."

The clerk nodded. "'Tis good to have confidence." The man reached under the desk and pulled out a form. My name be Clancy. Clancy O'Malley. And what might yours be?"

He hesitated. "Uh...Joe."

Lies came too easily these days. He gazed past Clancy to the vast expanse outside the window. Lying to the Kahills was the last thing he wanted to do, but what choice did he have? Heat crept up his neck toward his cheeks. What would Jed think? He knew exactly what that ol' boy would say. *Don't ya be for lyin, Cannon Fox. Stand up and tell the dad-gum truth, man.* Maybe he should do that, just come right out and say who he was and why he was there.

"Well, me good man, so ye be Joe? Ye mean you're only havin' one name? Or do ye have a last name?" Those green eyes twinkled, radiating more cheerfulness than he had ever seen.

He smiled. "Sorry, it's...it's Williams. Joe Williams. *He must think I'm an idiot who doesn't even know his own name.*

"Take this to a table over there, fill 'er out, and we'll go from there." Clancy handed him the application and they shook hands.

Joe Williams? Nice name but it doesn't match my social security number. The name thing hadn't even occurred to him. He walked to the table, silently cursing himself for being forty-seven kinds of a fool. *I've got a better chance of catching a bat in a flytrap than landing this job.*

He took a seat at the small round table by the window, dropped the application, and looked out. The hill, bare of trees, offered a clear view of the ski slope that cut a swath into the depths of the valley. Snowflakes big as cotton balls drifted lazily toward the ground. Heavy clouds floated overhead, depositing their load as they crept along. The more fresh snow on the ground, the better it would be for lodge business. But the thought of Jed buried in the cold ground bothered him until he remembered his friend's words on a fine spring day. They were sitting on the bench in the cemetery, their usual meeting place, when Jed spoke up. "Someday when you and me are reunited, we'll remember sittin' here in the breeze, beatin' up our gums." His booming laugh rang through Cannon's head. "Mind you, I'm not hopin' that'll be soon, but time has a way of catchin' up with us, and I've been borrowin' it for some years now." *It was too soon for you to go, ol' friend.* He hung his head, stared at his application, and tapped the table with his fingers.

He looked at the information required. Name, address, social security number. Name? Address? Social security number? He brought a hand up and pressed it against his forehead. *Why didn't I consider all these details in advance?* He sat there for several moments, considering the matter. Something he'd had to memorize back in his school days came to mind. Poet Sir Walter Scott could not have more accurately stated his predicament.

Oh what tangled webs we weave,
When first we practice to deceive.

He wrote his assumed identity, Joe Williams, and jotted down the address of the little place he had just rented. It was in a respectable neighborhood and certainly more acceptable than Skid Row. Social security number? He frowned and rubbed his chin, then transposed the last two digits of his own number. Contact information? He could be reached day or night on his new cell phone.

A few minutes later, he gave Clancy O'Malley a big smile, another handshake, and his completed application. "This is a great place. Your visitors look quite content, and you're the best advertisement going. I've never felt more welcome anywhere than I did when you greeted me a little while ago." A brief memory of all the times his brother had ordered him away from Fox Run flitted through his mind.

"I thank ye kindly, sir. It's been me pleasure to meet ya. And who knows, we may be seeing lots more of ye around here."

Cannon gave him another smile. "I hope so." He squared his shoulders, turned, and walked out.

The call came two days later.

"Mr. Williams, this is Dawson Kahill at Willow Walk Ski Lodge. I want you to know the job here is yours if you still want it."

"You bet...I mean, yes, sir, I do."

"Clancy seemed to think your pleasant personality would be a good fit with us here, and that won you the job over our other applicants. Working with the public demands a friendly smile and a good attitude, no matter how trying the circumstance or the day."

"Thank you, sir. I appreciate the chance to prove Clancy right."

"Just call me Dawson. We're far removed from formalities around here. You'll train with Clancy for a couple weeks—maybe three. We'll see how you do and then move you to the night shift, three o'clock to eleven o'clock. Come in Monday morning for the seven o'clock shift. Wear dark trousers and a white shirt or sweater. Any questions?"

"Not at present. Thank you again for hiring me, Mr. Kah...uh, Dawson. I'll do my best to fulfill your expectations. I'll be there at seven o'clock Monday morning."

"We'll see you then. Good-bye, Joe."

He flipped his cell shut, swirled around, and whooped. "I wish you could see me now, Jed. I got the job! Maybe there's hope for me yet." Life was looking up. He would do all he could to keep it that way.

He went straight to the kitchen to make coffee and then headed for his closet to see if he had suitable clothes for his new job. The things he'd retrieved from Fox Run were old, dingy, and several sizes too large. *I can't use any of these things and go to work dressed like I live in a homeless shelter. Tomorrow, I'll buy a couple pairs of trousers, three or four nice white shirts and maybe a sweater for really cold days. I want to look like I belong behind that registration desk.*

Monday rolled around before he was ready. He arrived at the lodge ten minutes early and was welcomed by Clancy's grin and a hardy pat on the back. He learned the basic workings of the cash register, how to check guests in and out, how to process a credit card, and the importance of being polite. Learning to smile even when someone gave you a hard time didn't always come natural, but it was the way things had to be done. The cardinal sin when working the desk, according to Clancy, was to make a guest—even an out-of-sorts one—feel unwelcome.

A nice looking fellow relieved him at three o'clock. His resemblance to a young Jedediah had him doing a double take. Maybe he was a relative. It wouldn't surprise him. The Kahill family could fill a football field with relatives.

"Joe," Clancy said, looking at him. "This is Cable Kahill, Dawson's brother. We call him Cabe."

"Don't you mean half-brother, Clancy?" Cable grinned. "Nice to have you aboard, Joe. You listen to Clancy here, and you'll get along fine."

"Away wid yerself, Cable. Half brother, whole brother, don't matter a flip. Ye think God doesn't look over both of ye?"

Joe looked confused. Cable caught his eye with a wink.

"Thanks, Mr. Kahill. I'll certainly do my best," He gave Cable a crooked smile, not sure how he should react.

"We're on a first name basis around here, Joe. Call me Cable. This overgrown Irishman has a heart as big as New York and a temper to match, just like my Grandfather's. So you'd best be warned upfront."

Suddenly, Cannon recalled Jed's telling him something about Clancy. Now he understood why the big Irishman seemed familiar.

"Stall the Ball, Cable, me bucko. Mine be the temperament of a *lover*." Clancy rolled his eyes first at Cable, then Cannon. A smiled tugged at the corner of his mouth. "If me ol' side-kick Jeddy were alive, he'd set ye straight, he would all right."

• • • • •

Two weeks passed. Glad that he'd not totally pickled his brain with the cheap anesthetic in a bottle, he caught on to his duties fast and was ready to start the night shift on his own. He was closing out the register and preparing the daily report under Clancy's watchful eye when Dawson walked up to the desk.

"Hey, Clancy." Dawson refilled the bin of folios. "Kat's flying home today. She said the weather is horrendous in New York, but the flight was still scheduled to leave on time. She's going to do a little shopping in Pittsburgh before she comes home. I wanted to meet her but she said she didn't want to be worried about me waiting for her while she shopped."

"Well, ye know how that goes." Clancy said.

"Yeah. She hates flying anyway."

"Ye fret, me boy, when ye shouldn't."

"I hope you're right."

Clancy picked up the phone. "Willow Walk Ski Lodge. Top o' the mornin to ye. How may I be of service?...Yes, he's here. One moment." He handed the phone to Dawson.

"Hello. Yes, this is Dawson Kahill."

The words on the other end of the line almost stopped his heart. He fumbled to re-cradle the receiver and dropped it on the floor. Fear exploded in his middle and traveled like shrapnel along his veins. He turned to face Clancy and Cannon and tried to speak. No sound came out.

"Might ye tell us what's wrong, Dawson? You be as white as a snow cap mountain. What is it, me friend?"

His mouth trembled. His eyes gleamed with unshed tears. "It's...it's...there's been an accident. Kat is...Kat's in...in Allegheny Mountain Hospital outside Pittsburgh."

Chapter Nine

*P*eople groaned, moaned, and waited in wheel chairs, fidgeting, wiping their eyes, and slumping against those sitting next to them. Allegheny Mountain Hospital's ER waiting area overflowed with sick and injured folks.

Dawson's heart pounded. His stomach lurched. He couldn't go through this again...couldn't lose her. He headed straight for the line at the receptionist's window.

A nurse approached. Not waiting for his turn to speak with the receptionist, he touched her arm. "Could you tell me where my wife is? Katerina Kahill? She was in the plane wreck. I've driven in from Wheeling, and..." A fresh wave of tears filled his eyes. His voice stuck somewhere in his vocal cords and refused to continue.

Her stressed look mellowed into a compassionate smile. "Follow me, sir."

"Thank you. I—"

"I understand, sir. When you're worried about a loved one, trying to get where you need to go in a strange hospital is like losing your way in a maze. We're trying to put the injured passengers who have been sent to us together with family. I'll be glad to help you find your wife if she's here."

He wished her feet would move along as fast as her mouth did, but she seemed to have only one speed...slow. He followed closely on her heels through a set of double doors that led them into a room partitioned off into numerous cubicles surrounded with muslin curtains. Medial workers scurried in and out, carrying trays of medical instruments, saline bags, oxygen tanks, and more. Urgent as their deliveries might be, they all served to delay his finding the person who meant the most to him in the whole world. He wanted to call out, *Kat, where are you?*

"Wait here, sir. I'll have someone take you to your wife." She left him standing beside the nurses' station. *That must mean she's alive.* It seemed like he'd been there for hours, but it couldn't have been more than minutes.

The nurses' station buzzed like a beehive, but no one seemed to notice him. Precious moments passed. For all he knew, they could have been Kat's last. He'd had enough waiting. *I'll find her myself before it's too... No. I'm not going to lose her.* He looked first one direction, then the other. *Which way?*

A gray-haired nurse approached. "May I help you?"

"I'm trying to find my wife. She was in the plane accident."

Standing on one foot and then the other, he listened while she asked him a million immaterial questions. Name, address, telephone number, everything except *do you wear jockey or boxer shorts*? He would have been happy to give her that information if he thought it would get him to Kat any faster.

"Ma'am." Dawson clenched his teeth to keep from showing the animosity that was rapidly building within him. "I'm not answering any more questions until I've seen my wife. She could be dying, and you're asking me questions that I can answer later, *after* I see her. I mean no offense but *please* take me to her... *now*."

Clearly taken aback by his tone of voice, she gave him a blank stare that after a moment softened into one of concern. She even managed a sympathetic smile as she motioned for him to follow her.

Disconcerting sounds invaded his ears as they passed one cubicle after cubicle. He heard murmurs, metal clanking against metal, cries of pain, and beeping monitors. He did *not* hear the only sound he longed for...Kat's voice. She was in the last cubical on the right. He caught only a glimpse of her before a state trooper barred the way with one robust arm.

"Hello, officer. I'm Dawson Kahill. My...my wife is in there."

The trooper laid his hand on his arm when he stepped toward the opening of the curtain.

"I'm Officer Striker. Nurses and doctors are working over your wife now. I'm sure they'll let you know when you can see her." The officer's robust, tin-soldier stance seemed to tower over Dawson's six-foot, two-inch height.

"Sorry, I can't wait for them." He took a breath and let it out, forcing the agitation in his voice to relax. "Please, I really need to see her. I've almost lost her once. I just need to know that she's going to be okay. *Please...*"

"Be patient, Mr. Kahill." Striker held fast to his arm. "I'm sure you don't want to get in their way."

Standing motionless, he glanced at Striker's hand on his arm. *Be reasonable. Demands won't get you in to see Kat any sooner.* "No...no, I don't. But someone needs to tell me what's going on." He stepped back, trying to forestall the flow of tears that paraded down his cheeks.

"I'm sorry, Mr. Kahill. I understand your frustration. They're doing all they can. You came from Wheeling?"

"Yes...from...from Wheeling. What do you mean, they're doing all they can? That sounds bad."

"As far as I know, they're still doing tests. I'm sure the doctor will be out to talk to you as soon as he knows something. It's a long drive from Wheeling under these circumstances."

"Longer than you can possibly imagine."

"Mr. Kahill, please, sit down over there." Striker pointed to a chair against the wall. "The doctor will be with you shortly."

Sit down? At a time like this? Yeah, right, a long drive and now sit down and wait. What did they think he was made of? He always thought of himself as a strong man. Granddad Jedediah had taught him well. But now...Kat could be dying. He wanted to collapse, but he could almost hear what Granddad would say. *Sonny, get hold of yourself. You're acting like a weakling. This is not how you were taught. Let the doctors and nurses do their jobs. Have faith, son. Have faith.*

"I know you're right." He replied aloud to Jed's imagined words that could have just as well been meant for Striker and sniffed. He trudged to the chair against the wall, sat down, and nodded at the trooper. "Can you tell me anything about the accident? How did it happen? *Where* did it happen?"

Striker's gaze traveled to the floor then back to Dawson. "The cause of the plane crash has not been determined. We understand the plane skidded about halfway down the runway, looped on the ground, and started going backwards over the hillside. A few hundred feet farther and it would have plunged off into a much deeper ravine. Three fatalities. Several critically injured. The rest had mostly minor cuts, bruises, and bumps. It was a miracle that so many survived." He paused and looked hard into Dawson's tear-filled eyes. "I know how hard this must be for you, Mr. Kahill."

"Is my wife one of the critical ones?"

"I don't know. But I do know you can be thankful she wasn't killed."

"I am *very* thankful."

Striker patted him on the shoulder. "I hope she'll be good as new real soon."

Officer Striker walked away, and Dawson's legs almost buckled under him when he stood. He leaned against the wall hoping, it would hold him up. When the shaking in his legs didn't subside, he sank back onto the chair, bowed his head, and covered his face. Fresh tears punctuated his prayer. "Dear Father, why didn't I stop her from going...or driven her to New York myself?" he whispered.

"You had no way of knowing something like this was going to happen."

He looked up to see Striker standing over him again. "I just found out the cause may not have been an icy runway. A passenger said he heard a loud pop that might have been a tire blowout. Another said he noticed no plane sag that would indicate a tire blowout. It's all speculation right now, of course. The investigation will uncover the truth about what happened."

Dawson leaned his head against the wall and closed his eyes. "I just can't believe this has happened. As much as she hated it, she flew so she could get back to us quicker. I don't..."

The curtain swooshed to the side. He forced his shaky legs to push him into a standing position and held his breath.

"Are you Mr. Kahill?" A nurse spoke to him from the opening.

"Yes, ma'am."

"Please come in."

Officer Striker reached into his shirt pocket, pulled out a card, and handed it to him. "I can be reached at this number if you have questions or just need to talk. I don't give this information to many folks, but I really want to know how you wife gets along. I'm sorry, Mr. Kahill. I wish you both the best."

"Thank you, officer." Dawson stepped inside the cubical. Stifling the gasp that rose in his throat, he stared at his wife. She looked like a science experiment from a thriller movie. Her face, bruised and swollen, barely resembled the woman he loved more than life itself. Tubes and wires ran from her body to monitors and bags of fluids suspended from mobile IV stands. A monitor attached to her chest beeped to the tune of her life. He wiped away more tears.

He laid his hand gently on her shoulder. "Kat, can you hear me? Sweetheart?"

She didn't answer or open her eyes. Her black hair against the white pillow framed her unrecognizable face. He gazed upward to the steel and concrete and closed his eyes. *Don't make me live without her. Please, God, don't let her die.*

"Mr. Kahill, I'm Doctor Hamilton."

Dawson turned toward the voice behind him and reached out his hand. It trembled despite his supreme effort to stop it. He strained to hear above the drumbeat of his pulse in his ears.

"Hello...uh...Doctor Hamilton, was it?" He cast a painful look over his shoulder at Kat. "Is she going to be all right? It's taken so long to get to see her."

"I'm sorry. It takes time to perform the tests. So far the examination shows a concussion, which we expected. How severe it is, we don't know yet. We did a CAT scan, and that indicated no bleeding or bruising inside the brain. Her memory and ability to concentrate are somewhat impaired, as are her reflexes and balance. Again, to what degree we can't be sure yet. These are normal symptoms of a concussion. We haven't found any internal problems or broken bones, but we will do some further testing. We'll keep a close watch on her for a few days, but the signs at this point are all good. The baby seems fine. That's as much as I can tell you for now."

"The baby?" *What baby!* "Oh...oh, yes, the baby. That's great news." The doctor's voice droned on, but he heard nothing more. A hundred thoughts raced through his mind. *That's what she kept trying to tell me before she left, but she was afraid to say anything because I kept spouting off about no more babies. She thought I wouldn't share her enthusiasm. I'm not sure I do. Having a baby could cost her life. But this accident nearly did that. It could have taken both of them. I can't lose her. I can't lose either one of them.*

The doctor's voice stopped. Dawson reached out to shake his hand.

"Thank you, Doctor Hamilton. I appreciate all you're doing."

"We'll be moving her to a private room very soon."

If he's moving her to a private room, she must not be critical. Otherwise, he'd put her in intensive care...wouldn't he? He dared to breathe a small sigh of relief. The medical personnel moved out of the cubicle, and they were at last alone. The anticipated homecoming—Joey and Molly waiting at Willow Walk with cupcakes and balloons—wasn't going to happen, not today anyway. Disaster had struck like a cyclone out of nowhere, and he was catapulted into a world of unknown conditions. *A baby? I can't even think about that right now. I wish you'd told me, Kat. I understand why you didn't, but I still wish...*

His fingers curled around the bed railing and tightened until his knuckles were the color of the sheets. He stood motionless, gazing down at her. Her eyes blinked and opened, first one, then the other, as if in slow motion.

"Daw? Where am I? What are all these wires? Everything hurts. What happened?"

"You were in a plane wreck, sweetheart. You're in the hospital, but you're going to be fine. You're okay. The baby's okay. Everything's okay."

For a moment she stared at him. "Oh, Daw, you didn't know about the baby."

"I know now. The doctor told me."

"I'm...I'm sorry you had to find out this way. I was going to tell you as soon as I got home. Are you mad at me? Are you happy about the baby? Oh, Daw, I want you to be happy." Her eyelids snapped shut before he had the chance to answer her. "I can't seem to stay awake."

"What's not to be happy about? We're going to have a beautiful little girl as lovely as her mother." He reached out and gripped her cold hand. "I love you, Kat. You mean everything to me. You always have."

Her eyelids fluttered open. "I love you, too, Daw. I'm so happy to be having your baby again. It's a dream come true." She frowned. "Oh...oh...I remember now. Allegheny Mountain Hospital, Doctor...uh...I can't remember his name."

"Hamilton. Dr. Hamilton. It's time for you to rest. Orders from the doctor—and from me."

"I'm so sleepy. Please don't leave me. I...I..."

"I won't leave you, I promise."

He sat in a straight chair next to her bed until late into night, when a nurse and an orderly brought in a recliner. They apologized over and over for his long hours of discomfort as they situated the chair next to the bed.

As soon as they left, he sank into its overstuffed cushions and pushed back so he could stretch out. His eyes closed, but his mind refused to shut down. He had texted Bonny and Debbie during his hours of waiting for her to wake up. Debbie would contact Silka Sinclair and Lillian Rae of Wolf International Fashions so they knew to expect a delay in Kat's designs for the Paris show. All this business stuff seemed so unimportant, but she would want him to take care of it. The only thing that mattered was that she get well and that she...not lose the baby. If she did, she would be crushed. But if she didn't, he would worry the whole pregnancy. Everything would be all right. He must believe that. With a plea in his heart and a prayer on his lips, he fell into a restless sleep.

Kat awoke in the tangle of covers. "Daw, are you here? I can't open my eyes. Help me!"

His hand grasped hers. "It's alright, Kat. I'm here. Just be calm so you don't disconnect the monitors."

The sound of his voice broke through her panic. She took a breath, then another, and tried to force her eyes open. Slowly two slits opened enough for her to make out his face. Something like a mallet kept knocking her in the head. Her arms wouldn't move, and her legs felt anchored to the bed. She felt more than saw his penetrating gaze—wide, worried, questioning. His disheveled hair, wrinkled brow, and red eyes didn't look like her Daw. Was something more wrong that he hadn't told her? Was it the baby? Again, the panic rose to suffocate her. Her whole body began to shake. Why was she tied down?

"Daw, what's happened to me?" Her swollen mouth tried to turn up. Even that wouldn't work. Nothing worked. "Am I dying? I have to live so our baby can live."

He laid his hand over hers. "You're in the hospital, sweetheart. There was a plane crash and..."

"Oh...that's right...you know about the baby. I didn't want you to find out like this. I...I...can you forgive me?" She faded away. Faces with no bodies floated in gray fog, up and down and sideways, some coming so close she could almost feel their breath. Her head seemed anchored to the pillow. Whispered screams, including her own, filled the space and then dissipated. She felt like she was going to throw up.

Dawson watched her short, jagged breaths ease into regular, peaceful ones. What was going on in that head of hers that kept her so agitated when she was awake? He tried to accept what had happened, to look at the big picture. He couldn't. The one thought that recurred time and again and forced all others away was the baby. How could this have happened? Kat had been on the pill since Joey was a few months old. She shouldn't be pregnant—unless...no, she would never have gone off it without talking to him—would she? A cloud of bewilderment hung over him until he thought his head would burst. *Can Kat survive having another baby?*

She woke several times during the day, but only for brief periods. He kept the conversation light and each time reassured her that all was well with her, the baby, and everyone at Willow Walk. Putting her mind to rest about Joey seemed to soothe her most of all. He talked with Carla several times during the day, Deb and Bonny texted him every hour on the hour, and a nurse reported a call from a man who inquired about her condition but did not identify himself.

That night he awoke every time she moved or moaned. When someone delivered a breakfast tray, he bolted upright, groggy and disoriented. Moments later, Doctor Hamilton entered the room, freshly shaved and bearing a cheerful smile that could only come from a good night's sleep.

"Good morning, Mr. Kahill." He extended his hand. Turning to his patient, he added, "All the test results are in, and everything looks good. It will take time for the bruises to heal, and you may continue to have headaches for a few days. Make sure you get a lot of rest, especially since you're recuperating for two." He looked at Dawson. "If things go well today, she can go home tomorrow. She's been concerned about the baby, but all the monitored information indicates that little one's just fine. Her focus is coming back, and that's a good sign."

"Doctor, should we expect side effects from the concussion? Anything we should be on the outlook for, especially since her first pregnancy was difficult?"

"We'll discuss all that tomorrow when she's released. You'll need to get her to your family doctor and obstetrician soon as you get back to Wheeling. The nurse will get their names, and we'll send them our records."

"Hello. I'm still awake. I can hear you talking about me." Kat laughed as heartily as her aching body and bruised face would allow.

Doctor Hamilton smiled and patted her on the arm. "I know you're getting well now. You're feisty. Are you ready to go home?"

"You bet I am."

Kat gave Dawson a shaky smile after the doctor left, turned her head, and closed her eyes.

He searched her face, trying to grasp the reason for the sense of foreboding that kept creeping into his consciousness. Dread of something he couldn't name pooled itself into a glacial pond somewhere in the vicinity of his stomach.

Why? The doctor obviously thinks everything will be okay. You're feeling it, too, aren't you, Kat? I can tell by the frown on your face. What is it?

Chapter Ten

*C*annon fidgeted as he sat on the stool behind the reception desk. Staring at the folio he'd just processed on the register, he couldn't focus on what to do next. The little knot of muscle above his jaw jerked visibly, and the reality that his daughter could die before they ever met refused to budge from his mind. Now that he'd finally mustered up the courage to tell her all the secrets of the past. *Am I too late?* Unaccustomed as he was to praying, he found a prayer forming in his heart. *Dear God, if you're there and listening to this foolish old man, please give me a chance to make things right with my girl. I know I've been a fool and wasted my life, but that wasn't her fault. Please...let me try to fix things. Let me be a grandfather to her little boy because I was never permitted to be a father to her when she was a child. You know the reason for that, and you know I've made a lot of stupid decisions. I guess I'm trying to say I'm sorry, and I'm really wanting a chance to right the wrongs I've done. Please...*

"Joe, me good feller, would ye join me in a cuppa coffee? This new snow storm is makin' a chill run through me bones."

"How's that, Clancy?"

"I declare, me lad, what be on yer mind?" Clancy's rust-colored eyebrows shot up. "I was askin' if ye wanna cuppa coffee?"

Maybe a shot of whiskey would be better. "Thank you, Clancy. Believe I will."

The fresh hot coffee hit the spot. He looked back at the computer, made the necessary entries, and finished his daily report. The last guest had checked in, and he was ready to call it a night. He and Clancy refilled their cups and sat at a table near the front window. A few late-nighters gathered around the fireplace, chatting and drinking. He forced back his envy as he gazed at them. *I could be like that...laughing, without a care in the world...if I'd live my life different. I bet they don't have skeletons in their closets.*

"What's ailin' ya, Joe? Ye ain't been yerself here lately."

He turned to Clancy. "Just worried about Mrs. Kahill."

"True, 'tis a terrible shame, but she's a strong lady. She'll pull through this. Ye just wait and see."

"I'm...uh...sure she is, but a plane crash is a serious accident. Most people don't survive them. I'm just wondering why the doctors are keeping Kat... I mean... Mrs. Kahill...up there in Pittsburgh. How long has it been now? Seems like forever."

"Away wid yerself...'tis only ben a wee while. Two days now, but you're right about it seemin' like a long time. Ye bein' a might commiserate for someone ye haven't even met. One would think ye be her lovin' father or uncle or some other relative."

The words stabbed at his chest like a dagger. He looked down at his cup of coffee. "I just hate to see anyone hurt. From what I've heard, she sounds like a wonderful woman."

"Aye, that she is. No finer to be found. Be patient, me friend. There's nothing so bad that it couldn't be worse. I'm sure they be doing all they can to get her back home soon. Ye know that Dawson's been keepin' us posted on her condition."

"I guess you're right, Clancy. Is there any improvement at all?"

"She be stayin' awake more, but she's not havin' much of an appetite. Dawson says she's bruised up a wee mite, but that'll heal soon enough. I've heard it said that God prefers prayers to tears. If that be the case, she'll be home in no time. Say, Joe, why don't ye stay here tonight? Save ye a trip in this bad weather. Besides, Dawson's been meanin' to talk to ye 'bout moving in durin' the winter season. Ye shouldn't be travelin' that road back and forth. Get's pretty bad some days despite the city's effort to keep it passable."

"Hmmm...I'm not sure. Uh...maybe that's a good idea. It sure is a mighty generous offer." He nodded. Any word about Kat would come to the lodge first.

"'Tis past time for us to be retirin' for the night. Maybe tomorrow we'll have good news from the hospital. Now, go pick ya out a room, and be sure to turn the card over in the rack so ya don't have someone bustin' in on ye in the middle o' the night."

"Thanks, Clancy."

He didn't need to turn on the light. Dim shadows spilled onto the floor and walls. He'd been in the room before; it was the one he'd been shown on his tour of the place the first day he'd worked. Besides, the dark room suited his mood. With the lights on it would have been inviting, quaint, and cozy. Symmetrical, rough-hewn beams lined the ceiling, and a fireplace flanked by matching rockers stood in one corner. Brightly colored quilts adorned the queen-size beds, but their cheeriness contradicted his doleful mood. He pulled the rocker near the window and watched flurries of snow flutter to the ground. A sliver of moonlight peeked between the clouds to pierce the bare branches of the trees and sparkle like diamonds on the whiteness. In the silence, he heard his own thoughts. *If Kat doesn't improve soon, I'll be on my way to Allegheny Mountain Hospital, regardless of the consequences. I wanted time for her to get to know me, but if she's hurt too bad to come home... She needs to know I'm her father. Or does she? Am I being selfish to throw this at her when she's trying to recover? How can I think about what I want instead of what's best for her?* Layer by layer, he reined in his raw nerves. *I can't show too much concern about the boss' wife because nobody will understand. Blazes, this is not going to be easy!* He dropped his head into his hands. His concern for his daughter and his inadequacy as a father mounted until they almost suffocated him.

A sense of loneliness seeped into him. The cold outside didn't begin to match the iciness inside his heart. He walked over to the bed, covered himself with the quilt, and tried to sleep. Instead, he imagined Kat in her hospital room. Was her life hanging in the balance? He couldn't do a single thing to help her. Nothing. A bitter conscience filled him, burning like bile rising in his throat—a conscience he never knew he possessed.

He should have been there for her when her kite came crashing down. But he wasn't. He should have been there when she fell from her bicycle and skinned her knees, when she graduated from high school and college. But he wasn't. He should have put her hand through his arm when she walked down the aisle to marry Dawson. It was a father's privilege, but he knew he had no right to any honors where Katarina was concerned. He'd not been an honorable father to her. He'd dilly-dallied money and time on prostitutes, drinking, and living a wretched life because he'd not been man enough to face his responsibilities. Even though he'd promised never to see Suzanne again, he longed to know his little girl. After her grandparents died he could have gone back to her. But he didn't.

Maybe just one shot of Jack Daniels to lighten my burden and this nagging guilt that plagues me? He and Jed had shared many a bottle, but now he seemed to hear Jed's voice. *"No. No, Cannon. Leave that junk alone. Stay straight and you can make it. I know you can."*

"I'm trying, Jed. I'm finally trying to do what's right. But God help me, I'll never forgive myself if something happens before I get to tell her."

Chapter Eleven

*D*awson gazed down at Kat, sleeping peacefully for the first time. *Has it been just two days since the accident? I feel like I've been here forever.* His emotions played havoc with his mind. *Why is she pregnant? Did she forget to take her pill? Now I have to deal with a situation I don't have any control over. I can't protect her from what's already happened.* Tears sprang to his eyes. Had he been lying to her about not wanting another child? In his heart, did he want this baby?

His mental turmoil drove him to walk the hospital corridors while she slept. Stepping off the elevator, he turned to see the nursery. *Funny, I don't remember coming to the maternity floor.* He stood at the window and looked at the babies. A little one wrapped in a pink blanket yawned and turned to stare at him. Her thick, raven hair matched her almost-black eyes. He gasped. She looked so much like Kat that she could have been hers...theirs. A tall, dark-haired man and a biracial woman in a hospital gown and robe walked up to the infant and lifted her gently from the bed. The baby's gaze remained transfixed on him until he was no longer in her line of sight. His breath caught in his throat. *Except for her racial background, she could be ours.* Casting one last envious glance at her adoring parents, he headed back toward the elevator. The recurring questions came back to mind. *Have I been honest with Kat and with myself? Have I been so afraid for her life that I ignored her desire for another child? Do I really want this baby?* The elevator door opened. He stepped inside. *Yes, Kat, I do want our baby.*

They would have to talk with Doctor Morgan to make sure every precaution would be taken to protect Kat and the baby. He shuddered. Was it already too late? He'd take whatever steps were necessary to assure that she'd be as safe and unstressed as possible, and he'd begin right now.

He walked into her room and found her in tears. After wiping them away, he lowered his eyes, then looked straight at her. "Why didn't you tell me about the baby, Kat?"

"You didn't want one, that's why. I didn't know how to tell you that what I had for you was not something you wanted."

"That's not true. I want a baby, like we talked about. A little girl we can call Willow. Or a boy, no difference. I want you both to be healthy, but I'm afraid childbirth isn't...right for you."

"Daw, will you stop trying to be the doctor here? Doctor Morgan said, with the right precautions, I should be able to have a normal delivery this time."

"Well...what does he know anyway?"

Her mouth flew open. "Excuse me?"

"Just kidding. I guess I should listen to him. Okay...that's it. I believe him."

"You do not. You're making fun of me."

"Sweetheart, have I told you this morning that I love you? And believe me, I am happy we're having a baby. You must promise me you'll be careful and take care of yourself."

"I promise. And I love you, too."

"What's it going to be? A sister for Joey? Or a brother?"

"Well...yes, one of the two, I would imagine." She giggled. "It's too early for the sonogram." He patted her stomach and kissed her forehead.

Early the next morning, Kat pushed herself into a sitting position. She bit her lip to keep from crying out in pain and glanced at Dawson, who was stretched out in the recliner next to her bed. He snored softly. Inching her legs toward the opposite edge of the bed, she let them dangle toward the floor. The closet couldn't be more than four feet away, but suddenly it might as well have been at Willow Walk. The room began to spin. She gripped the rail on the side of the bed and steadied herself. Her heart pounded, and her head throbbed.

"Let me help you dress, sweetheart." Dawson's strong arm slipped around her waist.

"Thanks, Daw. I wanted to surprise you and be dressed when you woke up, but I'm a little woozy. Must be from the concussion. Could you get my clothes for me?"

He nodded. "Don't you move, you hear?"

"I hear."

He handed her the plastic bag that contained the clothes she wore on the flight. She opened it and frowned. "These seem to be a bit bloody. I'm not sure I want to put them on."

"Would you like something clean?" He gave her a sly grin.

"Does that mean you're going out to buy me some?"

He coughed. "I wouldn't dare. But I did drive down to Willow Walk while you were sleeping last night and brought you some fresh ones to go home in. That's why I didn't wake up early this morning."

She reached out and gave him as big a hug as her bruised body would permit. "You're the best, Daw. What would I ever do without you?"

"I trust you won't have the opportunity to find out any time soon." He handed her another bag he retrieved from the closet. "Now why don't you let me help you? I don't want you to have another dizzy spell and fall."

"You worry too much." Kat eased her sore body into her jeans and sweater before stopping for a quick kiss on the cheek.

Getting dressed and into a wheelchair for the ride downstairs to Dawson's truck required more energy than she ever would have imagined. By the time she was safely buckled into the passenger seat, all she wanted to do was sleep. They had so many things to discuss, but she needed to close her eyes for just a few moments.

Now that Dawson knew about the baby, she felt more at ease. After her brief rest, they talked about everything from the plane crash to what had been happening at Willow Walk, how Joey was getting along, whether Debbie had kept in touch with Lil and Silka to make sure Wolf International wasn't adversely affected by the accident.

"Is Carla taking care of everyone?"

He reached over and patted her knee. "You know Carla. Willow Walk is running like a well-oiled machine."

She laughed a little, then winced in pain. "How's your new employee working out, Daw?"

"He's doing real well, Kat. Learns fast and has been extremely concerned about you. Seems strange since he hasn't even met you yet, but then again, he shows interest in everything. He's the kind of guy you like but can't quite figure out exactly why. He seems to have fallen right into place around the lodge."

"I can't wait to meet him. Are the reservations showing up as scheduled?"

"Yeah. I wish Granddad were here to enjoy it with us. Although if he had been here, I'm afraid he would have had a heart attack when you crashed."

She looked away from him and out over the sweep of the land approaching Willow Walk. Across the valley, everything had changed. The patches of green in the meadows had disappeared, and the wooded slopes above stood like black cutouts against an ominous lemon sky.

Dawson stopped the truck and helped her up the steps onto the large front porch. Crossing the threshold into the grand entrance hall, she gazed into the parlor. She stood still for a moment, looking at the small part of the world she had occupied during the most chaotic and the most exulting times of her life. Two days ago, that life had flashed through her mind in a random collage of vignettes as the plane skidded out of control toward the precipice she had seen out the window as they landed. Those same memories came again, this time in order and peace as her mind reconstructed the puzzle of her life—her childhood years in Mama Suzanne's loving care at Willow Walk, the early days of their marriage when life was always happy, the terrifying circumstances surrounding Joey's birth, the dark day when Dawson almost lost his leg and the devastating months that followed. His bitterness toward her in particular and life in general had driven her from her beloved home to work for Wolf Fashions International in Paris. The hectic excitement of the Paris fashion show gave her relief from Dawson's anger and brought her full circle to face her own. When her resentment at Dawson's treatment put her in a compromising position with an attractive man, she suddenly had faced the challenge of choice. Would she succumb to the kindness of the handsome and caring Dr. Mason Leblanc, or would she fight to save the marriage that had meant everything to her up until a few short months before? Even now, the temptation that had almost overcome her sent a chill up her spine.

Dawson helped her remove her coat and hung it on the hall tree in the corner. She had never been happier to be home or more grateful to be surrounded by those she loved. Willow Walk wrapped the arms of its safe haven around her, and she basked in the security that only her beloved home afforded.

Joey ran into the parlor as Kat eased herself onto the couch. "Mama's home!" He made a full-speed beeline for her lap.

"Joey, no!"

The little boy skidded to a halt mid-stride and looked up at his daddy. "Ooops! Carla said I wasn't s'posed to run around and jump and stuff until you got all better. You okay, Mama? Your face looks kinda funny, like you hit the door or somethin.'"

"I'll be good as new very soon. Now come here, you little urchin."

Joey climbed on the couch so gently that the cushion barely moved. "What's an erchimp, Mama? Is it some kinda monkey? I don't think I wanna be one."

Carla appeared in the doorway. "Lunch is read if you feel like eating a bite before you lie down to rest."

Kat tried to push herself up from the couch. "Ouch!" She sank back.

Joey's eyes grew wide. Dawson reached out and helped her to her feet and into the kitchen. Joey gripped her other hand as though he was afraid she'd get away.

A bright bouquet of flowers sat in the center of the table. Around it, Carla had placed a bowl of chicken salad and a basket of freshly baked croissants wrapped in a heavy napkin. An apple pie cooled on the stove.

"Carla, this looks absolutely wonderful. I can't wait to get back in the kitchen and help with the cooking."

The stout housekeeper put her hands on her hips and gave Kat the look that she previously had reserved for Granddad. "You just take it easy and let me do my job."

Dawson took a big bite of chicken salad spread generously on the melt-in-your-mouth croissant. "Mmm. This is perfect, Carla, but I need you to save my piece of pie until later. I'm thinking I could have it a la mode after a low calorie salad for supper." He grinned.

Shaking her head, she covered the pie with plastic wrap. "You know, Dawson Kahill, you're getting more like Jedediah every day."

He stood up and bowed. "Why, thank you, Carla. You couldn't have given me a nicer compliment."

"Humph. I was speaking of his conniving ways, not his redeeming qualities—which, by the way, he did have—in great abundance, I might add."

"Yes, he did." Dawson turned to Kat. "I'm going up to the lodge for a while. I want you to take a nap while I'm gone."

"Don't be silly, Daw. I'll go with you. I'm curious about our new employee who's so concerned about my welfare." She laid her napkin beside her plate and forced her body into a standing position. The room began to spin. She grabbed the edge of the table and closed her eyes.

"I don't think so. You're supposed to take it easy and not go traipsing all over the countryside. You have to follow Doctor Hamilton's orders until we get you in to see Doctor Morgan. You need to call this afternoon to make an appointment."

"I hardly think a short trip up the drive to the lodge is traipsing all over the country. My goodness, you'd think I was heading off to Egypt or something. I appreciate your concern, sweetheart, but please don't treat me like a baby. I won't overdo, I promise. And thank you for caring so much. But I'm still going with you."

"Listen to me, Katarina Kahill. You're staying right here and rest. If you want to stretch out on the sofa in front of the fire in the parlor, that's fine." He turned and pointed his finger at her. "You know as well as I do what the doctor said, and you promised me that you'd take it easy."

She gave him a pouty look. "All right, Daw. I'll keep my promise, but if you're not back in an hour, Joey and I will come looking for you."

Joey threw his arms in the air. "You listen to Daddy, Mama, you hear?"

"Yes, little man. I hear every word Daddy says." Kat turned her head away and tried not to a laugh.

"Joey, I'm putting you in charge of taking care of your mother. If you think she's not behaving herself, you tell Carla. Is that a deal?"

"Yes, sir. I'll take real good care of Mama cuz I'm a big boy now."

Dawson shook hands with his son and gave Kat a light kiss on the cheek. "Now lie down, get your feet up, and cover yourself with something warm, Mrs. Kahill. You've got valuable cargo to protect. And don't forget to call Doctor Morgan."

Chapter Twelve

*B*y the time Clancy made his third trip past the continental breakfast bar, the number of donuts and pastries on the large, covered tray had dwindled significantly. He turned around just in time to see Cabe, a big grin spreading across his face, come along behind him with new platters piled high with their patrons' favorites. Giving him a nod, Clancy filled his coffee cup and headed to the empty table by the window where he'd already devoured a plate full of eggs, toast, and sausage.

He chewed a caramel apple pecan swirl to the steady rhythm of the rustic lodge. Its pulse beat to the tune of laughter and chatter, while guests filled their plates from the wide selection of breakfast choices that ranged from simple donuts or waffles and coffee to bacon and sausage and hash browns and eggs to the Sunday champagne brunch that included prime rib and delicate soups in addition to traditional breakfast fare. Many guests booked rooms for a month or more and would stay or travel back and forth, depending on the weather. Regular visitors reserved rooms and kitchenettes early in the fall to get a choice of units.

Clancy washed down the last of his donut with coffee. A wave of awe and gratitude washed over him as it often did when he felt the heart of the lodge. The coincidental meeting of Jeddy at Joey and Molly Anna's births sparked a chain of events that had changed his life forever. He couldn't even imagine where he would be now had it not been for that fateful meeting.

The big double doors opened, and Dawson entered, Kat clinging to his arm. Clancy nearly choked on his last swallow of coffee when he saw her bruised face and the way she leaned on her husband. The competent, robust lady he knew bore little resemblance to the fragility he saw in her hesitant steps.

She smiled when she looked up beyond the cedar beams and said a silent thank you. It's good to be alive.

Dawson broke into her reverie. "Come on over here, honey. I want you to meet Joe, our new man."

Kat ambled over to the front desk and stopped short when she saw Joe. She squinted as if her eyes were not focusing well.

"You okay, Kat?"

"Yes. I...I feel a bit of a chill."

"Sit down over here." He pointed to a chair near the fireplace.

"I'm fine now, Daw." She put out her hand to Joe, and he took it. "So nice to meet you, Joe. I've been hearing a lot about you."

He smiled from ear to ear and nodded without answering. His hand squeezed hers so tight the ring she wore bore into her finger. *Strange. You'd think I was a long lost relative or something.* She flinched just enough to let him know what she was thinking.

"Oh, I...I...I'm so sorry, Kat...I mean, Mrs. Kahill. I didn't mean to...to... anyway, it's wonderful meeting you. It will be great getting to know you. I mean...everyone here is so nice and makes me feel right at home."

"Getting to know you will be my pleasure, Joe." She wasn't sure she meant that. "Have you been here in Wheeling long?"

"I've lived in West Virginia for most of my life. Wheeling was my home during my early years, and I spent considerable time on the Island."

"Small world...my parents lived on the Island. The Masons. Have you heard of them?"

"Mason? No...uh...I don't think so. Well...I better tend to my duties." His voice sounded strained.

She smiled and turned to Dawson. He guided her to the chair by the fire. "Nice fellow but a bit odd. I thought he'd never let go of my hand. But he seems real nice."

"I think you'll like him once you get to know him."

A tiredness washed over her. Was it due to her injuries or something else? She forced herself up from the chair. "I'm going to sit at the table by the window for a while, Daw. I just want to take in the ambiance of this wonderful place. Would you get me some hot chocolate, sweetheart."

"Sure. How 'bout a donut?"

"Are you kidding? After that big delicious breakfast you fixed me? Are you trying to make me and the baby fat?"

He gave her an evil grin. "I noticed you have put on a few pounds—with my help of course."

"That's the understatement of the year," she mumbled.

"What'd you say?"

"Nothing, Daw." She gave him her sweetest smile and maneuvered her way around several tables until she ended up at the little table for two by the large plate glass window overlooking the hillside. Clouds hung low in the space where clarity had opened the morning. Big white flakes swirled downward and sideways, looking for a place to land. For some inexplicable reason, her thoughts reverted to the man behind the desk. She turned. Her gaze met his and locked. *This is crazy. What is drawing me to this man that I don't even know?*

She slid back in the chair but kept her eyes on Joe Williams. He busied himself filing folios and checking reservations for the day.

Dawson had been in such a hurry to get to the lodge that she let her hair hang loose, something she seldom did when going out. Reaching into her bag, she pulled out a barrette and tried to clamp it back, but her coarse mane was too much for it. The clasp gave way, launching the hair clip on a haphazard flight across the room. It landed on the floor in front of Joe.

She covered her mouth with her hand, looked down at the barrette on the floor, and raised her gaze to meet Joe's. His face held the biggest grin she'd ever seen. Suddenly, they both burst out laughing.

"I think you dropped something, Mrs. Kahill." Joe walked over to her with the barrette in his hand.

"Thank you, Joe. And please call me Kat. If you want to, that is."

"Oh, I do...I will."

"That never happened before. My barrette sailing through the air, I mean."

"I wish we had a picture of it." He laughed again.

"Me, too." She hesitated for a moment. "Do you have family here? I mean... are you married?"

"Not now. But I was some years back."

"Any children?"

"Two girls. Two beautiful girls."

"Are they here in Wheeling?"

"Yes."

"It's good they're close by."

"Closer than you imagine, Kat." His voice turned melancholy. "And you, my dear? I know you have a little boy. A darling boy, too. And his grandfather, Jedediah Kahill, what a good man he was."

"Did you know Jedediah?"

"Uh...I've heard so much about him that...you understand."

She nodded. "He was well loved around here.

"Are your mother and father living?"

"Mother died when I was six, and I never really had a father. I mean he... he...I never met him. My step-father didn't deserve to be called 'dad.'"

He fixed his steady gaze on her. His eyes, the warm gray of old pewter, filled with sadness. "I'm so sorry, Kat." He turned his head toward Dawson, who brought hot chocolate on the table.

"Have you any pictures of your family, Joe?"

"Yes, I do. One of my daughters." He reached for his wallet and opened it to a picture of Maggie.

"My, she's very pretty. Looks about my age. What's her name?"

"Maggie. I call her Magpie. She's just like the black and white crow who chatters all the time and collects things that have been discarded by others. She's as sweet as she is pretty."

"You said she lives here in Wheeling?"

"Yes, she does."

"Please bring her by to meet us someday." Dawson joined the conversation.

"That I will. For now, though, I'd better get back to my duties before the boss fires me."

They all laughed. Joe went back to the front desk, and Dawson sat down with Kat.

"He seems very fond of Maggie. I wonder where his other daughter is. I must ask him sometime. I think I'd like to go home now, Daw. I can't believe how tired I am."

"I'm not surprised. The doctor didn't tell you to take care of yourself and rest just to hear himself talk."

She stood to leave and caught hold of the table to keep from falling. Dawson grabbed her arm and held on.

"I'm okay. Just a little dizzy."

"Let's get you home to bed."

"Yes. Please let's go." *I've never felt this weak and dizzy before. Must be the concussion. Or...or... No... Please, God, don't let anything be wrong with the baby.*

Chapter Thirteen

*S*he awoke as the first hint of morning turned the sky a pearly gray. Pushing her hair out of her eyes, she swung her legs over the side of the bed, slid into her slippers, and slipped on her white terry robe. The aroma of fresh-brewed coffee wafted up to meet her as she traipsed down the stairs to the kitchen. Dawson and the coffee would be waiting.

"Morning, hon." She poured herself a cup and flopped down at the old round pedestal table that had been in the family for generations. The rest of the kitchen had been updated several times, but the oak table remained in its appointed place. She might as well have been invisible. Dawson remained engrossed in the notebook he had found at the cemetery. "Morning, hon," she repeated a bit louder. Dawson waved with one hand, his gaze locked on the little black book.

"Huh? Sorry, Kat. I've been thinking about the stranger at Granddad's funeral and where this book came from."

"Oh?" Kat sat across from him, watching his eyes move back and forth across the page. "Found anything significant yet?"

He handed her a small photograph. "This was stuck between the pages. Looks like a photo taken at a carnival or street fair, where you step into a booth and take your own picture."

"Yeah, like we used to when we were kids." She reached for the photo. "I don't believe it!" Her mouth opened slowly; she covered it with her hand, squinted, and stared at the picture.

"What is it, Kat?"

"It's...it's...the girl in Joe's wallet."

"What are you talking about?"

"The girl in Joe's wallet. His daughter. This is her."

Dawson shook his head. "That doesn't make any sense. Probably just someone who looks like her."

"No, Daw. It's her. A little younger than in the one Joe carries, but it's her."

"If this is his daughter, this notebook must be his."

"Of course. Do you know what this means? Joe's the stranger at the funeral."

"Not necessarily, Daw. Remember that you said the book had been there much longer than just that day. Maybe there's some writing on the back." She turned the picture over. "There's something here, but I can't quite make it out. See if you can."

"Hmmm...looks like a name. Mag...Maggi...I don't know. She's lovely. Beautiful black hair and olive skin."

"Maggie. He calls her Magpie. You know, like that black crow? That's Joe's daughter's name." Kat bit her lip and rolled her eyes to the side. "What's do you make of this, Daw?"

"A little too coincidental to my way of thinking."

"If I hadn't promised Bonny I'd be at the boutique to help her today, we'd go talk to Joe about it right now. Or...maybe we should just wait and see where this is going. It's all too crazy. Something is up with this Joe guy, mark my words."

"Maybe. And then again... Let's just put it on the back burner, put some thought to it, and we'll talk about it when you get home. I won't say a word to anyone."

"Good. Give Mr. Williams enough rope, and we'll see if he hangs himself."

"Don't be too down on him yet, Kat. We don't know that he's up to no good. Let's not make a rush to judgment."

"You're right. Where did I ever find a great guy like you?"

"I know what you mean. They don't come along every day."

"Daw, you beat all." She picked up her coffee and headed upstairs to dress. "Mum's the word...remember."

"Sure you feel good enough to go to the boutique?" he hollered. "You know what I told you about overdoing..."

She knew what he was thinking. "Listen closely, sweetheart. I *know* my limitations."

"What? What'd you say?"

"Never mind."

The warm shower didn't take her mind off the mystery of Maggie and Joe, but it eased the remnants of her soreness from the accident. In less than half an hour, she was ready to head out the door.

"I'm off to the boutique." she called to Dawson when she reached the bottom of the stairs. No answer. The notebook seemed to reach out and grab her as she started for the door. She'd take one more look at the picture before she left and then get her mind off this perplexity and on to the matters at hand.

So many things had sidetracked her from the boutique in Wheeling that she had to give it her undivided attention now.

Bonny was removing garments from boxes and placing them on racks and shelves when Kat walked in the door. "Hi, hon, how are you doing?" Bonny stopped working and hugged Kat.

"Doing good, Bon."

"Been working on some ideas for our spring show. Are you going to be up to doing the Wolf International show in January?

"I hope so. Lillian and Silka can handle the bulk of the work, but I should at least make an appearance. I'm just not sure I can force myself onto a plane again."

Bonny grinned. "Have you considered hiring someone to run Wolf International, Kat? It's just too much for any one person to do. The stuff here and in New York is enough for anyone."

"Lillian and Silka get along superbly and are doing a great job. They've mentioned teaming up and buying Wolf International, but—I don't know how Rebecca would feel about that. She's getting more involved in running the company again."

"By now they should know all there is to know about the company and how to run it. Ironic, isn't it, that Lillian—Lincoln Wolf's former mistress—might now own the business he stole from his wife and from which he fired her as a model. I guess she got even with him." Bonny grinned.

"Yes, and I love it. Lil deserves the last word."

"Let's sit down and talk, Kat. It's been a while. I'll get us some coffee."

Bonny pointed to the wicker couch in the main room of the boutique, which had been designed for patrons and their significant others.

"Thanks, Bon." Kat sank onto the plush cushion and gazed around the shop. *What a long way you've come, Katarina Kahill. I still pinch myself whenever I walk into my boutiques. Even now, it seems like a dream.*

Bonny returned and sat down beside her. "You know, Kat, this may not be any of my business, but since when do I keep my mouth shut on that account?"

"Truer words were never spoken." They both grinned.

"It wouldn't be in your best interest to return to Paris, whether you hate flying or not. Dr. LeBlanc would surely come into the picture. He's probably still in love with you."

"Bonny, I never..."

"I know you never gave him reason to think you could be anything other than friends, but you don't need to go gallivanting all over the globe anymore."

Kat stared into space, her brows tugging together in concentration. "Oh, sweetie, I know what you're saying. But that's not the only reason to sell Wolf International Fashions. Dawson doesn't want me to go to Paris even though he knows nothing about Dr. LaBlanc. I saw no reason to even mention the situation to him. Besides, I hate flying more than ever now, so why not sell? I'll get in touch with Rebecca tomorrow. She loves Lillian and Silka, so it may be a done deal."

"Good. Now you've made up our minds."

"I feel like a huge weight has been lifted off my shoulders. I don't have to fly anymore. I can drive to New York but not to Paris. I may miss Lil and Silka and the hustle and bustle of Wolf International, but I'll never miss those flying machines that can fall out of the sky...or slide into a ravine when they're on the ground." She hesitated. "Now I have another surprise. I'm...pregnant."

Bonny's eyes grew wide. She gave Kat an up-and-down look. "You're kidding! I thought you'd put on a few pounds, but I never dreamed it was a baby."

"Daw didn't know until the plane crash. The doctor told him before I had a chance to."

"Uh-oh. How'd he take it?"

"Better than I thought he would. Now he's turned into Father Hen, and he's making me rest and do all the good things for myself that I never do."

"Good for him! And believe me, Debbie and I will be in his corner all the way to the delivery room."

Kat giggled. "I kinda figured that would happen."

"Now, I'm ordering you to go home, get your feet up, and have a cup of warm tea."

"Yes, ma'am." She shrugged into her coat. "I'm on my way."

She turned onto the road leading to Willow Walk. What a good feeling it was to be able to concentrate on the baby and help Dawson with the lodge. She said a silent thank you to Bonny for helping her come to a decision. Selling Wolf International Fashions would mean no more flying.

Snow had begun falling by the time she drove up the lane to the house. The skiers were arriving in droves now, and the white, cottony cover would add to the growing base depth. As for Joe and Maggie, she felt content to let that scenario play out without any nudging from her. Joe had said he would bring Maggie to meet them someday soon. The answers to the questions that danced around her head would no doubt come out of that. She stopped the car and looked toward the mountains to the west that were casting long shadows and tall silhouettes.

A twinge in her swollen stomach startled her. As she stared out the windshield into the distance, a cold shiver raced up and down her back. It was way too early for the baby. The pain stopped almost as soon as it started. She refocused her mindset. Everything was good. The weather was perfect for the lodge, she was recovering from the accident, and the baby was growing by leaps and bounds if her swelling belly was any indication. Nothing was wrong, nothing at all. Things were almost perfect...too perfect. Maybe it was her growing anticipation of the baby she wanted so desperately. Maybe it was Joe Williams and his daughter Maggie. Maybe it was the notebook and its unexplained connection to them. Or maybe...

Icy fear crept out of her heart and wrapped itself around her. Something wasn't right. *What's happening? I can feel it weave itself into the fabric of my being, but I can't see what it is. Please don't let it be anything bad. Please...*

Chapter Fourteen

$\mathcal{T}$hough he held the doorknob firm, he couldn't bring himself to turn it. Raising his hand, he started to knock as he had always done. No one dared to enter Jedediah's room without a proper invitation. *Lifelong habits die hard.*

He lowered his head, breathed deep, and squinted hard. Trickles of tears rolled down his cheeks. This time the voice he longed to hear seemed to echo from within. "C'mon in, sonny boy." He smiled and remembered back to the first time he entered this room. Now, with a trembling hand, he turned the glass knob and stepped inside.

How well he remembered this space. Many troubles had been solved right here; many problems and hurts and bruises were tended to. Granddad had a way of making everything right. On the far side of the room, an inconspicuous door made of unadorned pine led to a portion of the attic partitioned off—his grandfather's most private quarters.

Dawson had to stoop as he stepped inside. Jedediah had purposely crafted the door to be short. He said it lent itself better to a secret hideout. He'd not paid much notice to the height when he was growing up, but he noticed now. Standing very still at first, he felt warmth embrace him as he looked around. *This is where Granddad's dreams originated, developed, and materialized. Here is the place he came when he missed Grandma Emma and wanted to write in his journal.*

His gaze went straight to the center of the small room and a large, torn, upholstered chair. For as long as he could remember, it had wrapped its arms around his granddad, supplying comfort and peace of mind. The family had laughed when Jedediah claimed he and the chair had a lot in common. Dawson could almost hear him crowing, his eyes twinkling, "This old chair and me is well used and worn around the edges, but we'll never break down or wear out."

What a blow it had been to the family when Jedediah placed their present of a new chair in his bedroom instead of replacing the old chair in the attic. "No way," he said. "Thank ya all for this lovely leather recliner, but I'll just put it in the bedroom by the window."

He spied Granddad's coffee mug on the end table, always ready, ever flavored with a touch of brandy, awaiting the master to come home. Next to it was a pipe rack, still holding Granddad's favorite pipe. The sweet fragrance of Captain Black Cherry Pipe Tobacco lingered in the dust, the spider webs, and the faded muslin curtain over the small attic window that overlooked the south side of Willow Walk gardens.

How many times had Jedediah told him about his secret meetings with his Emma Baby? He had said he knew the visits were imaginary—his memory tricking his mind into believing she was there—but sometimes they seemed so real. Then he threw his head back and laughed. Now the chair Jedediah had imagined his Emma sitting in when she visited was vacant, but the impression in the cushion sank into the bumpy upholstery, a remnant of the many years when she had sat in that same chair in front of the fireplace in the parlor before they took both chairs to their secret room. Granddad wasn't crazy. He was a sentimental old man who had dearly loved and missed his wife.

The thought that he could lose Kat when the baby was born suddenly overwhelmed him. His eyes filled with tears as he ambled across the old creaky floor. Granddad was gone. Grandma Emma was gone. His parents were gone. He couldn't bear the thought that Kat could be gone, too. Then the subtle aromas of Granddad's tobacco, the brandy in his cup, and his cologne indelibly embedded in the old chair comforted him. Something of Granddad was there, something he'd left behind. He let himself bask in the familiarity of the mingling smells.

Pulling back the curtain at the tiny window, he looked out across the spacious grounds. Sleet tapped, then popped, then slapped against the window. Everything was colorless like the day of the funeral.

The leather-bound journal that he caught Jedediah writing in so many times lay on the end table, where he left it for the last time. Dawson picked it up and swept his hand slowly over it. "My Emma's Visits" the cover read. Dawson sat down in the chair that for so many years had brought Jedediah comfort. His tense body relaxed, and he knew why Granddad had come here. The chair seemed to welcome him, even embrace him, and soothe the turmoil he felt inside.

"How I wish you were beside me, Granddad. I need to know about so many things. I miss you more than I can ever say."

"What didcha say, Daddy?" Joey's voice broke the spell.

Dawson scowled. "You know better than to enter this room without being asked. That was Grandad's rule, and it still stands."

Joey poked out his lower lip. He stood shadowed in the doorway.

"I'm sorry. But...but...but the door was open and..." Joey's eyes turn glassy. "Great-grandaddy loved me, too, didn't he, Daddy? Don't ya think if Grandaddy was here, he'd say what he always did when I knocked?" Joey made his voice sound gruff. "Okay, my little Indian, come on in."

Shame washed over Dawson. How could he have put his own mourning for his grandfather ahead of his little boy's? "Of course he would, son. Come on in."

Head down, Joey meandered over to his father, his foot kicking out like he was playing kick-the-can. Dawson wanted to hold him tight and never let him go.

"Can I play with Great-granddaddy's cane? Please, can I?" His hand reached out to touch the cane that was propped up beside Jedediah's chair. He stopped inches away from it, his blue-gray eyes widening as he looked as his father.

"Yes, son, you can play with it but be careful. It's very, very old."

"Just like Great-granddad?"

"Yes. Now go on and play. Daddy wants to read."

Joey paused. Tears sprang from his eyes. He threw his arms around his daddy's neck and sobbed. "But...but I sure do wish Granddaddy was still here cuz I miss him lots and lots. How come we have to get old and die? I don' wanna die, Daddy." He leaned back and looked Dawson straight in the eye. "Are you and Mama gonna die and leave me, too? Then I wouldn't have nobody no more."

Dawson's breath caught in his throat. Thoughts of Kat and the tiny life growing within her—the life that could take her away from him and from Joey—again ran through his head. Tears that matched his son's threatened to spill down his cheeks.

"Daddy? Are you okay? You ain'...uh...aren't dyin', are ya?" Joey's round eyes filled with fear.

"No, Joey, I'm not dying. I just miss Granddad, too. He lived more than ninety years, you know. It'll be a long time before Mama and I are that old. By that time, you may be a granddaddy yourself."

The little boy climbed down from his lap and picked up the cane. "I guess I'd better hurry and get growed up so I can marry Molly Anna and have some kids, else I can't be a granddaddy." He laughed and mimicked his great-grandfather as he limped around, singing to the tune of "Old Dan Tucker."

"Ole Granddad Kahill's a fine ole man.

But wouldn't wash dem pots and pans.

Got himself married, took him a wife,

Now he's havin' a happy life..."

The words faded away as Joey hobbled around the room.

Dawson sighed and opened the faded leather-bound book. The first page caused his heart to skip a beat.

Emma's Visits

I waited for Emma Baby this afternoon, but my little lady didn't show. Guess I wasn't focusing hard enough, because my mind just kept wandering to something else that's been heavy on my shoulders. I sure was hoping she'd come in that blue dress I bought her, the gingham one with the little white collar and white cuffs on the sleeves. Pretty as a picture she was every time she wore it.

I was wanting to talk to her about Willow Walk and the kids and all sorts of things that happened long ago, the good as well as the not-so-good, including that dark secret involving the Fox family. We were sworn to secrecy from the beginning, but it never quite seemed right. Like it or not, we Kahills always keep our word, and our love for Dawson and Kat has kept us quiet all these years. The truth bein' known might just devastate them. I know they'd be angry that no one told them, and they'd have every right to be. Well, it ain't up to you and me. It will come out in time, if need be.

Well, Emma Baby, I gotta go. And I was thinking about the kids when they were so young and innocent. What was it Kat and Dawson used to call those kisses they blew off their fingertips to each other? Oh yeah, butterfly kisses. Here you go, honey. Catch it. I'm blowing this butterfly kiss over to you. She smiled that wonderful smile, and...oh, how I wish I could hold her just one more time.

Dawson reread the part about the Fox secret. His brow wrinkled. A shiver swept over him. Suddenly, he realized he was holding his breath. *Granddad and Grandma Emma must have befriended someone in the Fox family. But who? And why?*

His mind scrambled for answers, but all he could come up with were odd pieces to the puzzle that didn't seem to fit. *Could this have anything to do with the stranger at the funeral? What about the notebook I found at the cemetery?* He remembered the photograph they found in it and Kat's insistence that it was Joe's daughter. The notebook must have belonged to Joe. *I'm not much of a detective, but I'm certain there has to be a connection.*

He was about to flip another page when Kat's call floated up the stairs.

"You and Joey wash up now. We're going to the Ski Lodge for supper. Polly and Bonny are cooking a big meal, and we'll be meeting Joe's daughter, Maggie."

"On my way." Dawson left the journal open. He would be back to read more. For now, he wanted to meet Maggie and observe Joe more closely. *Somehow, somewhere, that man is connected to Willow Walk.*

"On my way, Mama." Joey repeated. He leaned Granddad's cane against the chair where he had found it. Giving Dawson a quick glance before he dashed through the little door, he beamed at his daddy's smile of approval.

Chapter Fifteen

*C*annon's smile spread so wide it almost hurt when he saw Maggie walk through the double doors at the lodge. He wrapped his arms around her in a huge bear hug.

"Follow me, sweetheart. We'll sit over there at the corner table. You look pretty—and a bit nervous."

"Of course, I'm nervous, Daddy. Katarina doesn't know who you really are, and that scares the devil out of me. I don't think she's going to take it kindly. Are you sure this is the right time to tell her?"

"No...I'm not sure." He pulled the chair out for her as she sat down. "Don't know if there will ever be a right time. But come what may, I can't hold back any longer. It's not fair to you, Kat, Joey, or me. If ever I can make up for the past, it has to be now." He patted her on the arm.

"You're right, Dad. There's no time like the present."

"Here they are now." Cannon nodded his head toward the front entrance and waved Kat and Dawson over to their table.

"Kat, Dawson, I'd like you to meet my daughter, Maggie. I call her Magpie because she's like that beautiful bird."

Maggie stood up. "Oh, Daddy, that's so silly. Me a raven?" She blushed and rolled her eyes.

"How nice to finally meeting you, Maggie. We've heard so much about you. Your dad is very proud of you." Kat extended her hand.

Maggie reached out and clasped it. "The pleasure is mine. I've heard so much about *you*—how pretty you are and how sweet. I feel like I know you already."

"That father of yours is...tops. Excellent employee and now a friend, too. I don't think we could get along without him. The kids are crazy about him." Kat sat down next to Maggie.

"I think all these kind words are going to my head. Might have to buy me a new hat." Cannon smiled.

"Nice meeting you, Maggie," Dawson said. "Are you as efficient as your dad?"

"I'd like to think so, Mr. Kahill." Maggie smiled.

"Please, call me Dawson. These are our children. Joey, our son, and Molly Anna, Clancy's daughter. They were born the same day, so they have a lot in common. In fact, they say they're going to get married when they grow up—next year."

Maggie smiled and shook hands with them.

"You're pretty. Your hair is the same as Mama's." Joey knitted his brows and gave her a serious look. "You look like Mama, too."

"Yes, you're very pretty," Molly said. "Can I be your friend?"

"Thank you. Yes, of course, and I would love to be your friend."

"She's *my* friend, too, Molly." Joey shot Molly Anna a she-was-my-friend-first look.

"I know, Joey. I was just sayin'—"

Maggie wrapped an arm around each of them. "There's plenty of me to go around. I will be friends with *both* of you."

Polly rang the dinner bell. "Time to eat. Come and get it."

Dawson led the way. "If any of us get away from the table without weighing five pounds more, we'll be lucky. Polly's cooking is beyond belief."

The round table brimmed with Southern fried chicken, mashed potatoes and gravy, lima beans, leaf salad from Willow Walk's hothouse garden, sliced tomatoes, and homemade applesauce. Happy chatter around the table continued throughout the meal.

After peach cobbler with a huge scoop of vanilla ice cream on the side disappeared, the children ran off to play, and Polly and Cabe began clearing the table. Clancy moseyed off behind the desk to straighten the disarray of paper work for the night and set up the morning check-ins. Dawson and Kat, Maggie and Joe moved toward the circular sectional around the fireplace.

"If you don't mind, Joe, I'd like to ask you something...in private. Let's all head to my office instead. Bring your drinks if you wish."

Kat sighed, cleared her throat, and picked up her coffee.

The office offered comfortable chairs for everyone. Dawson poured brandy for Maggie, Joe, and himself and sat down.

"What was it you wanted to ask me, Dawson," Joe said. "This isn't the part where I get fired, is it?"

"Naw...you've been a godsend to us."

Dawson looked at Kat and gave her the go ahead. Groping in the vast depths of her tote, she pulled out a small camera, a sketchbook, some odds and ends, and the notebook.

"We found this in the cemetery the day of Jedediah's funeral. It has a picture of Maggie in it, and we figured it might belong to you, Joe."

The color drained from Cannon's face. After a moment, he reached for the notebook, took it, and ran his hand across it.

"Yes, this is mine. I wondered where I lost it. I was there in the cemetery the day of Jed's funeral—at the place where Jed and I met so many times before he died. We used to gab a lot. He said I was the only one who could almost outtalk him." Cannon paused. "We had a good snort of brandy on cold days and wine on warm ones. Jed and I were best friends all our lives. I shared the Fox secret with him many a time. I know you don't know about that."

"I'm not sure I understand." Dawson sat back in his chair and eyed the man across from him.

Kat frowned. "I think I might...Joe is a Fox not a Williams. And he's a *fox* in more ways than one." The rest of them grinned, but she did not.

"That's right, Kat. I'm Cannon Fox. I grew up five miles from you. My brother Nicholas and I—"

"Why the pretense, Joe...I mean Cannon? What is it you want from us? Why didn't you make yourself known at Jedediah's funeral?" Dawson asked.

"Several reasons—and I'm not sure how to explain. Most of all, I wanted to get to know Kat. And I wanted her and Maggie to get to know each other. I was frightened... Hell, I was scared to death to tell Kat—and you, too, Dawson. Working here seemed to be the best way to bring it on gradual for me until I felt the right time had come."

"Tell Kat *what*? Why didn't you just come up to us and say you were one of the Foxes, a neighbor, and a best friend to Jedediah, instead of all this phony baloney. I don't understand. What's the big secret?"

I'm more than a neighbor, Dawson." Joe's face flushed. He wiped beads of perspiration from his forehead and cleared his throat.

"What do you mean, *more* than a neighbor." Kat's throat tightened. Heat rose up her neck and scorched her cheeks.

"I knew Suzanne Helen...your mother... back when...back before you were born. She was my sweetheart. We wanted to marry, but her parents wouldn't allow it. They took her away to France until after you were born."

"Wait just one doggone minute here! Are you saying what I think you're saying?" Kat stood up so fast it made her dizzy.

"Kat, sit down—and calm down. Let Joe finish, sweetheart."

"Yes, please, sit down, Kat" Cannon paused. "We tried to get together when she came home, but it was impossible. It almost killed me."

"Almost killed *you*? What about my mother?" Her pitch rose a full octave. "You left her to raise an illegitimate child alone."

"I loved your mother with all my heart and being. But your grandparents took out a restraining order against me when they returned from France. When your mother married Cable Kahill, I couldn't live with losing her. Beside myself with grief, I left Fox Run. I had to get away. I knew I wouldn't be able to handle living so close to them ...to you. So, I drifted—bummed around. I couldn't stand myself or the situation as it was, so I gave myself to booze and drugs, hoping to deaden the pain. All it did was make me hate myself more. From there I went further downhill, if that's possible, until Jed's death. As I stood there on the day he was buried, I heard his voice in my head, and he told me to straighten up my life and expose the secret. I heard his gruff voice say. "Come clean, my dear friend, and at least try to make things right."

Her voice took on a hard edge. "Is that supposed to warm my heart or something? You're looking at someone else who hated you. And I suppose Maggie is my sister? Let's see...that would make us...half-sisters, right? What a dandy mess your family is. Oh, pardon me, it's *my* family now." Bright red circles rose in Kat's cheeks. "So...Jedediah knew?"

"Yes, Jedediah knew, but your mother made him promise, on her dying bed, that he would never tell you. He loved your mother more than he loved his own son, Cable—your step-daddy at the time. Besides that, he said it was my responsibility. And he was right, as usual."

"Since you've proven yourself anything but a responsible person, I can see why you never told me. Until now that is. And by the way, why *now*?"

"I feel you and Maggie have the right to know each other."

Kat gave Cannon a long slow look before she spoke. "Oh, I see. And you?" She forced the words out between locked and grinding teeth. "Do you have the right to know me? Or is there something you want from the Kahills."

"No, Kat. I want nothing from the Kahills. Only for you to give me a chance to be the father I never was."

She glared at him. No defense. No explanation. No panic. He looked at the floor, then raised his gaze to meet hers. She stared into his deeply troubled eyes. "You'll forgive me if I don't say thank you."

"Kat, I've told you the truth, and that's all I can do. I didn't expect you to forgive me, but I did hope you'd be open-minded and try to understand." His voice seemed to plead for some small ray of hope.

"Kat," Maggie chimed in, "whether you forgive our daddy or not, our feelings toward each other should not be affected. We have nothing to do with the fact your mother didn't want you to know, or your father didn't tell you, or Jedediah made a promise he wouldn't break or...anything else. Just look at how things step up. One thing led to another until Daddy couldn't win for losing, no matter how hard he tried to make things right."

"You're right about us Maggie. As for you," she pointed her finger at her father, "I wouldn't count on having a place in my life."

The room felt like an out-of-control carousel. She wanted to scream, but she couldn't. Her fists clenched. Her face burned. Her life fell apart, shattered like fine china dropped on a concrete floor. It had been a lie from the beginning, when her mother allowed her to believe Cable was her biological father. She had to escape. *Now*. She jumped up to run. The room moved in circles, and the floor rolled under her feet. Faces faded away. Her legs wobbled. Her jaw tightened so hard it hurt her teeth, and then it dropped open. Her hands flew to her face. *I've got to keep things together*. She swayed a little to the left. *Oh no...the pain*. The intensity of the cramp ripped the breath out of her and folded her in half.

Darkness swirled around, drawing her into herself—down, down, down. If only she could scream. She blinked and saw Dawson and butterfly kisses under the willow, their laughter, bright sunshine, and the leaves above dancing over them. Strong arms enveloped her. She knew without opening her eyes it was Dawson. Her Dawson. Her safety net. Her everything.

Chapter Sixteen

She opened her eyes on the couch in Dawson's office. Her tense body ached almost as much as it had after the plane crash. Dawson held an ice pack on her forehead with one hand and stroked her hair with the other. Maggie hovered nearby, but Cannon stood off to the side.

Nothing terrible had happened. No miscarriage. No terrible headache from the concussion. No physical damage beyond the stress of confronting a man she'd hated ever since she'd learned that Cable Kahill wasn't her biological father. Nothing more terrible than a fainting spell. More than likely, she had passed out from the tension, and why not? A father she'd never known flew into her life from behind the reservations desk at Willow Walk Ski Lodge like that clichéd bat out of hell.

"How do you feel, sweetheart?"

"I'm fine now, Daw." She blinked hard and stretched. "The shock just... caught me by surprise." She shivered and fought the urge to throw up.

"You gave us a scare, Kat. I think we'd better call Dr. Morgan."

"No. I'll be fine, honey. Please, don't worry."

"Then let's at least get you to the emergency clinic."

"No no. I said I'm feeling okay now, sweetheart. *Please* let's not make more of this than it is. I just reached an emotional breaking point, but I'm all right now. Besides I have an appointment this Friday. I think that will be soon enough to see the doctor."

Maggie stepped closer. "Would you like me to check you out? I'm a licensed nurse practitioner."

Kat looked up the woman, the sister she never knew she had, and shook her head. She needed some space. She needed everybody to quit hovering around as if she were the first woman in the world to have a baby.

Doctor Morgan patted her on the arm and smiled. "Looks like you and the baby are doing just fine. I want to see you again in two weeks. I know that may seem a little soon to you, but I want to keep a close eye on you this time. We don't want the same emergency delivery as we had with Joey. By the way, how is the little fellow?"

"He's...he's rambunctious, Dr. Morgan. Just as rambunctious as Dawson, and you had a good dose of him during my appointments." She laughed.

"Oh yes, He is an unforgettable character, all right. Now let's talk a bit more about you. So far things are going very well, but you must take it easy, mentally as well as physically. Please do as I say, Kat. I repeat—we don't want to deal with another emergency situation."

"I will. Thank you again Doctor Morgan."

Three weeks later Kat sat at her drawing board in her bedroom. It wasn't easy being forced into the slow lane, but she understood the reason. Her hand migrated to the budding bulge in her abdomen and received a solid kick. A smile teased the corners of her mouth. Except for being antsy from slowing down, she felt wonderful. She wanted a healthy baby and a normal delivery, so she would do whatever was necessary to make that happen.

Dr. Morgan had suggested she find something to occupy her time while sitting down. That wouldn't be difficult. In fact, it was the perfect prescription for playing catch-up on her design work. Now she had no excuse not to create a stockpile of phenomenal apparel.

The New York and Wheeling boutiques would get the best of her new designs. Wolf International would be decked out with the most exciting raiment she could create for the January show. Lounging around, sitting still, and barely moving, had never suited her. But the thought of designing first-class, show-stopping apparel did. Just thinking about it made her feel things couldn't be better. But her reverie was interrupted by a dark cloud that refused to go away. She put down her pencil and stared out the large French doors.

How can I ever forgive my father's heartlessness for deserting Mom and me so long ago, for being the sort of father no one in her right mind wants? Do I love him? No. Can I ever love him? I don't think so. Do I even like him? Not at all. Dear God, I feel so torn between such hate and cold indifference...which is worse? Am I being unreasonable? Unfair? Childish? If only—if only I could learn to forgive him. But how does one do it? She turned toward Dawson when she heard his footsteps on the polished hardwood floor.

"Daw, could you bring the large easel home from the shop for me? And a few other things, too? I'll make a list. I really need more of my design tools here at Willow Walk if I'm going to be confined to my room."

"Sure. I'll get them this afternoon. Will that be soon enough?"

"Yep. You're a sweetheart. Thank you."

"Then why are your eyes watering?"

"Oh, Daw, I need to come to terms with Joe. I mean Cannon. He's my father! I still can't accept it. And then there's Maggie, my half-sister. She's so darling, as pretty as a picture."

"No prettier than you. Joey was right. There's a definite resemblance."

"She's darker skinned than me, but our hair color is the same. And her big black eyes are fetching. Mine...oh I don't know what mine are."

"Yours are the ones I fell in love with long ago, the ones that still captivate me. Except for the color of your eyes, you two do look a lot alike."

"Yes, we do. It's almost surreal, having a sister after all these years. I don't blame Maggie for anything. We're both victims of circumstances."

Dawson came over to the desk where she sat working on a special design for the January show in Paris. He pulled up a chair and sat down beside her. He was unusually quiet while watching her draw.

"What's wrong Daw? Suddenly you're not talking. That scares me. You sure you're not sick?"

"Very funny. But now that we're talking family stuff, I have something to say you may not like."

"What's that?"

"I think you should give Cannon a chance. In a way, he's a victim too. He tried to marry your mama, but he was put out of your life by your grandparents."

"Yeah, right. He's a victim of his own mean doing. He had plenty of time to make himself known to me, married or not."

"Your mother asked him not to, Kat. She wanted you to believe Cable was your father. He told me there were other reasons for not contacting you, but he didn't say what those reasons were."

"Oh piddle, Dawson. That's such a copout. I don't forgive him, and I never will. There's no excuse."

"Kat, he only did what your mother asked."

"Yes, and it obviously suited him just fine." She jumped up and started around the drawing board, her small hands balled up and shaking.

"Kat! Honey, please sit down. I know this is hard for you...but remember the baby. You're getting all worked up for nothing. I am so sorry. I shouldn't have brought it up."

"Oh, Daw, I'm trying to... I'm trying as hard as I can." She flopped back down. "I want to forgive him, I really do. I just can't."

She leaned one elbow on her drawing board and laid her forehead in her hand. A moment later, she straightened up. "Sometimes when I hear his name, it almost makes me sick."

"I know. That's why I don't mention him too often. But I do have a problem and a favor to ask you." Dawson waited for a response. Kat gave him a weak smile. "I haven't found a replacement for him yet, and it won't be easy in the middle of the season. He's a wonderful clerk. And he's all set up in a kitchenette room at the lodge for the winter. I know he seems like a monster to you, but for me he's doing a great job. I'd like to keep him—at least until spring. Think you can put up with that for awhile?"

"I guess it's okay if you need him. And it's okay as long as he stays out of my way. Oh...I meant to tell you, Maggie's coming to visit today."

"You like her, don't you?"

"She's one of the nicest people I've ever met. And you know what? She's showing some talent in fashion design. She can't draw and sketch but she tells me her ideas, and then I do the drawing. We make a pretty good team."

"That's good to hear. Get me that list of stuff you want from the boutique. Want me to tell Bonny anything."

"Yes. Tell her the indigo gown we talked about the other day needs... something. I'll leave that up to her. If she has any questions, she can call me."

He threw her a butterfly kiss, and she blew one back. He gave Carla a quick smile as he passed her on the way out of the room.

"I came to see if I could bring you something." She looked over Kat's shoulder at the partially finished sketch.

"Just a cup of hot tea, Carla, if you don't mind. I'm sort of tired. Maybe it will pick me up or put me down to rest. Is Joey still napping?"

"Yeah. He told me he and Molly played all morning at the lodge." Carla laughed as she rolled her eyes. "You should hear their story. Molly is rich with a big house, the ski lodge of course, and Joey takes care of the chores around the yard and the house. She pays him five cents a week and gives him meals for his work." Carla paused for a moment. "I'm glad Dawson doesn't pay his help like she does. I don't think I could live on five cents a week." They both burst out laughing. "Those two kids are a riot. I'll get your tea now, Kat."

"They're that and then some. When Maggie gets here, will you tell her to come on up?" Angry as she was at Cannon, she found great joy in getting to know her sister. *At least he did one thing right.*

Thirty minutes later, Maggie rushed into the room. She hugged Kat with one arm and pulled a sheet of paper from behind her back. "Look here, Kat. I tried sketching this design, and I think I did pretty good. What do you think?"

"Why I...I...well...it's...it's different. Very nice."

"You don't like it. I can tell."

"No, sweetie, I love it. It just needs a little work. The design of the gown is fabulous. We'll work on it now if you'd like."

"Awesome, thank you." She sat down next to Kat and watched in silence for a few moments as her sister studied the design. "I know you don't like talking about Dad, but don't you think you could give him a chance? He tried to make things right in the beginning, but no one would let him."

"Give him a chance? Like he gave Mom and me? I don't think so." She fought to keep her voice steady. "What he did passes all human understanding as far as I'm concerned."

"I know. I know. And I hate to bring this up right now, but I need to...it's eating at me. I love you, Kat. I really do. We are so much alike, but in this we differ. I need to get this out, please."

Kat closed her eyes for a long moment. Then she opened them and nodded in silence.

"When Dad left Fox Run, I was heartbroken. I wanted to go with him. He told me before he left that he had to go away for a while, but he would be back. He wrote me letters and sent me gifts. He kept promising to come home soon, and I looked for him every day. Even though it seemed like forever, he kept his promise. About a month ago, after your grandfather passed away, he returned. But I didn't see him right away."

Carla walked in the room just then with the tea. "Would you like some tea, Maggie?"

"Please, if it's not too much trouble."

"None at all." Carla headed back to the kitchen.

"Dad was down and out. I mean *way* down and out. Living on skid row, for goodness sake." Maggie shivered. "He straightened up pretty good. Still not sure how I would respond, I went to meet him. When I first saw him, I ran into his arms. I forgave him for every tear I ever shed over him. I couldn't help myself. Then he...he...well, he told me the reasons he had to leave." She paused and dabbed at her eyes. "Look, honey, things look different to a man when he's lost and lonesome and...drunk. Your mom couldn't help herself either. Her mother completely controlled her."

"How do you know all this stuff, Maggie?"

"Dad told me. He knows a lot more than you think."

"Well...just don't blame it on my mom. Everyone has a choice. And what do you mean—granny was in complete control? What about after Mom died? Oooooh...I really don't want to talk about this right now, Maggie." Kat stood and began pacing.

"Okay, okay. I understand. Just one more thing you need to think hard about. Without forgiveness, Kat, bitterness is all you have left."

Carla returned with more tea. The girls settled in around the drawing board. Kat pulled out a fresh sheet of paper and laid it over her other drawings. "Now, let's see what we can do with your design." The girls were all giggles once again.

. . . . .

Maggie sipped her tea and watched as Kat interpreted the drawing she'd started. "Have you got names for the baby yet?"

"For a girl, yes. We thought about Willow. Not sure of the middle name yet. Do you like that?"

"Perfect. I love it. What about a boy?"

"No, not yet. If you have any ideas, we're open. I'm looking forward to my twenty-week ultrasound. Then we should know for sure." She made a goofy face. "That is, if I can talk Dawson into it. He's so old fashioned—he doesn't want to know...like it's going to make some kind of difference or something."

"Just like a man. Hmmm...a boy's name. Let me see. How about Walker? Walk for short."

Kat did the tart lemon squint and let her mouth fall open. "Walk? Walk! Oh Maggie, that's awful. Surely, you can come up with something better than that."

Her face brightened. "How about...Keller?"

"Killer! You're joking, right?"

"No. I said *Keller*. Not Killer."

Their laughter filled the room. They spent the rest of the afternoon drinking tea, eating cookies, working with fashion designs, and thinking of names for the baby. Maggie filled Kat in on events at Fox Run. "Uncle Nick is okay, but he goes around with blinders on and has more book learning than common sense. He lives in the old days and thinks everything should be just as it was back in the 1800s. He's extremely prejudiced, too, a trait I can't stand. He makes nasty remarks about blacks and foreigners."

"Is Cannon that way, too?"

"Not at all. He's just the opposite. He likes most people, no matter what color or nationality they are. I don't see how they can be brothers raised by the same parents."

"I take it our uncle doesn't top your favorite people list."

"I didn't say that. He raised me, so I shouldn't talk bad about him. Sometimes, he's just so irritating, so narrow minded, so finicky...did I mention mentally numb?" She stopped her rant, and her expression softened. "He can also be so smart and kind. In a way, he's a Jeckle and Hyde personality."

Kat sat back and took it all in. She and Maggie were alike in more than looks. Her baby sister had some fire in her, too.

"How come you never married, Maggie? If it's any of my business..."

"Never found the right guy."

"You will some day. You're too pretty and too smart not to get a humdinger of a guy."

"Yeah, right." She looked at her watch and stood. "Oh, my goodness. I had no idea it was so late. See you next week, Kat. And please, my dear hard-headed sister, mind the doctor and your husband and Carla and me and everyone else that tells you to *rest*." Maggie's eyes sparkled with delightful mischief.

"Oh, you are too terrible." She shooed her away like she was peddling snake oil. She could hear her giggling all the way down the stairs and out the front door.

Kat's gaze followed her until it flowed into the private theater of her mind, where she saw only half a battle won. So much had come at her all at once—the death of Jedediah, the plane crash, the appearance of her long-lost father, potential issues with her health and the baby, and a half-sister who was so much like her it boggled her mind. A sense of warmth and well-being she had never known before, even with Dawson, swept over her. The miracle of discovering a rare and priceless kindred spirit wrapped itself around her.

Once again, in the midst of her perfect day, the darkness flowed out of the box where she kept all the hurts and painful memories she feared and hated. Forgive her father? Not a chance. She wished she'd never met him.

Chapter Seventeen

*A*cross the valley, everything had changed. Green and yellow meadows lay robed in fresh, white snow. Most of the neatly erected haystacks were gone, along with the sweet smell of the hay laced with the earthy musk of late autumn.

Maggie never tired of her hometown—the seasons, the cornfields and pumpkin patches, the farmers in overalls and straw hats as they brought in the harvest. She even loved the scarecrows who dared defiant black birds to perch on their outstretched arms.

An apple orchard streamed past her. Beyond the owner's fence lay the last of the fruit where it had fallen—good enough for pies and cakes, but best for kids to grab in night raids when no one was looking. *Are they still as sweet as I remember?*

Pondering the changes in her life, she wondered why she felt so discombobulated, so lonely, so out of touch with life. This unpleasant feeling was new to her. She paused at the gate to Fox Run, where the road branched off into a fork. One led to Big Wheeling Creek, a tributary of the Ohio River. The other led to the main house. *Am I going to have to spend the rest of my life here, alone, childless—with Uncle Nick?* Her stomach turned flip-flops just thinking about it. She loved the old house that had always been her home, but what she wanted most was a pair of strong arms around her, someone well grounded in sanity, someone to hang on to...to catch her when she fell.

She could never thank her grandmother enough for leaving her financially comfortable. Grandma Gary showed her how to give love and how to receive love and taught her the importance of good common horse sense as opposed to book learning. She taught her to be respectful to her elders and to always be honest. She joked so often, "Now, Maggie," she would say, "honesty is the best policy...unless you're a crook." Then they both would burst out laughing. Her grandmother had been her confidant, her best friend.

Nicholas was reading in the library and puffing on one of his hundred dollar pipes when she walked into the room. *Nothing but the best for Uncle Nick.* She frowned. The only thing that interested her about the pipe was the special blend of cherry and vanilla tobacco he used. The smoke filled the room with a subtle sweet smell. She sank into a rocker adjacent to the slow-burning fire that radiated warmth and solace to her mood.

Shifting her eyes from the fire to Uncle Nick, she studied his features. He looked so much like her father, yet the multitude of differences between them collided most of the time. Nicholas made no friends for himself with his arrogant attitude. He pictured himself at the top of a great ladder of privilege and everyone else at the bottom. Her father, on the other hand, tried to make amends where he had brought pain to others. His humility in admitting his wrongs touched her heart.

She shook her head as she studied her uncle's pricey Magnanni calfskin loafers. Gucci and Armani suits, many investments, and plastic gold—that's what Uncle Nick was made of. He lived first class. Life gave him no challenges. What favors he couldn't acquire, he bought. *I'll give him one thing though; he's almost as good as he thinks he is.*

No pricey Italian shoes for her father. He wore old sneakers and thrift-store clothes the day he came back to Fox Run. He could never be accused of being pretentious. An ache flared within her as she recalled the many times he'd told her he was unworthy of his birthright because he had abandoned his home, his brother, and his children for the life of a vagrant and squandered a good part of his inheritance. The pain etched into his weary eyes, fueled by self-hatred, hollowed out his soul. He knew what it meant to be empty inside. Her heart crumbled for him. The fear that Kat would never forgive him shook her the hardest.

A smile warmed her once again as she remembered her grandmother's little poem about living in forgiveness. It had puzzled her when she was younger but now she understood how it fit into life.

> What's past is past, what's done is done.
> What's yet to happen has just begun.
> All is forgiven;
> Get on with your livin'.

Her daddy's words after he returned took the edge off the chill in her heart. *Maggie, I think my new attitude is demolishing my old way of thinking and creating new ways of reasoning. Wouldn't that be a first? Even though I'm not living at Fox Run yet, I'm glad to be home. I'm glad to be able to spend time with you face to face instead of by mail. Don't fret none about us not living under the same roof. My time will come to move back to the old homestead. And I'll have earned the privilege.* Her heart swelled with pride. He'd come such a long way.

"Hello, Uncle Nick."

He grunted, never looking up from the book he was reading. "Why are you home so early? Thought you were going to Hill Country to see Lizzy Jones before dark."

"I am, as soon as I change clothes."

"Dinner's at seven o'clock, as usual. Don't be late."

"I know the drill, Uncle Nick." *Why can't he be warm and friendly like Daddy?* She looked into his face, and her disgust melted. Although his heart wasn't perfect, it wasn't rotten either. *Maybe I shouldn't be so hard on him...*

He remained lost in Tolstoy's *War and Peace*.

She changed into her jeans and a favorite tee shirt, adorned with a picture of a kitten and puppy on the front that she received from the Humane Society in thanks for her pledged membership. She put her medicine bag on top of a box of groceries and headed for the door. It wasn't a long way to Lizzy's place on the hill, but it was steep and winding. The roads were covered with snow. She had to drive carefully.

Lizzy's little shack was surrounded with snow-covered dirt and leaves that had stockpiled on the ground. Grass under the huge oaks in hill country just didn't happen. She stopped the car, opened the door, and stepped out. Even when the mountaintops gleamed and the rest of the valley glowed in warm sunlight, this particular patch of earth lay brown and sullen.

The acreage housed several shacks and their tenants, a little less than an eighth of a mile apart. Lizzy had told her once, "If'n I want t' scream and holler at my dumb chickens, I can. Nobody gonna tell ol' Lizzy ta shet 'er trap up."

The shanty's warped gray siding had darkened over the years. Missing boards on the porch left holes where holes shouldn't be. It was a wonder poor Lizzy didn't fall right through to the ground. The railing was so shaky that it wobbled when the wind blew. A lone wicker rocker sat crooked to the left of the front door, one side shorter than the other. The chair's lack of country charm didn't faze Lizzy, who had learned to balance herself perfectly while sitting in it. No one else dared touch it, let alone sit in it. Maggie favored Lizzy over all the other hill folk patients. She was a sweetheart. Old and impoverished, she was surprisingly healthy. Her sharp mind could equal or better the best of her more affluent neighbors down the hill.

The old woman came to the door of the shack in a coat three sizes too big for her, a dirty, gray scarf around her neck, and a knitted toboggan hat that her neighbor had made for her. Her back was bent slightly, her stringy gray hair stuck straight out from under her hat, and her shoes were full of holes. Despite all the raggedy clothing, Lizzy greeted Maggie with a toothless grin as wide as the Mississippi River.

Her watch-chicken stood at her side, raising a fuss with its cock-a-doodle-doing until Lizzy gently nudged it out of the way with her foot. She opened her arms wide and welcomed Maggie with a huge hug.

"Lawdy, my lil darlin', you come in dis house rat now. It's blue cold out thar. Sit down over thar by the fire, honey." Lizzy pointed to a high-back wooden chair beside the river rock fireplace. "Whar you'n been, missy?"

"I had to finish the courses so I can be a nurse practitioner. Just got word that I passed the state exam, and I'm working under Doctor Baker. Now I can officially continue my visits up here in hill country as a bona fide homecare nurse and do more than bring a few groceries for the table, bandages to bind up wounds, and any medicines the doctor has prescribed. Don't want to be confined to an office. He said I could work with him, and I jumped at the chance."

"Oh, you mean Doc Baker? Right nice feller. He come up now and then to see us'n in hill country, 'specially when you was in school. But you take the bestest care of us folks. I sure 'm glad youse back now, Maggie honey."

A loud bang in the back room startled both of them.

"Roper!" Lizzy turned her head toward the noise behind the closed door. "Lawdy, boy. Whatcha doin' back thar? Ya tearin' up yer Granny's lovely house?"

"No, Granny, I'm looking for the lovely wash basin."

"Oh, never ya mind rat now. Git yerself out here and meet m' best friend."

"Lizzy, you didn't tell me you had a grandson."

"Yes'm, I do. My grandson come in from the army last night. He was one o' dem field doctors—a medic or somethin'. He be a captain, too."

"Uh...that's nice, Lizzy. Will he be staying here with you?"

The door squeaked on its hinges as Roper opened it. "Not for long." The dark, resonant voice had a natural air of authority about it.

Maggie turned to see a muscled man not quite as tall as the doorway, rather bulky in build, and surprisingly handsome smiling at her. His hair, the color of butterscotch, and eyes like the night sky without stars gave his good looks a unique twist. He projected confidence without arrogance, and his tee shirt fit so snug it could have been skin had it not been white. Heat crept into her cheeks. She realized she had been holding her breath.

"I'm Roper Jones," He strolled over to her and extended his hand.

"Nice to meet you, Roper. I'm Maggie Fox. I visit your grandmother on a regular basis."

"She told me all about you."

The warmth in Maggie's cheeks began to burn. "I...uh...enjoy visiting the hill folks."

"Granny said you bring her food and medicine. That's real kind of you, Miss Fox. Not many folks from the valley wander up this way."

"It's...it's not much. I just bring a few things now and then."

"That's not what I hear. Is there something I can do to help you?"

"I do have a box of groceries in the car for your grandmother." She paused, looking down at his firm, gentle hand still holding hers. "Would you mind getting it for me? It's a little bit heavy, so I'd appreciate that."

He released her hand and gave her a look that was warm but unreadable.

She turned to Lizzy. "Have you been feeling well?"

"Felt so-so last week. I was gittin' better, but I've took a backset. This flu is right down mean to git rid of, I'm tellin' ya."

"I've got medicine here in my bag that Doctor...uh...Doc Baker sent to help you. I'll write down how you are to take it. And Lizzy, take it *exactly* like I say. You must stay in bed, keep warm, and drink lots of fluids. I brought orange juice and an electrolyte drink. You take them and water and leave your tonic alone."

"Oh, honey, can't not take my tonic. That would sure as snuff kill ol' Lizzy."

"No! You stay off that moonshine. Listen to me now. I won't be able to help you anymore if you don't pay attention to me and do as I say. And that comes straight from Doc Baker."

Lizzy's head hung down. Her lips pooched out. "But honey, it makes me feel good. And at night time, it makes me sleep sound as my old hound dog I use ta have."

"I'm not going to argue with you. I'll stop coming if you don't mind me. I'm not just your friend, I'm your medical caregiver and I took an oath—"

"Okay, honey. Lawdy, what would I do without ya?" Her hat fell down over her eyes as she got up to stoke the fire. She slapped it back up with a frown and a sneer and poked at the uncooperative fire. When it didn't respond, she spit a well-chewed chaw of tobacco into the hot coals. With a sudden crackle and a sputter and a pop, the fire spit back at her. She turned away just in time as a steaming chunk sailed over her shoulder, landing with a splat on the right toe of Maggie's new boots.

"Eeewww."

"Sorry 'bout dat." Lizzy turned her attention back to the fire, but not before Maggie saw the smirk of mischief on her face. "Good thing dem boots er plastic or whatever." Then she bent over and wiped it up with the end of her scarf.

"Thanks." Maggie's stomach lurched, but she forced it to calm down. No way could she be upset with the dear old soul.

"I won't spit no tobaccer in dat fire no more. Looks like it might be dangerous." She hung her head and stuck her bottom lip out like a scolded toddler.

"No harm done, Lizzy. Now getting back to Doctor Baker, he has your best interests at heart. He's a true old-fashioned doctor, and those kind are almost extinct these days. He's getting up in years, but he still remembers the name of babies he's ever delivered and keeps their pictures on his bulletin board. He's even got a picture of my nephew, Joey. We need more like him."

The front door swung open, and Roper toted in the big box of groceries. Maggie jumped up to close it behind him.

"Thanks." He nodded and set down the sizable box that all but covered the small tabletop. "I want to find another place for us to live as soon as possible, but ..." Roper looked at his grandmother sitting by the fire. "Granny, tell Maggie what you said about moving."

"Now don' you start that thar fiddle-faddle again. This won'erful place been my home for nigh onto forty years. Next time I move, I'll be six foot under and covered with good ol' hill country dirt, maybe even some grass on top o' me."

"See what I mean?" He grinned. "I'll bet you she has money stored away somewhere in this house because I don't see where she's spent any of what I've been sending her." Roper grinned at Lizzy. "Do you, Granny?"

"I don' need nothin', but if'n ya want me ta lend ya some money, I kin."

Roper laughed aloud. "No, thank you, Granny. I'll keep that in mind though. Just don't go and tell anyone you have it. Can't trust some folks these days."

"Do tell, boy. Last week I made some nappies and put 'em out dar on the porch t' cool. When I come out to get 'em, they was gone. I'm a bettin' it wuz Minnie next door. She jest loves my nappies. Once I caught her pilferin' 'round in my yard after dark. Next time I makes 'em, I'm a gonna fill 'em with pepper and let 'er chew on that. Bet she won' be stealin' no more nappies." Lizzy's eyes twinkled as she gave them a toothless grin.

"What are nappies, Lizzy?" Maggie's curiosity got the better of her.

"They be dough rolled out'n spread with lotsa butter, brown sugar, and cinnamon. Then I roll 'er up like a wagon wheel and cut into pieces 'bout the size of two big toes. Put 'em in a pan, bake 'em till they git light brown, then eat 'em. My granny taught me how to make 'em."

"Hmm...sounds good. I know you like it here, Lizzy, but don't you think it'd be nice to have someone help take care of you soon?" She realized at once that she shouldn't have said that.

"What youse talkin' 'bout, girl? You'n are here, ain't ya? And my grandboy, he's here now, an' him wantin' t' do the work like you does an' all. Lawdy, ya two got ol' Granny in dat six-foot grave before'n it's time."

"Didn't you tell me once you had a girl in California and a boy across the river here? Surely they help out."

"Naw." The sorrow in her voice caught Maggie by surprise. "They ain't been t' see me in many moons. Got an idear they don' much like me. Only family what care fer me is Roper here."

Silence hovered over the room as an image of her father flashed through her mind. Here was another scared but unbeaten soul who wanted to live life on her own terms. She resigned herself to helping Roper take care of his grandmother any way she could. No other way could she leave Lizzy her dignity.

Roper broke the silence. "Mom's out west. She's never been much of a daughter—or mother, for that matter. But I won't go into that."

"I'm sorry, Lizzy."

"Aw...don' ya go feelin' sorry for ol' Lizzy. I've had a good life. Two eyes to see with, ears to hear with, arms 'n' legs to git around, roof over m' head, groceries on the table, good health, friends, money aplenty, and this fine boy o' mine." She looked up at Roper with as much love as Maggie had ever seen radiate from another human being. He took hold of her extended hand and smiled down at her with wet eyes. "What more could anyone want?" She laid her cheek against his hand.

What an amazing woman! Lizzy has it all in the things that really count. Next to her, Uncle Nick's a pauper. "And what will you be doing, Roper, now that your home from the service?"

"Go for the medical field, I think. I had extensive medic training in the army, so that should be a good start. I'd like to be a physicians assistant. Don't know for sure yet. Depends on money and time, but that's my goal."

"Sounds wonderful. I love the medical field."

"I see we have something in common, besides Granny, that is."

They both laughed.

"Now listen, here, you two whippersnappers, I gotta see w'at's in that thar box." Her eyes grew wider as she rummaged around inside. "Why, I wish you'd lookit thar. 'Taters, 'maters an' ingems."

Maggie's eyebrows shot up. "Ingems?"

"Onions," Roper translated.

"Bread and...what's this? Aw...candy. My favorite." She paused and looked at Maggie. "Whar's the tobaccer?"

"Now what did I tell you about chewing that tobaccer...uh... tobacco?"

"I know. Ain't no good for what ails me. But...but..."

She couldn't maintain the tough-gal image. "Dig a little deeper, Lizzy."

Lizzy rummaged about in the bottom of the box, moving cans and boxed foodstuff to the side with all the grace of a hound on the hunt until she finally found it. A slow smile spread across her face. She pulled her prize out of the box and held it high.

"Looky here what I done found." Catching her breath, she wiped away a tear. "Aw...if ya ain' a darlin'. I jest luf ya ta pieces, Maggie, me sweetie." She hugged her neck so hard Maggie almost lost her balance.

"I brought you a little, but you have to make it last a long time. I'm not going to be bringing you that terrible stuff every time I come up here."

Lizzy tore open the package and scooped out a chaw, popping it into her mouth amidst coos of delight and slurps of savor.

"I'll see that she makes it last." Roper exchanged glances with Maggie.

"I have to go now, but I'll see you next week. You, too, Roper, if you're still around."

He studied her up and down. "I'll be around."

Those sultry eyes would raise the pulse rate of the most resistant heart. Only when the lingering silence became awkward did she turn to leave.

"Goodbye, dear Lizzy. Do as I told you now." She hugged her and patted her on the back.

"Sure will, deary. I'll be a-workin' on savin that thar tobaccer. Thanks for ever'thin' an'..." Just then a bird flew in the house. "Oh, Lawdy in heaven! Git dat bird outta here, Roper. Hurry. It be a bad omen. I don't keer t' die t'night." She waved her arms around like she was shooing away a swarm of hornets.

It didn't take long for Roper to chase the frightened bird back outside. Maggie was in her car and starting down the road as Lizzy closed the door to the shack. She paid as much attention to what she saw in her rear view mirror as she did the darkening road ahead. Roper stood on the porch, watching until she was out of sight.

Hill people have so many superstitions. She hoped Lizzy wouldn't agonize over the belief that a bird in the house meant a member of the household would die that night.

Such a silly fallacy.

Chapter Eighteen

What a beautiful, star-filled night! Maggie held the curtain back and looked out the window. Fleets of clouds floated in front of the little, thin moon. Thoughts of Lizzy and Roper and how they seemed like such decent, down-to-earth folks skipped through her mind. She knew Lizzy was a fine old lady, a real survivor, but she didn't know Roper well enough to form an opinion—other than he was handsome and his grandmother obviously adored him. The latter in itself seemed a powerful recommendation. However, a man's good looks didn't mean his character matched his physical attributes. She'd been fooled before.

She giggled at the moon and was sure it winked at her before she closed the curtain and crawled beneath the covers. Visions of Roper skittered through her mind and disappeared in the mist of sleep.

Maggie wrestled with the pillow just long enough to open both eyes. She rolled over, sat up, and yawned. Her first thoughts echoed her last ones before falling asleep. Tall, broad shouldered Roper framed in the doorway, then comical, sweet, Lizzy appeared in the window of her mind. Maybe the first of next week she'd go to hill country to visit them again.

Wiggling her feet into her fuzzy slippers, she slid into her terry robe and shuffled downstairs. Today she would visit her sister again. *Sister.* The word seemed to echo all around her. *What a difference she's made in my life already.*

Cup of coffee in hand, she stared out the kitchen window. Large snowflakes swirled around and down until they congregated on the ground. As a child she had never understood why some grownups complained about that gorgeous soft white snow. Now she knew. Driving in it was no fun.

Just around the bend sat Willow Walk. *Another grand house on a hill*, she thought as she approached. The blare of a siren and flashing lights startled her and stole her breath. Her right foot darted to the brake. She pumped it up and down to avoid sliding. An emergency vehicle shot out of the driveway. Her heart flip-flopped.

It must be Kat and the baby. What else!

She stopped her car and ran up to Carla, who stood on the porch, tears streaming down her face and waving a tissue in the air.

"Oh, Maggie! I'm so glad you're here. I was about to call you. Let's go in the house." She took Maggie by the arm and led her through the front door.

"What happened, Carla?"

"It's Kat. She began bleeding, and Dr. Morgan insisted they get her to the hospital right away. You know the trouble she had with Joey."

"Does he think it could be the same problem?"

"They don't know at this point. Dawson is with her."

"Oh my. I wondered if she was trying to do too much." Maggie shook her head.

"She's been pretty good. She wants that baby so much and knows she has to be extra careful."

"Even with the greatest care in the world, things sometimes happen. Listen, I'm going on to be with her. Wheeling Hospital, right?"

"Yes, and please call me as soon as you know anything. I'm so worried"

"I will. Just you keep things going smoothly here. Where are the kids?"

"They're with me. They'll be fine...the little urchins." Her nervous laugh didn't hide the concern in her eyes. "To make things more stressful, Conchita and Cabe are moving into Willow Walk's guest house on Friday. Kat is so excited that she wants to dig in and help with the preparations. You know how she likes to do everything herself, no matter how much help she has. She's a bit hardheaded, but you know that."

"Yeah, I know. I take after her."

She turned to leave. "I'll call you as soon as I find out something. And don't worry about the family moving into the guest house. I'll help you get ready."

"Thanks, Maggie. You're a dear heart. Maybe one more hand in the helping pot will be enough to keep Kat in bed or at her drawing board."

Maggie gave her a quick hug. "Everything will work out, Carla."

The drive to the hospital seemed endless. All the way there, she fought against the terrible possibilities her training in the medical field brought to mind. Bleeding, though not considered normal during pregnancy, is not uncommon in the first trimester. Kat, however, was well into her second trimester.

She arrived at the emergency room and was directed to the area where her sister had been taken. She slipped into the cubicle to find a doctor talking with Dawson and Kat. All three nodded to Maggie.

The doctor continued. "Our first goal is to make sure there's no ectopic pregnancy. Although it's a bit late in the pregnancy for this to be an issue, it's not unknown to happen. We'll do laboratory and ultrasound tests. We'll also check for placental abruption, particularly with your history. We're retrieving your records now, and Dr. Morgan has been notified." The doctor gave her a reassuring smile. "Any questions?"

"Ectopic...that's a tubal pregnancy, isn't it?" Dawson asked.

"Typically, yes. A small percentage of these pregnancies occur outside the fallopian tube, but that's quite rare. I really don't think that's what we're dealing with here. The sonogram should tell us much of what we need to know, so let's get you started right away, Mrs. Kahill."

"Thank you, doctor."

Maggie stepped over to the bedside and kissed Kat on the forehead. "How are you doing, sweetie?"

"I'm scared, Maggie." A tear rolled out of the corner of her eye and down toward the pillow. "If anything happens to this baby, I'll just die."

"The possibilities mentioned by the doctor are potentially serious, but it's a little early to start worrying about them. They always check out the worst scenarios first, but they're often not the problem."

Kat grasped her hand. "I'm so glad you're here."

"Would you like me to go with you and Dawson for the sonogram?"

"Please do." She looked at Dawson. "Is that okay with you, sweetheart?"

"Absolutely. We'll have our own interpreter of the medical jargon."

"Honey, don't you worry until you know there's something to worry about, okay?"

Kat frowned. "I can't promise I won't worry, but I'll try to be optimistic. I'm just so...so...to tell you the truth, I'm terrified."

Dawson stepped up, and Maggie stepped back. "Honey, everything is going to be okay. Remember when we were kids? When I told you something, you believed it, right? You had all the faith in the world in my words. Don't stop after all these years."

"You're right, Daw. I love you so much."

"Yep, I'm *always* right." Dawson's eyes lit up. "Be sure you remember that."

"Oh, Daw, you're so bad." Their laughter stopped when two orderlies walked in.

"All ready, Mrs. Kahill?" Maggie and Dawson stepped away from the gurney. The orderlies began to wheel her out, jabbering the whole time and not waiting for Kat to answer their question.

"No! I'm *not* ready." Kat hollered loud enough for the whole ER to hear. The orderlies stopped talking and gave her a stunned look. "I'm sorry, but when you ask someone a question, it's customary to have respect and courtesy enough to wait for an answer. I want to speak with my husband and my sister for a moment. I won't take long."

"Yes, Ma'am."

She reached out for both their hands. "You are coming with me, right?" Her gaze moved from one to the other. It will be so much easier for me if you're there." With a nod toward the orderlies, she smiled. "Thank you. *Now* I'm ready."

"Looks like our Kat got the last word." Maggie giggled as she whispered to Dawson.

"She usually does."

When the elevator door opened, Dawson took her by the arm as they hurried after Kat and the orderlies. As they strode down the hallway, Maggie wrestled with herself over the issue that remained foremost in her mind. Kat needed to know the real truth about her father...soon. But did she need added stress right now? *If I tell Dawson now then he can choose the time to tell her. The turmoil in her mind suddenly ceased. This is the wrong time to bring Dad up. Dawson's dealing with the potential loss of his baby and a threat to his wife's life. Dad won't be high on his list of priorities right now. Still...*

"Dawson, sometime in the near future I have something I need to talk to you about." Dawson's frantic expression startled her. She wanted to bite her tongue. Years had passed without their knowing the truth; another day or week wouldn't matter.

"For heaven sake, Maggie, what is it? Is there something more I need to know about Kat's condition? Did you understand something from the doctor's words that we didn't?"

She sighed and looked at Dawson with tears in her eyes. "It's...it's...this is not the place or time to talk about it. Let's just concentrate on Kat right now." She laid her hand over his that still gripped her arm. "Please?"

"Okay. I can't think about anything other than Kat right now anyway. If something happens to her or the baby, they might just as well put me six feet under."

She gave him a warm smile. "Think good thoughts. Have a little faith, and say a prayer. The doctors here know what they're doing."

"I know that, but..."

"No buts about it." They followed the orderlies into the room where the sonogram would be performed. "When we're finished here, maybe we can get some coffee. Kat might like some, too, with the doctor's approval, of course."

"Good idea." Dawson paused. "Thanks for being here, Maggie. I had no idea what it would be like to have a sister-in-law, but it's a good thing. Kat is overjoyed to find out she has a sister. Your visits are a breath of fresh air for her, especially when she's confined to the house. I don't know how she'd be handling this situation without you."

"You know that's a two-way street, Dawson. Believe me, I'm equally blessed by our wonderful new relationship."

They took a chair on the opposite side of the room while a nurse helped Kat onto the table next to the ultrasound machine. A moment later, Kat's doctor walked into the room.

"Hello, Dr. Morgan." Dawson stood and extended his hand. "Maggie, this is Dr. Morgan. He delivered Joey and saved Kat's life. Maggie is Kat's sister."

Dr. Morgan gave her a questioning look. "I thought—"

"It's a long story," Dawson interrupted. "We'll explain later."

The doctor shook Dawson's hand and then reached out to Maggie. "Nice to see you both. The ER doctor called me. I came right over."

"Thank you. How's Kat?"

"That's what we're here to find out. We'll do the sonogram. Then we'll talk."

Dawson frowned.

Minutes ticked by after the technician spread the gel over Kat's abdomen and began running the transducer slowly back and forth across her skin.

"Look!" Maggie pointed to the screen at the side of the table. "There's your baby."

Dawson leaned forward. "You mean that little thing moving around on the screen? Oh, oh...I see her head."

"Did I hear you say 'her,' Dawson?" Doctor Morgan grinned at him.

"Yes, but...but that's because we'd like a little girl. Of course, a boy would be fine, too. We just want it to be healthy...and Kat to be healthy."

"Chances are very good both wishes will be granted. So far, we don't see a problem, and your little girl looks like she's going to be a lively one—like her big brother, I hear."

"It really is a girl?" Kat's words were barely above a whisper.

"I'm ninety-nine percent certain. She's not a bit shy about showing us who she is, so I think it's a safe bet to pick out a girl's name."

"Oh..." Kat wiped away a tear that trickled down her cheek. "She's okay then?"

"She looks good to me. Now we just have to keep her that way until she grows up enough to live outside the cocoon of your womb."

"What does that mean?" Dawson walked up beside Kat's head. "I thought you said she's okay."

"She is...but we do have a situation here—the same one we had with Joey, but less serious at present."

Kat gasped. Dawson grabbed her hand. "Why is this happening again?"

"It could be because Kat's more prone toward Placental abruption. Or it could be a result of the plane crash. Both she and the baby took a terrific jolt, and this could have caused the small separation we're seeing." He pointed to the screen. "While we don't want to take this lightly, we also don't want to get overly concerned. Kat, your mental and emotional health are very important right now. It's vital that you keep a positive outlook because your little girl will be affected adversely by any negativity."

Kat began to sob. "I can't lose her now. Please tell me that won't happen, Doctor Morgan."

He patted her arm. "You know there are no guarantees in any pregnancy. But we're on top of this, and we have a good chance of controlling things so you can carry her to term." He paused and pointed again at the monitor. "Now let me show you something."

The baby, moving her arms and legs just moments before, lay very still. Her tiny heart pounded in her chest and on the screen. Maggie stepped up for a closer look.

"When you get upset—like you did just now—she feels it. She doesn't know what's happening, but she knows something is. And she reacts. Keeping yourself calm and positive keeps her calm and creates an environment in which she can thrive. This is very important, Kat. Do you understand?"

"I...I think so."

"I don't." Dawson frowned.

"Maternal stress can create a hostile intrauterine environment. This, in turn, can cause preterm labor. That's a situation we want to avoid."

"We don't want another preemie." More tears cascaded down Kat's cheeks.

Maggie took hold of her hand. "I'm going to help you avoid that," she said in a soft, calm voice. "We're going to make that little girl very happy where she is so she wants to stay there until it's time for her debut."

Kat smiled through her tears. "I'm so glad you're here, Maggie. I don't know what I'd do without you right now."

"I'm glad I'm here, too. Finding you has been one of the highlights of my life. Now look around you, Kat. We're all part of your team. Together, we're going to see this through, and you're going to have that beautiful little girl that Jedediah wanted so much."

"How do you know he wanted it?"

"He used to talk to Dad about it. That was the only thing missing in your granddad's life, Dad told me."

Doctor Morgan nodded. "I'm going to keep you here for a few days, Kat, just to be sure that separation doesn't get any larger. Then you can go home if you promise not to do *anything* strenuous or go back to the boutique. We want to be sure we deliver a healthy little girl."

Kat looked from one to the other to the other of them. "I promise."

"Good. The orderlies will take you to your room now. I want to talk to Dawson and your sister for a moment. They'll be up to see you shortly."

They all followed her out of the room, and Doctor Morgan ushered Maggie and Dawson to an office down the hall.

"I'm sorry, Dawson. I know this is upsetting to you, and I know this is why you didn't want Kat to have another baby. I really believe this time it's from the plane crash. The amazing thing is that she didn't lose the baby. Two other pregnant women were on that flight. One of them was killed, and the other one miscarried. With lots of TLC and absolute obedience from Kat, I think she can carry this little one long enough for the baby to survive. However, she *will* need help at home for the rest of her term."

Maggie spoke up before Dawson could respond. "I'll be taking care of her, doctor. And, I might add, keeping her down. I've just passed the NP exam, so I'm anxious to put my new skills into action. Right now I'm working under Dr. Baker. Not in the office, but as a visiting nurse for the hill people."

"Very interesting, Mrs. Fox—or is it Ms. Fox?"

"Ms., for now anyway." She shrugged her shoulders. "But please call me Maggie."

"Okay, Maggie, I'm very relieved that a nurse practitioner will be looking after Kat. With that in mind, I'll probably be able to release her a day or two sooner as long as she's stable and the bleeding has stopped. I wish you much success in your profession. I hear Doctor Baker is getting ready to retire."

She nodded. "Yes, I'll be looking for someone to work under when that happens."

"Please, come to see me then. It's rewarding to know someone that wants to help the hill people. They need care—better care than their one-hundred-proof home remedies give them."

"Thank you, Doctor Morgan. I'll do that."

Dawson fidgeted. "If that's all, I'd like to see Kat now."

The doctor reached out and patted his shoulder. "Go to your wife, Dawson, and keep her calm. We've got a fighting chance here, but as your sister-in-law said, it's going to be a team effort."

Maggie followed him to Kat's room. As much as she wanted to believe everything would be all right, her training dampened her optimism. *If Kat carries this baby to term, it will be nothing short of a miracle.*

Chapter Nineteen

*J*oey sat on the back porch steps. His elbows rested on his knees, and his chin was cradled in his hands. The red snow suit he couldn't live without—the one that had a picture of Bat Man on the front—must have shrunk, he had complained to his daddy, because it felt too small. He stared at something in the big weeping willow tree just a few yards to the right of the porch.

Dawson smiled and watched through the glass in the door, wondering what his little boy was thinking. Joey regularly held long dialogues with birds and squirrels.

The conversation carried on several moments. His head cocked to the right and then the left, and occasionally he would laugh. Then Joey looked up into the sky and waved. Dawson cracked the door open slightly so he could hear what he was saying.

"Hello, God. I wan' to talk to you if you listen to li'l kids. I think you knew my great-granddaddy, and you also know he got old and died a li'l while back. I sure do miss him, God. Now, my mama's jus' come home from the 'ospital, an' she's upstairs in her bed. I'm real skeered cuz I don' want her to die, too. She's gonna have a baby, an' I git to be a big brother. I really wanna be a big brother, but I need my mama cuz I'm not growed up yet, not till next year...or maybe the year after that. An' my daddy needs her, too. He'd be awful sad if she don' git well. Then I'm skeered he'd die, too, an' I'd have nobody 'ceptin' Molly Anna, an' she's too li'l to take care of me. So please, God, if you can hear me, make Mama better for Daddy an' me an' the li'l baby what's growin' inside her. I need Mama an' love her lots, and I love my baby sister...an' I love you, too. Amen."

All of a sudden, a loud bang came out of the kitchen. *What was that?* Dawson spun around as Carla dashed into the mud room, a dish towel in one hand and a spatula in the other, both waving in the air. Strands of long hair that had been in a neat bun hung down around her face. She screamed at the top of her lungs.

"Help! A snake...in the cupboard...under the sink...He's huge. Hurry!" She threw the dishtowel down, grabbed Dawson by the hand, and pulled him into the kitchen. She stopped several feet from the cabinet that housed the interloper.

He wasn't surprised. The gardener had seen a couple small ones beneath the hedges on the side of the house. They'd decided to leave them alone to do their job—catching field mice. Another scream bounced off the walls.

"Calm down, Carla. You're gonna have a stroke."

"I threw a pan at him, but he didn't move."

That explains the big bang. "Is he dead?"

"I don't know. I thought I saw his tail move."

Joey ran into the kitchen. "Saw *whose* tail move? What're you doin', Daddy? I's outside, an' I heard this awful loud noise. I tho't the house 'sploded."

"Don't come in here, son. There's a snake under the sink."

Joey shot past him, kneeled down, and stuck his head under the sink. He reached in and pulled out the snake.

"Joey! Throw that snake down right now." Dawson ran to him and snatched the snake out of his hands. His mouth flew open. He held the snake at arm's length and stared at it.

Carla gasped and stepped back.

"Aw, Daddy, Rambo ain' gonna hurt nobody! He's just a toy. Mama got him for me when we went to town." Joey paused. "You and Carla wanna see my frogs? I got six of 'em." Joey's voice rose with excitement.

Dawson couldn't contain himself any longer. He opened his mouth and howled at the top of his lungs. Hoping Kat, who was comfortably situated in the master bedroom upstairs, hadn't heard his raucous laughter, he stared at Carla sitting on the kitchen chair, legs outstretched, head resting on the back, and her apron hanging halfway off her shoulder. Eyes closed, she tried to fan herself with her hand. *Poor dear, she looks like she's been bleached.*

"*What* is going on?"

"Kat, honey, what are you doing down here? You're only supposed to use the stairs when it's necessary."

"Necessary? I thought I was going to have to run for my life. How could anyone not be frightened half to death with that loud bang a minute ago? I thought the water heater blew up."

"Well..." He was still laughing. "Sit down here, and I'll explain our morning's experience with wild animals and crawling things." He recounted the incident while Joey stood in front of them, holding his snake.

Kat threw her head back and roared. "What's wrong with you all? Don't you like Rambo?"

"Of course we like ah...Rambo. He just scared us a bit." Dawson said

Joey scowled at them. "Why are you all laughing? Mama likes him. He's not real, Daddy, don't you know that?"

"I do now." Dawson and Kat started laughing again

Joey stuck out his bottom lip and stomped out of the kitchen. A moment later, the screen door slammed.

"I'm afraid we hurt his feelings, Daw."

"We shouldn't have laughed, but I couldn't help it. Especially after seeing Carla's white face."

"Maybe you should apologize to our zoo keeper and explain that you also believed Rambo was the real thing."

"I remember once when I was a kid, Granddad and Suzanne Helen took me to town for new shoes. You were with us, but I doubt you remember. Anyway... we passed a hardware store called Kelly Brothers. I leaned up to the front seat of the car, and said 'Look, Granddad, there's Kelly Bros.' Granddad looked at your mother, and they both burst out laughing. When they stopped, Granddad corrected me. 'It's Kelly *Brothers*, sonny, not Kelly Bros. You remember that now.' I shouted, 'But that's *not* what the sign says!' They laughed even harder. Their laughter hurt my feeling so bad I cried. I'll never forget that."

"I'm afraid that's what we did to Joey. Rambo's special to him, Daw."

"I think you're right. I'll go out and talk to him in a few minutes." He opened the fridge and retrieved a carton of milk. "Want a glass?"

"No, thanks. I'm going back upstairs to finish working on a new gown that will be featured in the show. It's a killer."

"Do you think you're doing too much again?"

"What do you mean? Doing too much wasn't what caused my problem. It was a little matter of a plane crash, remember?"

"Regardless, I'm sure your crazy work schedule didn't help matters."

Kat rose and started for the staircase, Dawson right behind her. "I suppose if I carry Joey's frogs and snake up to his toy box, I'll be doing too much."

"Kat, please. I don't mean to nag, but I worry about you as much as you would worry about me."

She looked at him. "I'm sorry, Daw. I'm just having a hard time with all the restrictions."

He looked at her out of the corner of his eye, a mischievous grin lighting up his face. "You used to do exactly what I told you. What happened?"

"I'm not six years old anymore." She smiled, twisted her mouth, and gave him an exaggerated wink. "Wish I could help with the preparations for Conchita's move into the guest house. I feel so left out."

"I know, sweetheart, but you know what's more important."

"Of course I do."

"Your idea of a big fruit basket and a bottle of champagne is great. I think most everything is ready. Carla has done a beautiful job."

"Still, I want you to check everything out in case she missed something." She looked off in the distance. "Make sure there are plenty of paper towels, toilet paper, garbage bags, tissues, and enough groceries to get them started. I put some of our last butchered cow in the freezer a week ago. I can't wait. I just love that prissy fireball, Conchita." She stopped again. "Remember, Daw, the time Granddad gave Cabe a hard time about stealing the money, and how she took up for him. What did she tell Granddad? *My Cabe talks to his brother at once when he returns and pays back some of the money he took. So why do you say such a cruel thing? No soy estúpida, y mi esposo no está estúpido. But you, Señor Kahill, are a stupid man. I will leave your casa because I will no longer be welcome, and I no longer want to be here. But I tell you that your prayer means nothing if this is how you speak. What kind of a God listens to a man who says one thing and acts...contrario?*

"I think that's the only time I ever remember Jedediah's face turning red. She was right, and he knew it. She put him in his place that day. He loved her from then on and even began to understand and forgive Cabe for stealing from us. I'm so glad your brother was man enough to accept responsibility for his actions. He's a wonderful addition to the family, and he's earned the right to call himself a Kahill."

Dawson nodded.

"Granddad thought Cabe was a bum, a thief, a no-good grandson, but he only took the money to help Conchita get away from her abusive father. The consequences of her staying in that situation could have been deadly."

"How'd you get so wise, lady?" Dawson wrapped his arm around her shoulder. "I know how much you want to welcome them home. Why don't you curl up on the couch in the parlor instead of going up to our room? I'll build a fire, and you can visit with everybody. Cabe left for the airport over an hour ago, so they'll be here soon."

Tears sprang to her eyes. "Thank you, Daw. I'd really like that."

Maggie came in from the greenhouse and set the last bowl of fresh flowers on the credenza. "Here, let me help you. I heard what Dawson said about your resting in the parlor. That's a great idea."

The sisters walked arm and arm to the sofa. Maggie arranged the pillows and covered Kat's legs with a cotton throw Grandma Emma had crocheted more than twenty years before.

"Thank you, Maggie. I've only known you for a few weeks, yet I can't even imagine life without you. Is it always this way with sisters, do you suppose?"

"Maybe not always. But for us, we didn't know each other for almost our whole lives, so we know how special sisters are."

"The Kahills have always valued family. The more, the merrier, Granddad often said."

"I wish the Foxes were like that. Are you glad Cabe's family is coming?"

"We've all missed Conchita and the twins. They've been in Mexico with her father. He drank and beat her while she was growing up, but he gave up the booze and begged her to come for a visit. He'd never seen the babies. She went for a week, and he got sick while she was there. She ended up taking care of him for longer. Now we can't wait to have them back. The halls of Willow Walk will bustle again with children and relatives. Granddad would have liked that."

"Twins! The Kahills get more interesting all the time. What are their names?"

"Officially, they're Carson Joseph and Emma Dee. To us, they're C.J. and Emmie." Kat paused. "It's hard to believe they're five months old already."

Cabe stopped just long enough at the big house to take the twins to the door and Dawson's open arms, then drove straight to the bungalow behind it. He ushered Conchita inside. She stepped into the kitchen and looked around at the fresh flowers on the counter, the two place settings on the table, and the stew simmering in the Crockpot.

"Who is living here, *mijo*? I think *esta es la casa* of somebody. We leave now before they find us, *si*?"

Cabe laughed. "*Mija*, this is our house. We're going to live here for awhile... if you want to."

"*¡Me gusta! ¿Pero por qué?*"

"I thought you'd like it." He slipped his arm around her waist. "As for the why, Kat wants us near the main house. She's expecting a baby in April, and she just survived a plane crash and is having some problems like she had when she was pregnant with Joey. She needs the family close by, and she loves you and the twins with all her heart. I think she just wants to be able to see you often, and she can't if you're at the lodge or in one of the cabins."

"I want to help her, but I think maybe *mi ingles no es bueno*. What if I no understand what she needs? I forget the words *en ingles, mijo*."

"It will come back quickly because nobody here but you and me speaks Spanish. Don't worry..." He turned her around to face him. "I missed you, *mija*. Every day seemed like a year while you were gone." He wrapped his arms around her in a huge bear hug and held her for a long moment. "Now let's go look at the rest of the house before you decide for sure."

"Okay, but already I know this is the place I want to live."

Cabe led her into the living room and bedrooms. "You think you will be comfortable here? Nothing's too good for my girl, you know."

"*Perfecto*. We go see Kat now and tell her *gracias por la casa hermosa*."

A baby snuggled into the crook of each arm, Kat looked down at them and smiled. "I can't wait to have a baby again, Daw. I'd forgotten how precious these beautiful moments are when they look up at you with trusting eyes and are totally content to be cuddled." Joey and Molly Anna scampered into the room, dashed around the sofa, and ran out the door. Kat chuckled. "But you have to enjoy them while they're small because they grow so quickly."

Conchita and Cabe walked in, and C.J. fussed for his mama the instant he saw her. Emmie gave her mother a quick glance and turned back to stare at Kat. Conchita reached out for her son, kissed Kat on the cheek and told her how much she had missed her, then turned toward Maggie.

"I am Conchita. *¿Cómo se llama?*"

"I'm Maggie, Kat's half-sister. I look forward to getting to know you, Conchita. I've heard so many wonderful things about you."

"*Muchas gracias*. Half-sister? Maybe I get to know how this happens later?"

"Yes, we'll talk later." Maggie covered her mouth to keep from laughing.

"Now, *por favor*, my babies and me, we need for to sleep. The airplane ride is very long, and we are tired."

"Yes, of course." Kat kicked off the throw and started to get up.

"No, no, *mi hermana*, you rest *también*...also. I come back tomorrow. I love you."

Cabe helped her put the babies down in the cribs Kat had ordered for the nursery. He took her hand and pulled her toward their bedroom across the hall.

She frowned. "No *es bueno* for my babies to be in a different room. What if I do not hear when they need me?"

He guided her back into the nursery and pointed to a small box on the table between the beds. "Do you know what that is?"

She shook her head.

"It's a monitor."

"I do not know this word...monitor."

"It lets you listen to the babies from anywhere in the house."

She gave him a quizzical look.

"I'll show you." He took her to their bedroom." Now sit here on the bed. I'll be right back." He left the room, and a moment later she heard his soft voice coming from the box on the table by the bed. When he returned to the room, she was smiling.

"You do this *para mi, mijo*?"

"I set it up, but it was Kat's idea."

"That Kat, she is thinking of everything. Now I hear them even if they..." Her brows knitted, then relaxed. "If they sneeze."

"Right. And there are monitors in the bathroom, living room, and kitchen. She even had one installed outside the back door so you can hear them if you step outside."

She gave him a big smile and took his hand. He tipped her chin and kissed her mouth. She shivered when he slid his hand down her arm.

"Ay...you are mine, *mi amor*. I miss you too much when I am gone." Turning down the spread, she slipped out of her clothes and under the covers.

Cabe pulled the shades, turned on the gas fireplace, closed and locked the door, and climbed into bed beside her. He pulled her into his arms and let the warmth of her body spread through him. For the first time since she left, he felt complete. *Life is good. I am a happy man.*

Chapter Twenty

*M*aggie stood in front of the parlor window. An ordinary winter evening with an ordinary winter sky met her gaze. She might as well have been one of the black shadows that formed on the snow, sliding and slithering away from the trees, silhouetted by the setting sun and disappearing in the coming darkness.

Under the emerging face of the moon, slivers of silver sparkled on the snow, urging her to head upstairs, dive under the covers, and pop out to a spring sunrise after a long winter's night. The lazy, falling snow made her want to snuggle close to the man of her dreams. She'd almost given up, but her heart continued to search for that special man, the strong one who would stand by her side to face whatever the world tossed their way. A smile played at the corners of her mouth. If he also happened to be tall, broad, and good looking, that would be fine, too. The loneliness in her heart bubbled over. *You're out there somewhere, my love—but I can't find you.*

Her eyes wanted to close. Was it to shut out the absence of a special love in her life? Or was it to escape the inevitable process of explaining to her sister why their dad left so many years ago?

Sighing, she moved from the window to the cushioned Boston rocker by the hearth and threw the small, handmade quilt of many colors and patterns over her legs. Her mama had made it for her when she was seven—a special just-because-I-love-you gift. She relived the memory in her head. Tearing the gift paper off, she opened the lid in slow motion and peaked into the box, then flung the lid off and pulled the quilt out. Tears filled her eyes. She ran to her mama, hugged her, and thanked her. It was the most beautiful thing she'd ever seen. What a day that had been. She still marveled that a card from her dad with a twenty-dollar bill in it to buy the Barbie doll she wanted arrived the very same day. She still recalled his words. *Thinking of you, Magpie. I can't believe you're seven years old now. You're getting to be an old lady. Stay as sweet as you are, honey. Daddy loves you and will be home soon.* Then she remembered how they had laughed about the old lady joke.

Her hand smoothed each square of fabric that had once been school clothes or a lovely Sunday dress. She didn't need photographs to remember the nice clothes her mama made for her. Her mind's eye recalled and cherished each one. Mama was the most gentle, most caring mother in the entire world.

When her father came home for her mama's funeral, he held her close while she cried in his arms. "Oh, Magpie, your mama wouldn't want you to be so sad. She'd want you to remember all the wonderful times the two of you had together, the times you talked and laughed and celebrated special occasions."

Her father had left in the middle of that night. The next morning she found a note.

> *Magpie, Sweetheart, I'll be back soon. There are just a couple more things I've got to do. I can't tell you the reason now, but someday I will. Please know that I don't want to be gone. Remember always that I love you. I'll write. Stay as sweet as you are now.*

His leaving left her heartbroken again, but she would wait...because that's what you do when your heart is full of love for someone.

From that day forward, she allowed herself to miss her mother, but she didn't cry over the loss. She laughed at the things they had laughed about and reveled in what they had celebrated. Her mother had given her a solid, loving start in life that she wanted to pass on to her own children. She just had to find the right father for those children...

The memories continued to flow. She had grown up with Uncle Nick at Fox Run, always believing that Dad would be home someday soon, and they would be together.

Frank Yerby's *The Foxes of Harrow* lay on the end table beside her. She picked it up, turned to the fourteenth chapter, and tried to begin reading where she'd left off. The distraction didn't work. Rubbing her forehead, she willed her mind to focus on something far more important than *The Foxes of Harrow*— The Foxes of Fox Run.

Time had come to unhinge the closet door and let the skeleton out. No more procrastinating, consequences or not. She changed positions in the rocker and reached for her cup of hot tea. Hoping for a good night's rest, she couldn't be sure if she'd sleep like a baby or howl at the moon like a wolf. The clock struck eight, not too late to call Dawson and make arrangements to meet.

She uncurled from the rocker and picked up the phone twice, then put it back down. *Are you going to go in circles all night, Maggie Fox?*

Dawson answered. She willed her voice not to shake. "Hi, favorite brother-in-law. I...I...just wondered if Kat was behaving herself, or must I come over there and straighten her out...again?" Her laugh came out phony, more like a hyena's than her own.

Apparently Dawson saw the humor in it. "Hey, I'm your *only* brother-in-law. No competition in that department. And Kat? She's being a good kid. She realizes the seriousness of the whole matter. But come on over anyway."

"It's a little late tonight. What about tomorrow? Will you both be home?"

"I don't know about me, but Kat'll be here. They need help at the front desk now with the number of guests we have. Mind you, I'm not complaining. This is shaping up to be one great season for us. People from all over are arriving in droves. I love it, but we have to cater to them if we want them back again next year. Don't want a job, do you?"

"Thanks, but I have the hill people to care for—which leaves me little time for anything else besides keeping tabs on my sister."

"Maggie, I commend you for the job you do. Nursing hill people can't be easy."

"No, but it's rewarding. They live in poverty, Dawson, but they're proud and mannerly. Most are good, caring folks who know how to love one another. Many of them don't realize they're poor. One of my favorite little ladies once said, 'We'ns have a roof over er head and pots and pans to catch da rain wit. We'ns have food on the table, chickens, rabbits, and quail that the menfolk catches. We'ns have warm beds an' ol' river-rock fireplaces to keep us'n warm in da white snow time. Gracious, what else is there, honey?' They keep me in chickens and produce from their gardens. Can't complain about that, and they feel good about being able to pay in a way for the services they receive."

"You're something else, Maggie."

"The reason I called is I need to see you and Kat tomorrow if possible. Dad and I have something ..." She took a deep breath and exhaled. "Something we need to tell you. It's been hidden too long now. It mustn't wait any longer."

"Sounds serious. I'll try to take a break early in the afternoon."

"Will Dad be able to get away, too?"

"Don't worry about that. I'll see that he's free."

"Tell Kat I love her."

She laid the phone in the cradle and sighed. *That's the beginning of the end of this nightmare. Maybe Kat will understand that this whole business is not her mother's fault, that her grandparents carried the big ugly stick.* Picking the receiver up again, she called her dad.

"You think it's wise to tell Kat now, after all her trouble with the baby? Do you think the shock will be too much for her?"

"She's got to know sometime, Dad, and I think it should be now. Sometimes I think we're pampering her too much. If it were me—I wouldn't want to be left in the dark. She's got to know about our other issue, also, but...one thing at a time. After the first secret's out, there's only one skeleton left. We'll cross that bridge when we get to it."

"All right. I love you, Magpie."

"Me too, Daddy. Sleep well."

Maggie walked into the parlor at Willow Walk and stopped to hug her sister. "Please try to understand what I'm going to tell you. I've tried to find the right words, but I can only tell it like it is." She sat in one of the wingback chairs flanking the fireplace.

"Sounds a bit urgent."

"It's just the right time, Kat."

"Before you start, tell me how your Hill Country patients are getting along."

Maggie gave her a searching look. *Is she trying to put off what I have to say?* "If you ask them, they'll tell you so-so, even if they're not? They're amazing people. I look around at all the wealth here and at Fox Run and wonder how they can be happy, living like they do. A couple magazines lie on their orange crate bookshelves, if they have any bookshelves at all." Her gaze traveled momentarily to the book-laden shelves that lay against the wall on either side of the fireplace. "Lizzy's house is decorated with a couple chairs, each with one short leg. She found them in dumps around town. They sit by the rough river-rock fireplace. Some of the shacks, inside and out, have a coat of powdered limestone mixed with water to make whitewash, slapped on here and there. What I can't understand is how they live with the mice day in and night out." Maggie grinned

Kat's eyes widened. "Mice? You can't be serious."

"I asked about those critters that were scampering across the floor one day when I was there because I couldn't see a trap anywhere. "'Oh, honey,' she said, 'they don't eat much. And Sylvester is an entertainer. He does cartwheels and squeaks like he's singing. I love to watch him at night when the kerosene lamp is lit. He's my friend. He jest loves da cheese I feed him.'"

"With an attitude like that she'll never have a heart attack." Both girls giggled. "Maybe we should get us a couple entertainers for Willow Walk and Fox Run."

"But you know what else, Kat?"

"Don't tell me they have raccoons and possums for entertainers, too."

"They might. I don't know. Their medical bills never go unpaid. Sometimes they pay with chickens and sometimes with vegetables from their gardens, but they always pay somehow."

For a moment Kat was silent. "I can tell you think the world of them, Maggie. I'd like to tag along with you sometime when you visit."

"In the spring or early summer, I'd love for you to come with me. Lizzy will love you."

Dawson walked in, Cannon right behind him. The conversation came to a standstill.

Maggie watched Kat's face go pale as he came to stand behind her chair. She turned her head away from him as Dawson sat down across from Maggie. Silence hung like a black cloud in the room.

Dawson cleared his throat. "Maggie, what is so serious that you have to tell us?"

Maggie bit her lower lip and looked at Cannon for support. "I...I don't know where to start, Dad." A whisper of uncertainty tingled through her.

"Start at the beginning, Magpie."

She rose, walked to the large window, and turned to Kat.

"Dad left us when we were little girls, but not because he wanted to."

Kat's jaw throbbed visibly.

"I'll be brief and to the point to keep your stress to a minimum."

"It's already too late for that," Kat muttered in a low tone.

"Take your time." Dawson said.

"Thank you, Dawson. To make a long story short, he was forced to leave. It broke his heart but he didn't have any other option." She forced back the tears that filled her eyes. Suddenly her words rushed out like water over a dam. "Kat's mother had been ordered by her parents, the Masons, to have an abortion." A single tear escaped down her cheek, and she brushed it away with her finger.

Kat gasped. Her jaw throbbed harder.

Cannon spoke up. "Kat, would you like us to stop here?"

"I think not. Say what you came to say and get it over with."

"Stop now, Cannon." Dawson leaned forward in his chair and looked up at the man.

"No! Go on with the story. I'm okay."

Cannon looked from Kat back to Dawson. He picked up where Maggie had left off after Dawson nodded.

"Your mother was too young to defend herself. She didn't know how or what to do. Besides, she was terrified of her father. She told her parents we loved each other and wanted to marry, but they forbade it. Your mama pleaded with them. They refused to listen. They didn't want to hear, nor did they want an illegitimate child running around to sully their golden reputation." He paused as the color drained from Kat's face. "I'm sorry, Kat. I don't mean to put your grandparents down, but you didn't know them." Cannon began to cough.

"Water, Cannon? Maggie? Kat? Or maybe a brandy?" Dawson stood.

"Water, please." Cannon said.

"Water for me." Kat neither smiled nor looked at anyone.

"I wish a brandy, but it's a little early." Maggie thought a moment. "I guess one wouldn't hurt." She took a deep breath and blew it out rapidly. Dawson laughed. "Now you sound like Granddad. He always said a good stiff brandy never hurt *nobody*."

"I think Jedediah and I would get along like spit and tobacco." Maggie said.

"Maggie! What a thing to say. Spit and tobacco?" Cannon repeated. "That's terrible. Haven't I taught you better?"

"Sorry, Daddy. Uncle Nick always says it."

"Figures," Cannon mumbled.

Maggie took the glass of brandy from Dawson and gulped it down in one swig. "I know Jedediah was a wise old man. If he said it, I believe it." She opened her mouth, exhaled, and waited for the fire to shoot out and devour her family. When the sting eased, she relaxed, returned to the chair, and crossed her legs. "Thank you, Dawson. That will do nicely."

Everyone grinned except Kat.

"You're welcome, Maggie. Now you were saying, Cannon?" Dawson asked.

"I tried to see Suzanne many times, but the Masons ran me off."

"You mean my grandparents, not my mother, ran you off? Why did they want Mama to have an abortion? Why didn't they like you, Cannon?" Kat voice was barely above a whisper.

"Yes, they ran me off. The reasons we'll go into later. Let's get the basics out in the open first." Cannon paused. "You might as well know your grandparents were very old school—proud, self-righteous folks who tolerated no deviation from their standards and offered no forgiveness to anyone who crossed the line. They threatened to call the law if I ever came back. That didn't frighten me—but the terrible news I heard from my brother did. He learned about the plan to abort the baby—you. I went to plead with them not to do that. You were my child and Suzanne Helen was the first precious love of my life. The only other woman I ever came close to loving the same way was Maggie's mother."

Kat frowned. Tears welled up in her eyes and began rolling down her cheeks onto her neck.

"I still thought we could somehow sneak away and get married, but a week later, they took your mama to Paris, where you were born."

Maggie walked over to the couch and laid a hand on her sister's shoulder. "You okay, honey?"

Kat nodded. "Go on, Cannon."

"When I was talking to Suzanne's parents, I got huffy and said I would take you away from them. 'Go ahead and try it,' her father dared me, 'and you'll spend the rest of your life behind bars for kidnapping.' Then I said I would do anything they wanted if only they would stop insisting on the abortion. I begged, I pleaded, I even cried. The answer I got about killed me right there. Mrs. Mason spoke up—to this day I've never seen hate portrayed in such depth of ugliness in another human being. Her look of contempt was so intense, so... Please don't take offense at what I say, Kat. You never knew your grandparents and just as well you didn't. Maybe they meant well, but the decision they made was terribly wrong. You need to know the whole truth. Painful as it may be right now, it will serve you well in the future, I'm sure of it."

Kat's tears flowed down her face, streaking her makeup. Dawson handed her a box of tissues and squatted down beside the couch.

"Do you want to stop, Kat?"

She gave him an almost uncomprehending look. "No, Daw. I'm all right."

Cannon hesitated, then continued. "Then Mr. Mason said, 'Here's what you can do. You can leave Fox Run, get the hell away from Suzanne, and never see her again. Never contact her in any way. You're nothing but a lousy, no-good Fox. Take this money to seal the deal.' I told him to keep his money because I wouldn't want it if I were starving." Bitterness crept in around the edges of Cannon's voice. He bowed his head and walked to the window.

"Anyway," Maggie continued for him, "Mr. Mason and my—our—father shook hands. The deal was made. Your father agreed not to force the abortion if Dad left town and never tried to contact Suzanne in any way."

Cannon stopped his pacing at the window and walked back to stand behind the chair, his arms resting on its high back. He looked directly into Kat's eyes. "You see the choice I had. More than anything, I wanted you to live, even if I could never see you. You were my blood, my baby that I helped create. I would have done anything..." Cannon turned his back to the group, shoved his hands in his pocket, and looked out the window.

Maggie studied Kat's reaction, looking for some remnant of compassion, some sign of forgiveness, some willingness to share the suffering. She saw a blank expression, a tear-stained face, eyes devoid of emotion, and total indifference.

Chapter Twenty- One

*H*er sister's indifference grated on Maggie's mind like chalk screeching across a blackboard. She stood and walked over to her father. When she tried to look him in the eye, he hung his head—but not fast enough for her to miss the tears that tumbled down his cheeks. His anguish filled the room, triggering something so deep in her that she let out a gasp. This pain was going to end right now because she was going to end it. Quiet as a cat that brushes through long grass at night, she strode halfway across the room to stand in front of Kat.

"Listen up, Kat. Dad kept his promise so you could be here today. Your father, in preventing the abortion, lost all rights of ever seeing you. He loved Suzanne and you, even before you were born." She paused to let her words sink in. "I know what you must have felt all these years because I felt the same thing. I was abandoned, too, because Dad was afraid that somehow your grandparents would find out he was in the area. So look at it this way. You don't have to forgive Dad now because there is *nothing to forgive*. He saved your life. It's as simple as that."

A steady stream of tears ran down Kat's cheeks and dripped onto her lips.

Dawson kneeled and nestled her in his arms. "We had no idea. Why didn't someone tell us long before now? It wasn't fair to withhold this knowledge from Kat."

"You still don't get it, do you? This isn't just about Kat." Maggie bit the inside of her cheek, turned her back on all of them, and paced to the other side of the room.

Cannon walked from the window to the back of the chair where Maggie had been sitting. "I didn't want Kat to blame her mother for not standing up to her grandparents. And I didn't want to feel compelled to voice my opinion about how inhumane I thought they were for even considering such a horrendous thing. I knew she needed to know the whole truth and not just bits and pieces of it." He directed his words to Dawson, then turned his gaze to Kat. "I would rather have you hate me than your mother. Can you forgive me for not telling you sooner?"

Kat sat up straight, her rigid posture like that of a mannequin. Neither moving nor speaking, she looked at her father.

Cannon lowered his head. "Of course you know the rest of the story."

Dawson held Kat's hands with both of his. "Yes. We grew up knowing that Suzanne Helen wasn't my mother but believing the lie that Cable was Kat's biological father. Suzanne Helen wanted it that way, so we believed we were half-siblings...a terrible lie that almost kept us apart forever." He rose and began passing around coffee and hot chocolate from the tray that Carla had set on the table.

Maggie walked back over to her sister. "Now you know why our dad left us. I'm so sorry about the Masons. Maybe they meant well. If so, they sure went about it in the wrong way."

Kat remained almost catatonic. Her tears dried up. Her passive expression and unresponsiveness made it seem that she hadn't comprehended what she'd just heard. At last, she moved. Pushing herself to the edge of the couch, she looked at no one in particular and said nothing. Then she stood up, letting both hands fall to her side. Cannon stepped out from the back of the chair to face her. Their gazes locked. Her jaw throbbed visibly. Turning her back on him, she headed straight for the parlor door.

Maggie felt the blood drain from her face. A fire started in her stomach and worked up to her throat until she felt like spitting flames.

"Kat, wait."

Kat stopped short a step outside the doorway, her back to everyone.

"Wait just one damn minute." The blood that had drained away charged back. Her cheeks burned. She couldn't still her racing heart.

Kat turned with a start and looked at Maggie. Flashes of recognition lit her eyes, then disappeared. She stared at Maggie without emotion.

"You're going to walk out of here just like that? Not say one word about what we've told you, what Dad has poured his heart out about? Talk about unfair. Let me tell you something, Katarina Kahill. You're not the only one hurting here. We all feel the pain of this whole sorry mess. Dad was good enough to tell you why he left, but you seem to have blinders on. You're thinking only about yourself and how much you've suffered. Let me tell you something, girl. I missed having my dad around, too. You know why he wasn't there for me? He made a promise so *you* could live. Was this my fault? No. Do I blame you? Of course not. Just you remember this, missy. The hole in Dad's heart is as big as yours, maybe bigger. You've suffered because he left you...he's suffered because he had to leave you in order to save you. Don't you get it? You didn't hold it against me for what Dad did, so why then would you hold it against Dad for the sorry thing your grandparents did? Give the man a chance. He did the right thing—then and now. You're walking proof of that. And because he walked away, I have the most wonderful sister in the world. Can't you see that?" Maggie took a ragged breath and let it out. Tears coursed down her cheeks. "I thought I knew you, but now...I...I don't know."

Maggie threw her hands in the air. She had to get out of there before she exploded. Picking up her pocket book, she slung it over her shoulder and slid sideways through the door and past Kat.

"M...Maggie?" Kat's voice broke. The air sliced in and out of her lungs like the blade of a ripsaw.

Maggie stopped dead in her tracks and turned slowly, almost as if she might still decide to walk out of the house.

With tears rolling down her cheeks and soaking her shirt, Kat walked over to her, stared for a long moment, then threw her arms around her. For several seconds, Maggie stood there, arms at her side, before she returned the embrace. They rocked back and forth, holding onto each other as if life was ending—or beginning—right then. "I love you Maggie...I...mean...sis. I *do* love you." At last they pulled away, laughing and crying at the same time, then hugged again. "Now I have something else I need to do, sis. And I think it's well overdue."

Cannon faced the window, his hands in his pockets and his head cocked to one side. Kat walked slowly toward him. She stopped and whispered his name. He turned to her. The pain, defeat, and disappointment on his face stabbed her heart. Tears fell from his eyes. She stood before him, her lips moving but no sound coming from them.

Would I walk away from Joey or Willow and never see them again to save their lives? In a heartbeat, but I think I would die from the pain. Oh, Cannon...oh, Daddy...I'm so, so sorry.

"For so many years, I despised a man who didn't even care enough about me to tell me who he was, who never sent a card or a letter or brought me medicine when I was sick. I created him in my mind, and he was a monster. I knew if he ever revealed himself, I would scream at him about his despicable behavior and then walk away, never looking back, no matter how much he pleaded. And then I met you—the last person in the world I suspected of being my father." She shook her head and began to sob.

Cannon wrapped his arms around her and pulled her close. "It's all right, Kat. You don't need to say anything more."

She leaned her head back and looked up at him. Somehow he seemed a little taller. "Yes I do. I need you to understand the awful things that hate did to me." She sniffed. Maggie handed her a tissue. "The real story of why I grew up without a father is so different from what I imagined that I couldn't accept it. I had to blame somebody for the pain in my heart. Cable was not a nice man, and when he told me on his deathbed that he was in reality my *step*-father, I could only imagine my real one to be even worse. Otherwise, why would he have abandoned me?" Her body began to shake.

Cannon stepped to the side and wrapped his arm around her shoulder. "Let's sit on the couch. We need to take care of you and that baby." He led her to the sofa and covered her legs with the throw. Then he sat down beside her and reached for her hand.

"When I was young, I always wanted to be Daddy's little girl, but Cable called me names and spanked me for almost everything I did. Even as a child, I knew he didn't like me. Then he left and took Dawson with him. He didn't want me."

"Oh, my god..." Cannon wiped away a new flood of tears with the back of his other hand.

"So you see, my hate began long before I knew he wasn't really my daddy. And now, it's such a habit that it's hard to let it go. I don't want to hate you, Cannon. I just don't know how to love you. Please give me a little time to get to know you and come to grips with the *real* reason you weren't around. You've shown me today that sometimes the greatest love of all is the one that walks away. You did that for me, and I'll love you for it—really I will—but I just need to work through everything."

Her anger melted. She looked up at him and saw the man he was and the unselfish love he had shown to preserve her life. She saw his eyes, his expression, his pain—all so like her own. Out of the overflow of her heart, she whispered.

"Welcome home, Daddy."

Chapter Twenty-Two

*M*aggie heaved a huge sigh of relief, like the weight of the world had been lifted off her shoulders. The smile on her father's face when he and Dawson had headed back to the lodge made every hour, every minute of stress over his relationship with Kat so worth the wonderful final outcome. Now, glad to be on her way home to check on Uncle Nick, she would make him some hot tea and a pot of chicken soup to ease the flu he had diagnosed himself as having. For weeks he'd had dark circles under his eyes, no color on his face, and his clothes looked positively baggy. But he flatly refused to see a doctor despite her argument that many ailments had flu-like symptoms and self-diagnosis could be costly in the long run. *Why can't I shake the feeling that something else is going on here?*

Fox Run welcomed her with a warm and cozy feeling as she crossed the porch and opened the double doors to the grand hall. After removing her coat and scarf she headed for the parlor, where Nicholas sat reading, sniffling, and coughing.

"Hi, Uncle Nick. How are you feeling? You're still sniffling."

He scowled at her. "It's just the leftovers from the flu, Maggie. Don't make so much of it. It's got to run its course."

Well...hello to you, too. "The only flu symptom you have is a low grade fever off and on, and that could also be something else working on you. And that cough...I don't think that's from the flu."

"Listen." Nicholas pointed his finger at her. "You can't keep a Fox down with something as insignificant as a little cough. I told you it's from the flu I had a few months ago."

"What? Are you joking?" *A few months ago!* "Most coughs from the flu would be long gone by now." She shook her head. To bandy words with Uncle Nick meant losing a battle every time.

"What do you want me to do? Go to a hotel until it's gone so you don't have to hear me hacking?"

No use arguing with him. He listens to reason only when it's his reasoning. "Don't be sarcastic, Uncle Nick. You know I don't want you to go anywhere— except maybe to the doctor."

"I wouldn't put it past you or that brother of mine to put me out of here over a little cough."

"Why must you always be so hostile? You're the most argumentative man I've ever known."

"It's not my fault you haven't known many men."

"That really hurts, Uncle Nick. I don't deserve those nasty words. What's wrong with you lately?" She patted herself on the back for controlling her temper.

"I'm sorry, Maggie. I know I'm a real jackass sometimes. Only difference between me and other jackasses—I admit it."

"I can't argue with that."

"Maybe I should find somewhere else to spend the rest of this evening." Nicholas blew his nose and squirmed in his chair. He reached his left arm around and rubbed his back above his waist.

"Do you have pain?"

He squirmed again. "Just been sitting in one position too long."

"I don't mean to harp on it, Uncle Nick, but you can't be sure your diagnosis is correct. You need to see a doctor. My educated opinion is that it's something else working on you."

His expression changed to the one she loved best, that caring, loving look. "Maggie dear, sometimes you just have to believe in what you wish for."

What does that mean?

Maggie reversed her usual routine in the Hill Country, visiting all her other patients before she stopped at Lizzy's. She kept telling herself that she wanted to spend more time with the old lady to be sure she was doing as well as she claimed to be. Her heart chided her. *You want to spend more time all right, but it's not with Lizzy. You're smitten with her grandson, Maggie Fox, and you might as well admit it.*

Still, she stayed to visit after giving Lizzy a thorough examination. The woman was healthier than most folks who lived in the city and enjoyed all the advantages of civilization. Maggie and Roper sat on orange crates while Lizzy did a happy dance in front of the fire. She twirled around and around, stopped in front of them, and pointed a waggling finger first at Roper and then Maggie. The point of her little verse could not be missed.

"Holey Moley – Sudden Joy
Maggie Girl and Roper Boy
Like the cooing of a dove –
When you kiss, you'll fall in love."

Heat rose in Maggie's cheeks. *When did Lizzy become a matchmaker?* She wanted to look at Roper, but she didn't dare.

"You weren't supposed to say that, Granny." He gave his grandmother a half grin. "I haven't even asked her out yet."

"Tha's even more reason fer me t' light a fire under ya, boy. I jes' wanna be sure ar Maggie girl says yes. Never hurts t' bring yer feelin's out in the open, ya know."

"I'm only inviting her to supper and a movie on Saturday. That's no big deal."

Lizzy flashed a toothless grin. "Maybe not, boy, but the sparkin's jes' beginnin'. Ya wait 'n' see now. We'll be havin' a weddin' 'fore ya know it."

Maggie cleared her throat and sneaked a peek at Roper. His cheeks glowed a pretty shade of pink in the firelight. He turned to look straight at her.

"Granny spoiled my surprise, but I guess I'd better ask you here and now before she blows a gasket."

Maggie tried to suppress a giggle, but didn't quite succeed. "I'd be honored to go to dinner and the movies with you, Roper." His grandmother let out a whoop loud enough to travel the length of the mountainside. Maggie shook her head and rose to leave. Roper held her coat while she slid her arms into it. "And you'd best be letting other people handle their own affairs. You'll be scaring your grandson away if you keep that up."

"Oh, drat, don' wanna do dat."

She looked at Roper, raised her eyebrows, and tucked her scarf inside her coat collar. He winked. "Goodbye, you two. I had a great time and love those nappies, Lizzy."

"Here ya are, chile. I done made an extra batch for ya to take home. And youse be careful on them thar risky roads, ya hear me now?" Lizzy handed her a big sack and kissed her on the cheek.

"Thanks. I'll see you both soon." She looked at Roper. "Seven o'clock?"

"Yep. If I can wait that long."

Now it was her turn to blush.

"You stay in the house, Granny. I'll see Maggie to her car." Roper took her by the arm.

As soon as they were out of Lizzy's line of sight, Roper took her in his arms and kissed her. Time stopped. She lost herself in the moment. It almost hurt when he pulled away.

"Roper, I..."

"Hush now." His voice, low and throaty, caressed her.

She stared at him. Surely, he must hear the wild pounding of her heart.

"You're so beautiful, Maggie. I've wanted to kiss you since the moment we met."

"I...I better....be going."

"I take it we're still on for Saturday?"

"You just try to get out of it." *Can he hear my heart dancing?*

"Goodnight, lovely lady." He opened the car door. Before she had a chance to step inside, he pulled her close and kissed her again. "I think I'm falling in love with you."

Tucked up against him like a woodland creature seeking warmth, she burrowed her nose into the hollow of his shoulder. His arms curved around her like they belonged there. Every part of him imprinted itself on her brain. More scared than she'd ever been, she couldn't imagine letting go.

"I'm confused, Roper. I don't understand what's happening. This isn't my way. Never have I fallen head over heels for a man I've just met." She shook her head.

"Sometimes we don't need understanding. We just need to accept, enjoy, and..."

"...and hope for more?"

His deep chuckle sent shivers through her. "That's it...hope for more."

She slipped under the wheel and waved out the window. The butterflies in her stomach flew in a holding pattern long after the glow of the oil lamps in Lizzy's shanty disappeared from view. In a matter of moments, her life had done a one-eighty. Whatever lay ahead, she was ready.

Maggie Fox, step to the fore. Your love life is about to come into its own.

Chapter Twenty-Three

Maggie stood in the grand hall. The lonely quiet of the old house echoed all around her. Fox Run's solitude had never bothered her, but something tonight was different. She hung her coat on the clothes rack, laid her purse and car keys on the hall table, and walked into the parlor. Nick wasn't sitting in his usual chair. His book lay closed on the table beside it. The faint aroma of his pipe tobacco suggested he had not smoked in the room for several hours.

She sat on the edge of the rocker and warmed her hands by the fire, a fire he had no doubt started in anticipation of her arrival. Her eyes roamed. What was wrong with this forsaken place? It needed children romping from room to room, playing hide-and-seek. When did the music and the laughter disappear? The aroma of pies and cakes in the oven no longer wafted from the huge kitchen. She felt as though she were living in a magnificent mausoleum.

She should be married, bear those children, awaken Fox Run with laughter and energy. She could almost see a dog named Spot chasing a cat named Felix all over the house, squealing children right behind them. And when Joey and Molly Anna visited, Fox Run would be in total, delightful chaos, just the way it should be. Then there would be George, the gerbil, who escaped from his cage at least once a week and hid under the beds, scaring her to death when his furry little body brushed up against her toes. Fox Run cried out for someone to turn its gloomy atmosphere into a happy home.

Alone in the parlor, she paged through a magazine and visualized Roper sitting beside her. An advertisement with a little white house surrounded by green grass mixed with dandelions and a white picket fence caught her attention. She envisioned herself standing on the porch, waving with one hand and holding a broom in the other, a starched white apron covering her housedress. *Stop it!* She scolded herself for thinking of him *that* way. Her old-fashioned mama would say it wasn't nice, but she found it very nice, and oh, so natural. That's the way she wanted to live.

She laid the magazine down and wandered off to the kitchen to make coffee. She poured a cup, then added a touch of hazelnut creamer to it.

The fire crackling in the hearth created a wonderful sense of home, but it was also a harsh reminder that that she had no one to share it with. She drank her coffee, but she wasn't hungry even though she hadn't eaten anything except Lizzy's nappies all day.

Where's Uncle Nick? He rarely went out these days, and his absence worried her. His appetite had dwindled to almost nothing, he had little strength, and his endurance seemed to wane more every day. Her training had taught to diagnose and prescribe in many situations where a doctor wasn't present. Every ounce of book-learning, every clinical experience, every instinct screamed at her that influenza was the least of his problems. As though he had heard her thoughts, he appeared in the doorway, tottered across the room, and sank into his recliner that used to fit his form like a glove but now almost hid him in its folds. For a long moment he didn't move. Pain lines marked his face and showed in the wrinkles of his brow. The whites of his eyes had taken on a yellow tint. He held his breath at intervals and moaned low.

"Maggie, would you be a darling and get me a glass of water."

"Sure, Uncle Nick."

When she returned, he had straightened up and reached for the glass. He slipped something in his mouth and swallowed it.

"What was that you just took?"

"Just some over-the-counter cold tablets."

She knew better, but she could tell by looking at him that he didn't have the strength to argue. She also knew he would try.

He reached for his best pipe, the one he smoked on special occasions, put it in his mouth, and lit it. Keeping a pipe lit seemed to her like a full-time job, with all that huffing and puffing to keep it burning. Without a word he stared into the fire, seemingly oblivious to her presence.

She waited for him to speak, half expecting him to complain about how the traffic bothered him and how those inconsiderate teen-agers ought not be allowed to drive. Then his gaze returned from some distant place and focused on her for a long moment.

"I wonder what it feels like to die."

"What?"

"I said, I wonder what it feels like to die."

"No one knows that, Uncle Nick. Why such a question?"

"I'm dying."

"What did you say?" Her breath stuck in her throat. She squinted. *This has to be one of his morbid jokes.*

"I said...I'm dying."

"That's not funny, Uncle Nick."

"No... it's not funny...but unfortunately, it's true. I see your squinty eyes. You don't believe me, do you?"

She caught something in his fearful tone that made her change her mind. Her mouth was too paralyzed to speak, her mind too muddled to think. Uncle Nick never cried before, he wasn't the type, but for the first time in her life. she saw tears, bright and unashamed, in his eyes.

"Have you seen a doctor?"

"Yes. Some time ago. He gave me six months to a year."

"When was that?" She tried to push what he was saying out of her mind.

"Well over six months ago. The pancreatic tumor has metastasized. No surgery, no chemo, no nothing will get rid of the monster...or the pain—with the exception of morphine, which I've been taking for some time. Dr. Ross told me to put away the pipe. I asked him why I should put it away now. A few more puffs on my pipe won't change anything."

"Why didn't you tell me sooner? I'm going to check with your doctor tomorrow. You must have heard him wrong. I can't believe this."

"You mean, after all that fancy medical training, you can't see when a man is dying?"

"In this case, I don't want to see. And I don't want to believe it." She wiped away the tears that tumbled down her cheeks.

"Believe it." Nicholas puffed on the pipe and blew smoke rings in the air. "Don't say anything to Cannon right yet."

"Why not, Uncle Nick? Daddy's already suspicious. He keeps telling me to get you to a doctor because what you've got isn't the flu. I told him my hands were tied. You wouldn't listen to me or anyone else. He has a right to know. Don't you think so?"

"Yes...ater. I have some things about Fox Run that I'll talk to him about when the time comes. You know more about the estate than he does."

"I don't know what to say." She walked over to put her arms around him, laid her head on his shoulder, and wept. "How can I help you? I'll do anything... you know that."

"Thank you, but all I need from you is your forgiveness."

She felt the sobs he was holding back. "I don't understand. Forgive you for what?"

"Forgive me for all the years I peddled prejudice and pride and blamed you for what you couldn't help. I knew, and I closed my eyes and my ears because the one thing I couldn't stand was proof that my great-great grandfather Ezra had a sleepover party with his house servant, Pearl. Sheldon was the result of that frolic. Cannon saw to it that I got the proof I didn't want to face. But I still rejected it. Now, with what's happening, it doesn't matter anymore. Funny how you struggle through life one way, and then it means nothing because you die."

"But you told me when I was old enough to understand. That's what matters, Uncle Nick. I never could see any reason to be upset, and I never held it against my great-great-great-grandfather." She shook her head. "It may have been scandalous at the time, but it wasn't all that uncommon. Neither Dad nor I thought it was a big deal. That was then, and this is now. Times have changed."

"There used to be a saying among the colored folks, Maggie. I read it in Ezra's journal. 'When trouble comes, close your eyes, and the white people did.' Until recently, I lived in the past. Part of me still does. I'm set in my ways. My old-school thinking doesn't change just because times change. Before it became commonplace like it is today, it was an evil thing for Negroes and whites to mix. I was prejudiced, pompous, and so afraid of what people would think—*white* people, that is. I was afraid the precious Fox name would be blackguarded. So... I chose to close my eyes. That's when I realized what that saying meant."

"Listen, Uncle Nick. I forgive you—although I still think there's nothing to forgive." Maggie knelt at his feet with her arms folded and resting on his knees. She looked up at him, tears rolling from her eyes. "I'm just glad you told me when I was old enough to understand. The whole thing happened so long ago. I wonder how Kat will take it, though. Seems like one thing after another hits her. She's had so much worry on her lately. The baby, the plane crash, Dad coming forward, a new half-sister, and she hasn't even heard this yet. She's a strong lady with a lot of faith, but this...well, I don't know."

Her uncle patted her head and stroked her hair until she stopped crying. She stood and took a long, slow breath. Ambling toward the fireplace, she stared up into the eyes of her Aunt Sarah Fox. *What a beautiful woman—even though the painting doesn't do her justice. No wonder Uncle Nick never remarried after she died giving birth.* The loss of the only woman he ever loved had almost killed him. The premature boy baby lived only a week.

Nicholas made his way to the liquor closet, poured three fingers of peach brandy, and took it to her. He reached over and kissed her on the cheek. "Now I'm going to get a four-finger brandy for myself and disappear upstairs."

Her cheeks burned from the constant flow of tears. "Uncle Nick, thank you. You're a mind reader...and I *do* love you... but you're not supposed to drink while taking that medication."

"I know you love me, and I know I'm not supposed to drink with the meds. But what's going to happen to me if I do? I get a little drunk and land in bed? Honey, don't worry, nothing but this cancer will kill me."

"Maybe so...but...I just need to do something for you, and I don't know what."

"Contrary to brother Cannon's opinion, I love you—and I love him, too. If I don't get around to it, tell him that after I go. I'm not good at showing love or any sort of emotion like you two are. Now far be it from me to cry over something like dying. Spilled milk, maybe, but not dying. I have no intention of ruining my image." His lips smiled, but his voice fought for control.

"Please let me do something, Uncle Nick. Fix you a sandwich maybe?"

"No thanks." He hesitated. "Now don't you start babying me. When I go...I go...and I'm going right now to my room." One corner of his mouth curved upward into a slight smile.

"Yes, but...but..."

"Maggie, dear, don't worry. Whatever will be—will be. I don't want to die. I don't care if I'm bald or rude or mean or crazy or ugly. I don't want to die. For the first time in my life, I'm up against a firing wall, one gun loaded, and me in my stocking feet. I can't run from it, nor can I do anything about it."

He left the parlor, head held high. She followed him to the bottom of the stairs, where, walking perfectly straight, he headed up the steps as he'd always done.

Part of her wanted to cry; part of her wanted to fight. All of her wanted to kill the terrible cancer that was stealing him from her. At the top of the stairs, her room waited for her. It was her place of refuge from the rest of Fox Run, her private little corner of the world. She could lounge, work, play, or do whatever she wanted. Tonight she would cry for her Uncle Nick.

She turned the black and tan striped spread down, undressed, slipped into her flannel nightgown, and crawled under the sheet. She lay on her back and stared out the window at the starless night. The realization that her uncle was dying and she was powerless to help him smothered her in pain. She closed her eyes.

Father, I have a complaint, and I don't know where to begin.

Chapter Twenty-Four

*K*at was sitting at the kitchen table when Maggie arrived. Carla poured her a second cup of coffee and placed another cup and a Danish on the table for her sister.

"Thanks, Carla." Maggie shrugged out of her coat and hung it on a hook in the mudroom, then slipped into a chair across from Kat. She reached for the steaming cup and took a sip. "Mmm, this is so good and so hot. The snow's really coming down now."

"Hi, Maggie." Kat waved her hand without looking up from the paper she was staring at.

"What's got you so occupied, sis? You look like you're off in another world."

"Two things, actually. First, I have this great idea for the show, which we'll talk about later. And second, I want to throw a dinner party."

"You're kidding, right? How are you going to do a dinner party and stay off your feet at the same time?"

Kat gave her a big smile. "I'm going to ask my sister to help me."

"I see. Assuming that your sister has time in her busy schedule to do this, do you think she has the experience to create a worthy Kahill bash?"

"I think she'll handle everything just fine...because I'm going to teach her. And because I'm going to invite one elusive man friend I've heard about but never seen. What's his name? Rover? No, that's the dog. Roper—yes, that's it—Roper."

Maggie struggled to suppress a laugh, but it burst out despite her best effort. "Just what makes you think he'll come?"

"I have my wily ways."

"I should've known. We're both our father's daughter." She made a face.

"Are you suggesting that Daddy's *wily*?"

"I didn't suggest it. I said it outright." Maggie hesitated. "Are you serious about this?"

"You better believe it."

"Who else are you asking?"

"Daddy, of course, Cabe, Conchita, and the babies; Clancy and Bonny with Molly Anna and her older brothers who haven't returned to Ireland; Darrell and Polly Dee; and Nicholas...how's he doing?"

"Each day he seems a little weaker. Pancreatic cancer is such a horrific disease, and the cure rate is dismally low. He doesn't know I told you how sick he is, so keep that to yourself."

"Will do. I really hope he's up to coming. We can do it next week. You know, the Kahills and the Foxes haven't sat at the same table for a meal in...how long, do you think?"

"More than a hundred years, I'm sure, except for you. And you didn't know you're a Fox. Of course, neither did the Kahills—except for Jedediah."

"I'd like Nick to be part of this long overdue reconciliation. You've said he's not the ogre that Dawson and I grew up believing him to be. I'd want to see that for myself. After all, he's my uncle, too."

"It's going to be difficult for him to go out, Kat. I have an idea, though. Do you think the doctor would let you come to Fox Run if you stay off your feet during your visit? We can have this historic little get-together there, if Uncle Nick agrees, and I think he would be more comfortable. He could excuse himself and go lie down if he needs to. We haven't had much staff for years, but maybe he'd agree to hire someone to help me prepare the food."

"Or maybe Carla could do it." Kat cast a questioning look at the lady who was cutting up vegetables for chicken pot pies.

Carla chuckled. "I wouldn't miss this for the world. Count me in...if you can get Nicholas Fox to agree to it. However, I'm not placing any bets on your doing that."

"Don't underestimate my sister." Kat grinned at Maggie. "Maybe we could get Conchita to bring her famous peach cobbler. It's the best anywhere—and it has Granddad's seal of approval."

Decked out in a burgundy smoking jacket and charcoal-gray slacks and turtleneck shirt, Nicholas greeted each of the guests at the door with a warm welcome. Maggie watched him from a distance. *No one will ever know that he hasn't done this in my memory, if he ever did it at all. I wonder how much morphine he took to create his gregarious host persona.*

"So you're Roper." Kat smiled at the handsome man sitting next to her sister. "Maggie tells me you were in the military."

"Yes on both counts. I'm happy to report that part of my career has come to an end. I have my discharge and am about to go back to school to become a physicians assistant. I figure my medic training gives me a head start, and I liked that work in the army a lot. Never figured I'd take to doctoring, so my interest came as a bit of a surprise."

Kat shot a quick look at her sister. "Then you and Maggie could work together up in the Hill Country."

"I've been thinking that very same thing."

Nicholas stood at the door as the Kahills and friends filed out. Maggie marveled at his stamina. He had been a gracious host, and no inkling of past hostilities between the families surfaced throughout the evening. None of his trademark cynicism, no caustic remarks, no self-absorbed behavior had entered into the conversations. Nicholas Samuel Fox had gone all out to show his softer side and give the end of the Fox-Kahill feud his official seal of approval.

He closed the door. "I'm beat...but I made it."

"Yes, you did. And you did it with more grace and diplomacy than I knew you had, Uncle Nick. I'm really impressed. Now why don't you sit down in the parlor, and I'll grab us a last cup of coffee."

"Sounds good, but you better make mine decaffeinated."

"Have you given any more thought to telling Daddy?" Maggie walked into the parlor, handed him a cup, and set the other one down on the end table next to her chair by the fireplace.

"Some. I'm not quite ready yet. It seems so...final."

"He knows what's going on, Uncle Nick. Everyone knows. He's hurt that you haven't confided in him. I told him about the cancer when he cornered me about your losing weight and looking so ragged."

"I asked you not to tell anyone, Maggie. That's interfering in my business and disrespecting my wishes."

"He *asked*, Uncle Nick, so I told him. He loves you, and he wants the two of you to act like brothers. He knows he's going to lose you, and he's hurting."

Nicholas sighed. "Maybe I should talk with him tomorrow."

"Yes, you should. He needs that...and so do you."

"Okay, Maggie, if you do me one last favor."

"What's that? And don't tell me to get you a brandy. I won't be a party to mixing alcohol with your medication."

"Believe me, Maggie, there's not enough brandy in all the world to drown my problems. Bring me a nice cup of warm tea with a slice of lemon." He handed her his almost full coffee cup.

"Have you taken your pain medicine?"

"Yep, that's why I feel so good." He chuckled. "I took an extra dose. If I must die, I prefer to die happy."

"Uncle Nick! You are *not* supposed to—"

"Quit gabbing and bend down here so I can give you a peck on the cheek." Maggie shook her head and leaned over.

"I love you, Maggie girl."

"The feeling is mutual—even though you're insufferable. What in the world am I going to do with you?"

"The question is...what are you going to do *without* me?" He raised an eyebrow. "Right now, just be my favorite niece and get me that cup of tea."

"Your *favorite* niece? I won't tell Kat you said that." She placed both hands on his cheeks. "I love you, too, Uncle Nick, no matter what they say about you."

"No matter what *who* says about me?" He shook his head and laughed. "Whichever, get out in that kitchen and fix the tea before I die of thirst."

The kettle whistled and blew steam until Maggie closed her *Better Homes and Gardens* magazine that she had left on the kitchen table. Rushing to the stove, she turned the burner off just in time to hear Nick holler, "Get the kettle, Maggie. I might be ill, but I'm not deaf."

"I'm getting it. Sit tight and relax." She laughed at her uncle's budding sense of humor, something he'd seldom shown before. Congeniality had never been an obvious trait, but its last minute appearance would foster fond memories after he was gone. If only she could have seen this side of him in the past.

Picking up the tray, she started for the parlor and then put it down on the top of the table. The lemons! She reached into the fridge, pulled out the bowl of lemon wedges, and slipped one on each cup rim.

"Sorry it took so long, Uncle Nick. I forgot the lemon." She set the tray on the coffee table and turned to him.

He looked so peaceful she hated to wake him. He had reclined in the chair and stretched out his arms on the armrests. She watched him for a moment, waiting for his chest to rise as he took a breath. It didn't. Not a muscle moved—not a twitch, not a twitter from his closed eyes. She turned up the light and touched him. His face was strangely white. Her hand migrated to his carotid artery. He had no pulse.

Her hands slapped over her mouth. Then she reached out to caress his cheeks with both hands. "I love you, Uncle Nick."

Picking up the phone, she dialed nine-one-one. Then she called Cannon at the lodge and Kat at Willow Walk.

Uncle Nick was right. What was she going to do without him? He had been more of a father to her than Cannon, especially during her younger years. He raised her, took care of her, and taught her to be the person she had become.

Tears rose from her heart and choked her before cascading down her cheeks. Uncle Nick was dead.

Chapter Twenty-Five

*D*awson sat across from Maggie at the kitchen table. "I wish I would have had more time to get to know your Uncle Nick. It's sad for all of us that the Foxes and the Kahills tried to outdo the Hatfields and the McCoys."

"What a waste." Maggie shook her head. "I'm so glad we ended the feud before he died."

"Nicholas wasn't known for his charm and his captivating manner, but we couldn't have asked for a more hospitable reception the other night."

"Even I had never seen him play the role of the perfect host."

"He was Kat's uncle, too, and the dinner party was the only time she ever saw him. She feels a real sense of loss...or maybe it's deprivation. She never had the chance to be his niece in any meaningful sense."

"I guess she'll have to learn about him from Dad and me—and I assure you that she'll get two very different perspectives."

"Did he have any children, Maggie?"

"His baby boy lived only a few days after his birth—a birth that took my Aunt Sarah's life. Uncle Nick never remarried. As far as I know, he never had a girlfriend. He was a lonely man."

Dawson shuddered. He could relate to Nicholas' pain over the loss of his family. He'd come too close to the same himself—much too close.

Kat sat at her drawing board and began sketching the last few designs for the New York show. Everything had fallen into place now that she had no option but to sit quietly and give it her undivided attention. Still, she welcomed the occasional diversion, and she put her pen down when she heard Maggie running up the stairs.

"I can't stay long, Kat. Dad's alone at Fox Run. He took Uncle Nick's death even harder than I did. He wanted things to be right between him and his brother, and they were making progress in that direction. They just weren't quite there yet." She slipped out of her coat and plopped into a chair next to her sister. "I had a couple things to ask you about our theme for the show. I thought I'd work on it tonight if I can put my heart into it. Seems keeping busy is the best way to ward off the blues, and the show is coming up real soon. Dad and I will have a quiet dinner and sit around the fire, read, work on the show, or whatever."

"Why don't you two come over here for supper? Carla always cooks enough for an army. Good thing that woman has a way with leftovers that turns them into a gourmet meal the second and third times around."

"That's really nice of you, but I think Dad would rather be alone right now. On top of everything else, he has suddenly become the patriarch of Fox Run, and I don't think he's sure how to handle that. As for me...Roper's coming by later. He's been so supportive through all of this. I don't know what I would've done without him."

"I understand, sis. You've fallen for this Roper person, haven't you?"

"Why, does it show?"

"Not much. You just light up like a beacon when his name's mentioned. Is the feeling mutual?"

"I hope so. If actions really do speak louder than words, then I can say a definite, yes."

"Keep me in the know about what's going on with you two, okay? Now, what do you need to know about the show?"

"Since Over the Rainbow is our theme, I think it would be really neat to have Joey and Molly Anna as part of the background scene. What if they were having a picnic at one end of the rainbow? I know they've been taking tap and ballet lessons, and they're both quite good for their age. I'm wondering if we could get permission to use the song "Over the Rainbow" and have them dance onto the stage, set down a rainbow-colored tablecloth and picnic basket, and dance briefly around it before they sit down to eat—something simple and sweet and theme appropriate that their instructor could choreograph. It would be totally unique, and they could do it before the first gown is presented. Then they could sit and watch the show from that location. Their outfit colors, of course, should be taken from the rainbow. What do you think, Kat?"

"I...I...what a *fantastic* idea, sis! I'll start somebody on getting permissions to use the songs we choose this afternoon." She paused, looked out the window across the valley, and turned back to Maggie. "Yes, a little original ballet in the beginning. I don't think that's been done before in a fashion show—and I've been following the big ones for years. At the end, the kids could stand, pick up their stuff, and dance off the stage just as they came on. I think we could use a medley of songs that begins and ends with "Over the Rainbow.""

"Good. Then it's settled. I need to get back to Dad now. I'll talk to you tomorrow." Maggie gave her a quick hug and hurried out."

"Be careful driving, sis. The roads are still bad."

It was nearly noon. That meant it would be six o'clock in Paris. She wanted to talk to Rebecca about transferring ownership of Wolf International Fashions from herself back to Rebecca, and this should be a good time. Parisians ate very late in the evening by American standards. She dialed her number and waited, hoping the connection would be clear for a change.

"*Allo, je suis Mason Leblanc.*"

What was he doing there? Had she dialed the wrong number? Their names were close in her address book, so that was possible.

"*Allo,*" repeated the voice on the other end.

"Mason? Is this you?" *What a stupid question.*

"I think so." She could hear the laughter in his voice. "Do you want to speak to Rebecca?"

"Mason, don't you r...recognize my voice?"

"Kat? Of course I do. How are you?"

"I'm fat and pregnant. Dawson and I are expecting a little girl."

"That's wonderful. I'm very happy for the two of you."

"I...uh...am concerned because you are there. Rebecca's not had a recurrence of the cancer, has she? I just talked to her a month ago, and she wasn't feeling her best. I know you're not in the habit of making house calls, but..."

"No...no...Kat. She's fine. I'm just...uh...making a friendly visit."

"Oh?"

"I'll let her explain. It's so great to hear your voice. I never thought I would again. You take care of yourself. I'll call Becky now."

"Thanks, Mason. It's been g...good talking to you."

"Hello, Kat? Are you okay? The baby okay? The family?" Rebecca sounded breathless.

"Slow down, dear. Everyone's fine. But what is the good doctor doing at your place?"

"Oh, Kat, he's within earshot, so I can't talk right now. But I guarantee it's something wonderful."

"You're not going to get away with that, Becky Wolf. I will not hang up until I know at least a little of what you're up to."

"Then I must speak very softly. Can you hear me?"

"Barely. Go on."

"We're getting married. I wanted it to be a surprise."

"Married? Do you love him?"

"Of course I love him, silly girl. Why else would I marry him? We both have money, so it's got to be love." Rebecca burst out laughing. "Oh, honey, I have so much to tell you. Mason and I were just talking about the time you were here for the Paris show and how well you did with it when I was laid up with the cancer. We even talked about you and him. He was truly in love with you, Kat, but I helped him get over it. Oh, we'll have to talk again soon so I can tell you everything."

"Rebecca LeBlanc. That sings, Becky. Sorry to change the subject, but how are things coming along with the transfer of Wolf International Fashions from me back to you?"

"Papers are well on their way to completion. When you get them, just sign them in front of a notary and send them back. Then we'll be good to go."

"Perfect. Are you satisfied with what we're doing? Having Wolf International back in your lap again won't be too much on you, will it?"

"Kat, I couldn't be any better. Mason says my cancer will not likely return if it hasn't by now. And I'm so raring to get back into the Fashion business with Silka and Lillian. I've been working with them for awhile now, and we make a great team. They're accustomed to taking suggestions from you, but I have their blessing with this transfer. You know the show is in January, as usual. I don't suppose you'll be able to travel. You didn't sound good the last time we talked. Please tell me that everything's okay."

"It is now. I've had some ups and downs, but I'm taking it easy—doctor's orders. You know the story with Joey, so I've got to be extra careful. I hate not to come to the show, but I don't have a choice. I've got heaps to tell you, too. We've got to talk soon."

"I was hoping to help you with your show in April, but you said you had more than enough help. I'm here in case you change your mind. And I *have* known you to change your mind." She giggled.

"I'll be waiting for the papers. Tell Mason I wish you both all the happiness in the world. I'm so-o-o-o happy for both of you."

"I'll tell him. You take care, and tell that man of yours hello for me."

"What are friends for? And Rebecca, I know you'll be able to give Mason all the love he so desperately needs. Just one question…why did you wait so long to tell me?"

"It just happened a few minutes ago. You're timing is amazing, as usual. Right on the nose."

"Hmmm. I wonder how long it would have been if I hadn't called you? Anyway, I'm sending you both big hugs."

"Sure will. Let me hear from you soon. I love you."

Kat wanted to cry and laugh at the same time. Rebecca deserved a good man like Mason LeBlanc and visa-versa. They both needed love and all the trimmings.

Without Wolf International Fashions, her life would change. Now she could concentrate on her boutiques in Wheeling and New York and still have plenty of time to raise Joey and Willow. Her unborn daughter seemed so real that it was almost as though she were already here. It would be a little while longer, but not too much. April was just four months away.

She stood in front of the floor length mirror and ran her hand over her stomach. Cold shivers raced up and down her back. Everything at her last checkup had been great, so why the feeling that all was not as it should be? She forced the negative thought out of her mind. She was beginning to sound like Dawson. That would never do.

Chapter Twenty-Six

*R*ain, sleet, and snow pelted the earth from the low-hanging clouds, coating the ground and roads with a slippery white glaze. Cannon looked out the parlor window, drew the heavy drapes, and put another log on the fire. It sputtered, then blazed, sending a shower of sparks up the wide chimney. *This night's not good for anything but hibernating.* He shuddered and sank into the chair opposite Nick's and closed his eyes. Images of him and his brother darted back and forth in his mind.

He opened the journal and pointed to the account in Ezra's own hand. Nicholas grabbed the book and hurled it across the room.

"Liar!" he screamed.

"How can you say that? Ezra's words are right there in front of you."

"He's a liar and so are you! Now get this slanderous book out of my house! I don't ever want to see it again."

"Please, Nick, listen—"

"*Out,* I said!"

He snatched the book up from the floor and bolted from the room.

His eyes opened wide. The dream had been so real that he looked around the parlor for Nick. Ezra Fox's written account of the family history lay on the table next to his brother's empty chair.

Maggie must have brought it back to the house after Dawson returned it to me. Was he reading it? Did he get to the part where Ezra acknowledged his own responsibility for forfeiting the esteemed Fox name?

Nick, did I misjudged you?

Kat stood in the doorway of the master bathroom, watching Dawson shave. She tiptoed up behind him, put her arms around his waist, and kissed his neck.

"Hmmm...I don't know what that's for, but I want more."

"You have that three-little-pigs look. You're afraid to open the door, afraid the big bad wolf will get you." She giggled. "That's exactly the expression I see. What now do you have to tell me that I haven't already heard?"

"I didn't know it showed."

"Didn't know what showed? That you looked like one of the three little pigs?" Her smile broadened.

"No, silly. Oh, never mind." He turned and gave her a warm hug and kiss, transferring some wet shaving lather from his face to hers. She backed up and looked in the mirror, and they both grinned. The kiss, the lather, his playfulness, made her fall in love all over again.

"Now that's enough out of you, my big bad wolf." Dawson showed his teeth and snarled.

Kat shook her fist at him. "Oh, you! Kidding aside, I need to know what's on your mind. I always know when you're itching to tell me something."

"I found something unexpected when I was reading more of Granddad's journal last week. I can't figure out why we weren't told about this."

"I had no idea this family had so many secrets. What is it now? And what does it have to do with us?"

"Nothing bad in my opinion, just something that should have been disclosed long ago. I'm just not sure how you'll take it, and I don't want you upset anymore."

"Oh, piddle, Daw." She flipped her hair around her ear and walked to the other side of the room. "I'm doing fine now." She patted her stomach. Willow is kicking up a storm to let me know she's alive and well. You know...you've felt her. She's going to be a tomboy, I'm sure of it."

"Let's not give her any ideas she doesn't already have. I want a little lady this time. Molly Anna is all the tomboy we need. We're in line for a sweet, quiet, demure little lady."

"A lady she'll be then." She rolled her eyes when he wasn't looking.

"You know, my dear, that's why I love you. You're so agreeable... sometimes."

"I love you, too." Even though she shot him an evil grin, she couldn't imagine life without this man. "I'm not as fragile as everyone seems to think. I know you've always protected me from hurt, but you can't isolate me from life, Daw. Pain and sadness are part of what life's all about." She paused for a moment. "So what's the big secret?"

"Let's grab a cup of coffee and go to Jedediah's hideaway. Every bit of it is in his journal. I'll read it to you."

"Okay, but if you need any help, I learned to read in first grade." She gave him a wide-eyed look.

Dawson shook his head and gave her a peck on the cheek. "Silly girl."

"Sounds to me like you're procrastinating."

"All right, all right. Remember how everyone wondered about the Fox secret?"

She nodded.

"It's kind of a Kahill secret, too. But let me start at the beginning. Granddad and Cannon must have been very close—I'd say best friends—and no one ever knew it."

"You're kidding! On the other hand, that sounds a lot like something Granddad would do."

"You're right. Those two were thicker than split pea soup."

"Oh Daw, is that the awful secret? No, it couldn't be. Hmmm...let's see, someone had a baby out of wedlock? Or, one of the ancestors was in prison for theft...no, for murder? One of the son's are the son of the father who..."

"What?" Dawson glanced at her and frowned. "That's double talk. One of the son's are...never mind. Are you sure you're okay today, Kat?"

"Just kidding, Daw. I can think of some worse things if you want me to go on..."

"No no no. That won't be necessary. Let's go to Granddad's hideaway and find out before you guess it."

Dawson opened the little door, and they bent low to enter the secluded room. "Sit over there in Emma's chair, hon." He pointed and winked. "There's a lot here in Granddad's journal, but I'll read only—"

"The part you hate for me to know about, right?" She sent him a butterfly kiss.

"Granddad and Cannon shared a secret that dates back to the 1800s. It's about Cannon's great-great grandfather, Ezra Fox." He began reading.

"Fox Run will never overshadow Willow Walk in beauty or charm, but it is one heck of a pretty place. That's what I told Cannon when we gabbed in the cemetery last week. I was point blank with him, but he never minded. He said, 'No, Jed, it's just the other way around.' We laughed and punched each other, friendly like the way we always do.

"Emma and me was talkin' the other day 'bout some of the Fox ancestors that must've been morally unrestrained. Take Ezra Fox, for instance. He was hell bent on having his way, to hear Cannon tell it, and he did have his way with Pearl, a young black slave girl. Cannon even showed me the ol' boy's journal to back up his words. Funny how folks believed back in them days. Like the color of skin would wash off on one another. Nobody seemed to understand there's good and bad in folks of all colors.

"Personally, I'm colorblind when it comes to judgin' a person's worth. What's inside a person—there's the big difference. Values, moral soundness, knowin' right from wrong and doin' the right, that's what makes a man a man, not his color.

"Anyway...Pearl caught the eye of her master's son, Ezra, a year or two older than her, and she got pregnant."

Dawson sipped his coffee, looked at Kat, and raised both brows. She wrinkled her forehead and nodded. "Go on...I'm listening."

"Ezra's parents had a fit. To keep Ezra away from her and try to save face, they sold her and her younger brother Bo to Silas Kahill. Ezra said in his journal that Silas was a good and moral family man who cherished his life and property. Course, all us Kahills knew that."

Dawson stopped reading.
Kat looked at him. "That's all?"
"No. Granddad took a break for lunch."
"He wrote that he quit for lunch?"
"Sure did." Dawson pointed. "See. It's right here."
"But it's not time for our lunch, so let's move on."
"Okay, okay." Dawson looked down at Jedediah's journal.

"Sheldon was bi-racial born out of wedlock in the South at the time when slavery was still very much alive. In fact, he was born a slave right here at Willow Walk. Now comes the interesting part. Silas Kahill knew he was an illegitimate son. But he gave him his full name as Sheldon Fox, not Kahill as was the custom when a slave was born into one's household."

"Stop right there, Daw. Does this mean what I think it means?"
"I don't know. What do you think it means?"
"Am I descended from Sheldon or from one of the other Foxes."
"Unless I'm mistaken, Sheldon is on your list of ancestors."
"So...Maggie and I are part Negro?"

"That would be the case, but a very small part."

"I don't care about that. I'm in full agreement with Granddad that it's what's *inside* a person that makes them who they are, not the wrapping."

"I like your attitude—I just wasn't sure what it would be."

"How can you say that, Daw? You know I have almost as many black friends as white ones."

"That's not the same as being one yourself."

"Shame on you, Dawson Kahill! You talk like skin color makes a difference. You know better than that. Besides, we'll love our Willow no matter what color she is—look how beautiful Maggie is, and her skin is several shades darker than mine. I wish mine was the color of hers."

"That's another reason I love you."

"Because of my skin color?"

"Because of your beautiful heart, silly."

"Aw, that's sweet. Does Granddad say anything else?"

"Sure does, but not so much about the Foxes. You want to hear what he said about you?"

"What did he say?"

He changed positions in the chair and paged to the next entry. "When Sheldon passed in 1926, the last conspirator in the Fox family secret was laid to rest. All knowledge of the tainted blood vanished...well, almost all knowledge. Cannon knows. I know. That scoundrel Nicholas knows, too, but he ain't about to admit it. I think of our dear Kitten, who has no idea about her real heritage. I know Cannon would fight a lion with a toothpick if anyone tried to hurt her.

"That's enough, Daw. Let's stop here and be thankful for Jedediah Kahill. God threw away the mold when he made Granddad. I so wish he was still with us."

"In some ways, he is. His presence is so imprinted in this house that he seems to dwell in every nook and cranny. I can almost hear his cane tapping when I'm falling asleep."

"Honey, I just want to tell you, I think you've filled his shoes wonderfully. I'm so proud of you."

"Thanks, but no one could fill his shoes."

"It's not nice to argue with your wife. You're supposed to say, 'yes dear.'"

"Yes, dear." Dawson smirked. "I'll let you think you're right."

Chapter Twenty-Seven
Two-and-a half months later

Kat cupped her hand around her mouth. "It's show time."

A sound like the pounding hooves of horses racing up the stairs echoed through the corridor and into her room. Dawson, Carla, and Cannon shot through the door, almost knocking one another down. Their worried frowns dissipated when they found her seated at her drawing table, beaming with enthusiasm.

"You okay?" Dawson asked.

She nodded. "Gather around everyone, and I'll brief you guys on the upcoming show for Fashions by Kat, being held in the most renowned city in the world. Move over, New York...here come the Kahills and the Foxes.

She flashed a prom-queen smile to everyone in the room.

"I know how badly you want to be there, Kat," Carla said. "But, honey, you'll be able to watch the whole thing right here on TV. You can even communicate with Debbie the whole time if you need to. That's the next best thing to being there."

"I'm not complaining. I just hate not being there in person. The main thing I'm going to miss is working with Joey and Molly Anna. But it's for a good cause." She patted her rounded belly. "You'll have your hands full, Carla. Just don't let them out of your sight for even one second. New York City is *not* Wheeling."

"Stop worrying, Kat. You know you can trust me to watch over them like they're my own. Land sakes, what am I saying? They practically *are* my own by now." The musical tinkle of Carla's laughter flooded the room.

"They've taken to me, too, although I can't compete with Great-grandad Jedediah. Why, Joey and Molly Anna are both calling me 'granddaddy' now. I don't have words to tell you what it means to me to finally be part of my family, to be called 'daddy' and 'granddaddy.' In some ways, I wish I could go along, too."

Carla nodded. "Okay by me, Cannon...I mean...if it's okay with Kat."

"What do you think, Daw?"

"I think having backup for Carla is a great idea, but I also think having you here to watch it with Kat and me would be really special to all of us."

"Oh, it would be so-o-o special, Daddy. I want you here with me...us."

"Nothing would please me more." Her father's eyes glistened with tears.

"That's it then. Carla, I trust you implicitly, and you have a way with the kids that makes them behave. I think it's because you tell them one time what you're going to do if they don't mind, and then you stick by it. They know not to push you." Kat turned to Cannon. "Joey's so happy to have a granddad again. Every night, when he says his prayers, we kneel by the bedside, and he says, 'Thank you, God, for my other granddaddy who just found me. Please don't let him go away again. I still miss my great-granddaddy and love him lots. He was my buddy. But Granddaddy Cannon's my buddy now, too.'" Kat hesitated. "The fact that you can tell him stories about Jedediah that we don't even know is a big bonus in his eyes. It's almost like he has two grandfathers rolled into one. She hugged her father's neck and whispered in his ear. "Please Daddy, promise me you'll never leave me again now that we've found each other. This is one of the most important times in my life and I want to share it with you. I know we can never make up for lost time, but we sure can put a dent in it. I...I love you, Daddy."

He wiped away his tears. "I promise...and thank you, Kat. I can hardly wait to see the show. I'll love watching it here with you and Dawson." He stuck his hands in his pocket like a shy little boy.

She gave him a big smile. "Now that that's settled, let's get on with the show. Our title is *Over the Rainbow*." She went on to describe the show with pictures and drawings of most of the apparel, scenery, props, and choices of music to accompany the models as they stroll down the runway.

"Do you thing Joey and Molly Anna will be okay? They're pretty young. You don't think they'll get stage fright?"

Dawson laughed. "Joey get stage fright? That boy's pure ham."

"Molly Anna will follow his lead, so she should be fine. They've been practicing with their dance instructor for several weeks now. The little ballet she's choreographed for them is sheer perfection. And they're so cute when they do it. They're going to be the hit of the show. Nobody will even notice the fashions."

"Oh, I think they'll notice." Carla stared at the designs spread out on the work table. "These are absolutely stunning, Kat."

"I can't believe I was blessed with two such talented daughters."

"They're definitely that," Dawson agreed.

"Back to the show...Bonny and Conchita are helping Deb organize the details and keep things in order. They're already there. The kids will only need to be there a day before the show to practice on stage. Conchita's a bit nervous about modeling in New York and wants to familiarize herself with the runway before the other models show up. All runways are a little different."

"Does she feel intimidated because she lacks experience?" Carla asked.

"A little, I think, but she can hold her own. She's modeled for us before, and she has a real flair for it. She has two important gowns to model in the New York show, so she wants everything to be just right."

"Conchita will be just fine. That girl can do whatever she sets her mind to doing." Dawson put his arm around Kat and kissed her forehead.

"She's taking the babies with her because she's still nursing them." She looked up at Dawson. "I'd really like Cabe to go with her to help with the babies. With Dad here and the other help you have, do you think you could spare him for a few days? I know this is the end-of-the-season rush at the lodge, but it would help so much with the show to have him there."

Dawson raised an eyebrow and gave her a teasing smile. "I think we can manage without Cabe for a few days. He's been moping around because he wants to go but thinks we need him here. If things get really busy, I can man the desk myself for a shift. I think I remember how to do that."

Kat punched him in the arm.

Cannon glanced at Dawson and raised an eyebrow. "I already see you're a lot like your granddad. You're going to make a great patriarch, Dawson. Jed would be so proud of you."

"I can't wait. What fun this will be!" Carla clapped her hands. How 'bout some lunch? You guys hungry?"

"Thanks, but I've got to be going," Cannon said. "I'll be back for sure at show time. I don't recall ever having the opportunity to watch a closed-circuit television broadcast."

"I'm arranging for a special camera to record the children's performances. We should see some good shots during the show, but this will focus only on them with lots of close-ups. We'll get a tape of it after the show's over. I think you'll be bringing that home with you, Carla."

After Cannon left and Carla went downstairs to the kitchen, Kat turned to Dawson. "Why don't you go with Carla and the kids, Dawson? They'll be gone just four days, and I'll be fine here. If I need anything, Dad will be here to help. The baby isn't due for another six weeks."

"Don't even *think* about that!" Dawson raised his voice. "I wouldn't leave you now for love nor money...well...maybe money." He winked at her.

"You're a smart one. I give up. Maybe you're right—sort of. I'd be uncomfortable trying to give birth to Willow without you. I rely on you being there to remind me to push and breathe and all that stuff that I'll probably forget." She paused. "I hope and pray I can have a natural birth this time. I don't want another C-section."

He grinned. "I'll talk to Willow about that." He put his face down to within inches of her belly. "Listen, my little darling, please don't make a fuss when it's time to make your appearance. Mama wants to have an easy time with you. Daddy will buy you a pony if you promise to be good."

Kat laughed and hugged him.

Carla brought their lunch and set it on the small table near the fire.

"Where's yours, Carla? I thought you would eat with us." Kat's spoon hung in mid-air on its way to her mouth.

"I've got so much to do before the show. I need to get Joey and Molly Anna's things together and mine, too, because we're leaving in the morning. It's a long drive, so I want to get an early start. But thanks, honey."

Kat finished the last of her soup and put her spoon down. "Daw, are you sure Joey and Molly will be safe without us there? I have the utmost confidence in Carla, but she doesn't know New York City like I do. I've got myself in a pickle with this show. I should never have agreed to let the kids be in it. At the time I thought I would be there."

"Regardless, you've got to stop worrying about the kids, the show, and everything else. Control your stress, or you're going to be in trouble. Carla handles the kids even better than we do sometimes. Besides, you're forgetting that Bonny, Deb, Cabe, and Conchita will be right there with them the entire time. If five women and one man can't handle them, we'd better take a hard look at our parenting skills."

Kat nodded. "You're right. I know I'm a worrier."

"That's my girl. Now sit back and let the capable people you've put in place do their jobs."

"Easier said than done, but I'm working on it. Deb called earlier to tell me all of the preparations had been arranged and executed. The invitations went out on time, stage and props are all in place, fashions have been hung on racks, closed-circuit cameras are ready, and the models are all there. Everything's set to go."

"Sounds like your staff is very efficient."

She frowned. "Maybe they don't even need me."

"C'mon, Kat. Who do you think is the brains behind all this? Everything right down to the theme for the show—*Over the Rainbow* from Fashions by Kat—has been advertised on billboards and in all the prominent fashion magazines for over a month. I know you want the Big Apple with its many fashion houses to welcome you with open arms. It has before, and you already have a sizeable clientele. Your new designs are so classy and so innovative that you're almost guaranteed large orders. You've already established your reputation. This show's only going to enhance it."

"I guess I'm feeling down because I can't be there. I've sent out RSVP invitations to several buyers, as well as leaders in the garment industry, and nearly all have accepted. That alone gives me butterflies."

"Honey, the only butterfly you need is the one I'm sending you right now." Dawson blew her a butterfly kiss.

She wrapped her arms around him. "Thank you, for being my pillar of strength and support and my most adored fan."

"You're welcome. It's good that some of the most prestigious couturiers will be attending the show, Kat. You're being taken seriously in the fashion world, and you'll be giving the big boys a run for their money. How about ticket sales?"

"Debbie said they were going like hot cakes since we expanded our advertising to TV and the Internet. We'll have a full house for sure. I invited big department store buyers along with their assistants. I can't even remember them all. Another thing I'll miss is meeting some of them. That personal touch is so advantageous to the business, but I'm sure Debbie can pull it off with her charm and expertise. And Bonny can back her up."

"From the quality I've seen in your sketches, there may be an all-out war for exclusive rights to your creations."

"That remains to be seen, but I will be heartbroken if the show's a flop." She stared hard at the ceiling, trying to will that thought away. Experience had taught her that anything was possible in the fashion business.

Chapter Twenty-Eight

*D*awson pulled the big plate of miniature sandwiches Carla had prepared out of the freezer. She'd cut the cheese bites and put them in a plastic bag in the refrigerator. He chuckled when he looked at her drawing of how to put an olive on top of each bite with a toothpick. *Whatever would we do without Carla? She knows I'm a total klutz in the kitchen.* Her sausage balls would be wonderful if he heated them in the microwave, she had assured him. "You can do it, Dawson," she had said as she headed out the door with the children. "I have great faith in you."

"How's it going, Daw?"

He turned to find Kat standing in the doorway of the kitchen.

"Carla left all the food and information I need to make sure we have plenty of snacks while we watch the show."

"I can't believe the day of the show is finally here. I'm so nervous. It's really hard to be here when I want so much to be there." She sighed. "Just a little while longer and we'll be watching the show on TV." Kat walked over to the table and sat down. "Will you please pour me a cup of...ouch!"

"Are you okay?"

"Oh gracious! Kat took a deep breath and exhaled slowly. "I think Willow just kicked a field goal. Please tell me my dainty little girl isn't going to be a football player."

Dawson patted her stomach and gave her a peck on the cheek. "No no no. She's going to be a cheerleader. Now, I'm going to call and remind Clancy to phone me in case of an emergency. Otherwise, I don't want to be bothered today. He can handle things just fine."

Dawson turned on the closed-circuit TV. They took their seats on the couch in the workroom, where Kat's sketches were ready for her to make notes. She grabbed Dawson's hand and placed it on her abdomen.

"Something wrong, Kat?"

"No, it's just that little Miss Willow's complaining because she doesn't have the best seat in the house for the show."

"Gosh, what more does she want. She's got a water bed to lie on."

"Yeah, kids nowadays are spoiled even before they're born. She wants out and that's it."

"Kat! Don't scare me like that. I'm not ready. What will I do? I'm glad Cannon's coming over to watch the show with us."

"Honey, I told you everything to do. Don't you remember?"

"Yes, but—"

"Don't worry. This is probably just one of her not-so-demure moments. I think I heard the doorbell. Will you go open the door for Dad, please?"

His hand that rested on her tummy rose abruptly. "She's a back-talker, Kat. You think she's going to be a sassy little girl? I won't stand for that, you know."

"She can't be much sassier than Joey. Ooooooh, that was a ferocious kick. She's getting stronger and stronger.

"You know, sweetheart, this is one of the happiest times in my life."

"Me, too, honey. Now go open the door for Dad so he doesn't have to use his key. I don't want him to think he's not welcome."

Cannon came running up the stairs to join them. "I let myself in when nobody answered the door. Anything I can do, Dawson?"

"Just take a seat. The show's about to begin."

Kat changed positions. She rubbed her hand over her middle and winced. It didn't feel like the pain she had with Joey, but then her pain with Joey wasn't labor. This pain came and went, like a punch from a prizefighter. She looked down at her bulging belly.

Little Willow, if you're thinking about leaving your warm swimming pool and comfortable bed to venture into this hard, cold world, please wait just a little while until the show is over. It won't be long, I promise.

Willow kicked hard again, leaving no doubt that she wouldn't wait too long.

Chapter Twenty-Nine

The announcer took center stage. "Ladies and gentlemen, welcome to the fabulous spring collection from Fashions by Kat, designed by Katarina Kahill. Introducing our *Over the Rainbow* show, we have an original dance presentation by Joey Kahill and Molly Anna O'Malley, who will set the stage for the stunning things to come. Sit back, make yourselves comfortable, and enjoy this fantastic evening we have planned just for you!"

The houselights dimmed. Excited chatter in the auditorium hushed. On the darkened stage, a beautiful rainbow began to glow as strains of "Over the Rainbow" emerged from the silence. A pale ivory spotlight appeared and brightened below the arc of the rainbow, then moved slowly to the right. From behind the curtain a little boy and little girl attired in rainbow colors danced onto the stage. Holding the handles of a picnic basket between them, they stopped to the left of center stage, lifted the top off the basket, and spread out a tablecloth. Then, arm in arm, they skipped toward the runway that ran from the center of the stage into the audience. Stopping at the white gate at its head, the little boy opened it. He and the little girl, held hands and skipped down the white path to the end. He bowed to her. She curtsied to him. Then they bowed and curtsied to the audience. Turning around, they linked elbows and skipped back to the gate. He turned to the audience, smiled, and waved.

Kat laughed. "That wasn't in the script."

Dawson chuckled with her. "Maybe not, but it's typically Joey."

The curtain rose from behind the rainbow to reveal willow trees, their branches covered with tiny lights in different shades of gree. The children danced through the open gate to their picnic spot, which lay under one of the trees to the left of the stage. They sat down at the edge of the tablecloth and opened the picnic basket.

Cannon leaned forward in his chair. "I can't believe those two rambunctious little munchkins are doing exactly what they're supposed to—well, *almost* exactly. You can sure tell little Joey is related to his great-granddad."

"If I were going to guess, Dad, I'd say Carla laid down the law. You can bet that she's somewhere directly in their line of vision, watching their every move."

Kat leaned back on the couch as best she could. Willow's rhythmic kicks seemed to keep time to the music. Her eyes filled with tears. She wasn't sure whether it was the incessant kicking, anxiety over how her daring new designs would be received, or the impeccable behavior of the two beautiful children who couldn't have fulfilled their roles more perfectly. "Look at those two. What little hams they are. They just might steal the show from the models." She took Daw's hand in one of hers and her father's in the other.

"The kids were a fantastic introduction, but your designs will speak for themselves. You wait and see."

"You've always been my staunchest supporter, Daw." She turned her attention back to the TV as the melodic strains of "Over the Rainbow" flowed into the lively beat of Bill Haley's 50's hit, "Rock Around the Clock." The first model stepped through the open gate in a stylish pantsuit in shades of soft gray with a suede charcoal collar and cuffs. Under the jacket, a fitted pink silk scoop neck top hung slightly below the waist. The front of the shirt displayed circles of gray tones. O-o-o-ohs and a-a-a-ahs arose from the audience when the jacket was removed and the model retraced her steps up the runway. Four more pantsuits in various rainbow hues received similar receptions before the presentation of the dresses.

Kat glanced first at her husband and then at her father. *I wonder how bored they really are. Men are rarely thrilled with fashion shows.*

"I can't believe how talented you are. I'm so proud of you, Kat, that the buttons are about to pop off my shirt." Her father seemed almost to have read her thoughts.

Dawson squeezed her hand and looked at Cannon. "I don't think she has any idea how special she is."

"You two are hardly impartial judges." She gave them both an indulgent smile, but their words of reassurance spoke to her doubting heart. "It'll be over soon, and then you're both off the hook. You won't have to watch any more models parade up and down the runway."

"We're not complaining about the models, Kat." Dawson shot her a grin. "They're very...uh...watchable. Right, Cannon?"

"Tight...I mean *right*."

She rolled her eyes. "We're coming to the part that will determine whether the designs are a hit or miss for the spring season. The buyers will be noting every detail, accessory, and presentation. The future of Fashions by Kat is at stake from this point forward. This show's a little risky because I'm introducing some innovative styles with slit skirts and backless gowns. Look! Here comes the first of the gowns now."

The dress fit the model like she had been poured into it. "See, Dad, today's styles are less frilly. Straight, elegant lines portray class and glamour. This simple design in indigo brings a surprising element of excitement to the wearer because of the tight, slit skirt."

Cannon shook his head. "I never knew so much went into making a dress. I just thought—"

"The same thing I thought," Dawson interrupted. "Sew some material together, and it's a done deal."

"You two are impossible." Kat laughed, then cried out.

"Are you all right?"

"Your daughter refuses to settle down and go to sleep. She's been practicing her high kicks all afternoon."

"Why is it that she's my daughter when she's acting up and your daughter when she's behaving?"

Kat suppressed a grin. "That's just the way it is." She looked back at the screen. "Oh, look! Conchita's at the gate. She's wearing an updated and somewhat formal version of the little black dress made of sandwashed silk crepe. See how the fabric floats along with the model's movements. Note that the simple lines of the previous number are repeated here, but the two dresses are nothing alike. In the black version, the skirt is fitted from the waist to below the hip, where it flares to the knee-length hem to flatter the feminine figure. I designed it to be a bit orthodox and sassy at the same time. The bodice is cut very low—all the way to the waist—and held together with a row of tiny bows for a touch of sophisticated whimsy."

Conchita took control of the runway. The camera panned the audience for a brief moment, and every eye in the house was locked on her. At the end of the path, she smiled, did a full turn, and smiled again. She then made a half circle and shot a saucy look over her shoulder before walking back up the runway. The audience went wild with applause.

"A woman who wears this gown will own the night," Kat continued. "Its sweeping one-shoulder design and single flutter sleeve cascading to the front of the flared skirt flows like the wind."

Dawson raised his eyebrows and whistled.

"Do those bows come untied?"

"No, Dad. The dress has an invisible zipper in the back."

"Good! Otherwise, it might be a little...dangerous."

"That's enough out of you two! Now pay attention. Each of the next creations comes in one of the seven colors of the rainbow."

The first model in eveningwear appeared to the wonderfully rich voice of Judy Garland's signature song. The spotlights focused on the open gate, then followed her as she strolled down the lighted runway into the audience. A hush fell across the room.

Kat continued her description. "Her scarlet lamé gown drapes at the neckline from shoulder to shoulder with gentle gathering at the sides to make this gown softly romantic and definitively sexy at the same time. Spaghetti straps of garnet sparkling beads match the large garnet drop earrings to show off the gown. Her clutch is of onyx jeweled beads with a small garnet bow on the front, and her two-inch heels match it perfectly. The straight skirt shows a side-kick just below the knee on the left. This gown is just right for dinner or any festive evening.

"The second offering, a glamorous, streamlined gown of terra cotta crepe, is highlighted with a lustrous peach satin bow attached to one side and a flowing sash corded in chocolate brown. The floor-sweeping skirt has a high slit, and I've splashed the halter neck bodice with sparkling peach dust. The model's strawberry blonde hair twisted high on her head shows off the daring bare back that extends below the waistline. Long opal earrings and a cuffed opal bracelet complete the look."

"Wow, Kat! That one's really different."

"That's the idea, Daw. One of my favorites is coming up."

The third gown of jasmine yellow silk with an off-the-shoulder bodice is overlaid in ivory Chantilly lace as is the straight styled skirt. The backless gown and its slit skirt are part of my innovative design plan to bring new sophistication to the industry from Fashions by Kat. Shoes in pearl yellow covered in lace and a clutch to match finish the outfit."

"I'd love to see you in that one, honey. With your raven hair, you'd be stunning. It's such a sweet, demure look. It fits you." Cannon beamed at her.

She laughed and patted her tummy. "I think you'll have to wait a while before I can get into anything like that."

Next, a gown of Paris green adorned the fourth model to step through the garden gate. Fashioned with an A-line skirt, it sported tiny seed pearls adorning its bodice in a fleur-de-lis pattern. Appliqués of the same were interspersed throughout the skirt. When she turned at the end of the runway, the audience could see that the back was laced up to allow a more custom fit. A simple pearl choker and fleur-de-lis earrings completed her stunning look. "What do you think of that one, Daw?"

"I think it's even more magnificent than the others. You're knocking 'em dead, Kat!"

Blue, indigo, and violet gowns followed in order, each even more gorgeous than the one that had gone before. The applause grew louder and longer with each successive design.

"Is that all?" Cannon reached for the last of Carla's sandwiches.

"Are you asking about the food or the fashions?" She grinned at her dad.

"I was asking about the fashions. But if you weren't family, I'd be doing everything in my power to entice Carla out of your kitchen and into mine. Everything she fixes is amazing."

"Fat chance! Just one more—gown, that is—and it's the *pièce de résistance*. Shhh, here's the announcer."

"Ladies and gentlemen, that completes the seven gowns representing the colors of the rainbow. However, Katarina Kahill has one more gown to present to you."

The strains of "Over the Rainbow" flowed through the room once again, this time accompanied by Judy Garland's rich voice. Only the runway and tree lights illuminated the room until a spotlight brightened the garden gate. In its opening stood Conchita. She remained statue-like for several seconds before beginning her final trek down the runway. Her beautiful black hair was pulled over her bare shoulder. She wore a sheath of a cream-colored silk that hugged her body until it flared at the hips. The gown, long-sleeved on one side and strapless on the other, was adorned with a delicate Point de Lille lace shawl in matching ivory, clipped at the shoulder on the sleeved side with a delicate gold and black onyx pin in the shape of a willow tree, its opposite point flowing down the sleeveless arm.

At the end of the runway, she smiled at the audience, winked at the camera, slowly turned, and walked back to the stage. When she reached the gate, the spotlight faded. She disappeared into the shadows.

Thunderous applause erupted from the audience that rose in unison to give Kat a standing ovation. Several moments later, they sat down as the instrumental version of "Over the Rainbow" filled the auditorium.

Joey and Molly Anna stood as the spotlight focused on them. Joey placed his hands on either side of her waist. With her hands pressed together over her heart, she stood on her toes and did three full turns. Then she linked her elbow with Joey's, and they skipped down the runway one last time. When they reached the end, she curtsied and he bowed to the audience. Then they galloped back to their places. Folding the tablecloth, they put it in the picnic basket, and each grabbed a side of the handle. They made a full circle around the stage and skipped out of sight.

Another standing ovation continued for three full minutes. Tears streamed down Kat's face as Dawson hugged her first, followed by her father's hug and peck on the cheek.

"You did it, kiddo. I knew you could." Cannon gave her another hug.

"All that time you spent at the drawing board because you couldn't do anything else really paid off." Dawson's proud smile couldn't have been more welcome. "You're in the big league to stay now."

She wiped away her tears with the back of her hand and patted her round tummy. *Thank you for waiting until after the show, Willow. Any time you're ready now is okay with me. Daddy and I just want you here safe and sound.*

Chapter Thirty

Roper rolled over and pulled a light blanket up around his shoulders. It wasn't warm inside the shack, but neither was it cold. On nights like this, he wanted someone to rub his shoulders and share his covers, to warm his bed and ease his needs. The taste of Maggie lingered on his lips, and the feel of her molded against him still tingled throughout his body. Now, when dawn seemed a long way off, he wanted her forever. He wanted to go to her, touch her face, tangle his fingers in her hair, and never stop kissing her.

At night, when it was dark, he couldn't stop thinking about her. The weight of it pressed down on his chest. He could still hear the sound of her voice, smoky and low. She had taken a handful of words and touched something inside him that dipped deep and nameless. He wanted to make love to her forever, but was that what she wanted?

Their Saturday night dates had come and gone. The next level of their relationship loomed before him. He forced his thoughts back to the present, shaking away the fog that shrouded his brain. It wasn't like him to look back. He wanted her now, as his wife.

Tell her your feelings before it's too late, Roper Jones.

Orange and golden flames from the modest fire flickered and dimmed in the room where Maggie curled up in the rocker beside the hearth. But the fire in the hearth had nothing to do with the warmth that engulfed her whole being. She stared into the flames that crackled and rose up the chimney. By comparison, they couldn't come close to the firecrackers exploding in her heart.

She imagined Roper standing beside the mantle, clean-shaven, his hair wild and tussled. Her breath caught in her throat, and her heart kicked against her rib cage. All of a sudden, it hit her. *I love him.* She spent a whole moment digesting that, and then she remembered his warmth, his strength, how she fit against him perfectly, as if she belonged there.

But...but...can he give me his heart? Can I trust him with mine? She arched her brow and threw both questions out the window. *Love is like City Hall—you can't fight it.* He was all she would ever want.

Closing her eyes, she leaned back against the chair and tried not to remember the waves of longing that engulfed her when he came near. She couldn't quite manage it, and tears came from a deep well of loneliness within her.

The phone startled her.

"Maggie, I need to see you." It was not exactly a request, not quite a command.

"Now? You mean now?" She stared at the floor.

"Yes. Please say it's not too late for you. I'd like to come over." His voice was almost a whisper.

She forced herself to breathe. "Is anything wrong Roper? Is Lizzy okay?"

"Nothing's wrong. Lizzy's snoring away. I just...just need to see you."

"Of course...please come. I'll make us something hot to drink."

"Sounds great. See you in a little while."

His voice reached inside her to cradle a part of her that was being born, full-blown and mature. She went to the kitchen and waited in stillness for the coffee to finish.

The bell in the grand entrance hall rang.

She opened the door, welcomed him inside, and watched him remove his coat and place it on the hall tree. It all seemed to be slow motion because her heart pounded wildly in her chest. He turned to look at her, scarcely moving, yet his eyes danced to the beat of her heart.

"Maggie, I know it's late. I couldn't wait to see you."

The sleeves of her robe fell to her fingertips. He slid his arms, around her waist and gathered her to him, wrapping her safely in his strength.

She closed her eyes. His gentleness heightened her senses. His silence opened her ears.

"Are you sure nothing's wrong, Roper?"

"Wrong? I don't know yet. I need to know how you feel about me. I'm tired of guessing. I'm tired of Saturday night dates, and I'm tired of needing you and not having you."

"Oh!"

"Will you?"

"Will I what?"

"Will you marry me?"

"I...I...don't know if I should." *What a stupid thing to say. Of course I want to marry him!*

"Maggie, there are certain things you should never do. Don't try to lasso a tornado. Don't sneeze into the wind." He caught her shoulders. "Never say no to a marriage proposal from a man who loves you the way I do and knows you feel the same about him...you do, don't you?"

The pleading in his voice wrapped itself around her.

"I feel your heart beating in sync with mine whenever we are close, and we connect on some level so deep that it scares me. Our hearts know that we belong together, and tonight my head realized that you're the person I've waited all my life for. Now the big question is...what is your head telling you?"

She tried to look like she was contemplating his words, weighing them on the scales of reason, but she couldn't suppress the smile that leapt from her heart to her lips. Never could she say anything but yes. She had known since the first minute she set eyes on him that he was the one.

Laughter burst forth from her sheer joy. His mouth flew open, and his eyes widened.

"Yes, Roper. Yes! Yes! Yes! I've dreamed of this moment from the time we met. I'll marry you if you promise..."

"Promise what?"

"We don't have to have a big, fancy wedding."

He stood speechless for a few moments, then picked her up and twirled her around. Setting her down, he kissed her with more passion than she had ever felt before. "I hate big, fancy weddings."

Tears burned at the back of her eyes. "I love you, Roper. Never change. Stay just as you are right now."

He patted his midsection. "I don't know about that. I might get fatter with your cooking." He paused and studied her. "You do cook, don't you?"

"Well...with Cannon and you and Grandma Lizzy in the house, I guess I'll have to learn."

"You haven't learned yet?" He frowned. She giggled. "Wait! You mean you plan to keep on living here at Fox Run."

"Uh...that's what I'd like. I don't think the shack will be big enough for all of us."

"I planned to get us a house, Maggie."

"Look around you, Roper. Don't you think there's enough house right here for all of us?"

"I can't deny that, but I don't know if Lizzy will leave the shack. You know how much she loves it. She thinks it's a castle. And what about your dad?"

"Dad's living at the lodge right now. Whether or not he'll come back here, I don't know. Even if he does, he has his own wing of the house—just like we'll have. As for Lizzy, we'll talk her into it if we have to. I love her to pieces, and I have an ace in the hole, as the saying goes. I think she'll make a wonderful baby-sitter."

"Whoa! girl. Not for awhile."

"Why? I want babies *now*. We're not spring chickens, you know. I don't want to be too old to enjoy my grandchildren when they come along."

"Maybe you're right. We'd better get started right away. Come on."

She cleared her throat "First things first. *After* we're married...sometime next week."

Their laughter echoed through the rooms of Fox Run. "I guess that's soon enough."

They finally made it to the parlor to sit on the couch. The fire blazed low and mellow.

"Roper? Let's just go to the justice of the peace and do it."

"Do what, honey?" He cast a sidelong glance at her and smirked.

She sat straight up on the couch and cut him off with one not-so-feeble, waggling finger. "Oh, no, Mr. Jones, you don't get by with that. You're not changing your mind on me now. Daddy's got a shotgun right here in the closet, and Daddy knows how to use it."

His big face split with a grin. "I guess that settles it. Off we go to the justice of the peace next week. But I do want to talk to Granny. She'll be devastated if we don't tell her first before we tell anyone else."

"By all means. And talk to Cannon, too. I really do think Lizzy will move in with us if we promise her she can keep the shack. Fox Run is big enough for an army." She looked at him and squinted her eyes. "Just don't get any wild ideas about bringing all your old army buddies in here to play poker every Friday night."

"I'll try not to, but it will be a challenge. I have dozens of army buddies." A sly grin crept across his face. "If you wear your pretty underwear and sexy nightgowns, I guarantee you there will be no poker playing."

"Deal." She wiggled her torso.

"I wonder what Cannon will say about this arrangement?"

"Dad's so happy to have Kat in the family fold that he wouldn't care if all of Hill Country moved in."

She scooted back on the couch and snuggled into his arms. Heaven didn't have to be high above—it was right here beside her. Up until now, her geography had been all wrong. But she didn't have Roper until now. She closed her eyes and envisioned the green, rolling hills of her childhood, dotted with rainbow colors from spring wild flowers sprinkled across the ground and silent wooded areas where she and her friends had romped, then stopped on the way home to pick yellow and purple violets for their mothers and grandmothers. Many wonderful places surrounded Fox Run. She remembered growing up and loving the outdoor world of her ancestors. This was exactly what she wanted for her children.

Fox Run had been her hiding place from every storm of life. Now she would share her place in the sun with Roper, the most wonderful man in the world, with one exception—her dad. Those two ran a close race. She grinned in her half sleep.

Her dreams chased each other around her brain until she wanted to shake them out and live them one by one. Soon she would.

She and Roper married the following week with just Lizzy and Cannon in attendance. Lizzy had taken to Fox Run with far more enthusiasm than even Maggie had dared to hope.

"Law, honey chile, anybody who don wanna' live in a house like dis is worse than so-so." She tiptoed around the room, looking it up and down. "Ya know, some folks call us'n in Hill country...white trash. But we'n jest good ol' mountain hillbillies. We neber hurt nobody and we take care of 'er own. We cry and hurt and laugh and smile like the rest o' the folks what be rich. We mind our own druthers and don' get in da way o' nobody. Why they wanna' call us white trash, Roper?"

Roper and Maggie looked at each other and shook their heads.

Maggie wrapped an arm around her thin shoulders. "Lizzy, you've got more sense in your little finger than some folks have in their whole brain."

Roper nodded. "I guess, Granny, it's because they have no feelings for anyone but themselves. And they sure don't have any understanding either, or they'd realize that all people have value, whether they live on the mountain or in the valley."

"Least ways we tries t' live by that there Gold'n Rule."

"You sure do, Lizzy. You and the folks in Hill Country are kind and honest and don't go around calling people names. You're miles ahead of those folks when it comes to being a decent human being."

"Law, I think I done been rewarded for all that there good behavior. Why, look at these digs! And right now, I'm seein' the two o' ya hooked up and ready to make ol' Lizzy a great-granny. I done thank ya from da bottom o' m' heart fer inviten' me into yer home. And you, Roper Jones, you best be a mighty fine gentleman and don' put yer feet on da furniture and don' be bustin' nothin' in this house to flinders, either. Ya hear yer Granny? Most of all, I'm fixin' to thank ya-all fer lettin' Lizzy keep her lovely home in Hill Country. Minnie said she'd holp me watch over it if'n I promise to go hither and spend some time wit her. I be jest lovin' ta do dat, ya know?"

"I've been meaning to ask you, Granny. What happened about the nappies that Minnie stole from your front porch while they were cooling?" Roper asked. "Did she own up to it?"

"Law...I never tol' her I knew. Jest made them next nappies with a little skift o' pepper in 'em. The next time she stole 'em I 'lowed would be the last. She'd never eat another one o' Lizzy's nappies again unless we ate 'em together. But ya know, I got ta feelin' sad I done dat to my frien' Minnie. She din't mean no harm, and she gives me stuff all the time. So ol' Lizzy baked 'er a big batch o' nappies and left 'em on her windowsill one afternoon when she were takin' a nap. I guess she knowed where they came from, but she neber said a word—an' I neber said a word. We'n jest the bestest friends ever was."

Maggie gave her a big hug. "Lizzy, you're the greatest. You'll be the best granny ever to our babies."

"So I hope soon we git to move in here and you two whippersnappers git me a grandbaby dat I kin help wit."

"Slow down, Granny. We're getting to that, slow but sure."

"I knowed, sonny boy, but Lizzy's not gittin' no younger, an' I think ya better hurry that slow up. I wanna git to know dat great-grandbaby o' mine before'n I kick da bucket."

"Granny, don't say that! I promise we'll hurry up, okay?"

Lizzy stepped up to Maggie, stood on her tiptoes, and whispered in her ear. "My li'l missy, ya can't be too quick about these matters...so...you'n hurry. I ain't never been a great- granny before, so I be hopin' it's real soon now.

"I promise, Granny, but it'll be at least nine months."

"I'm a knowin' how long them little buns gots t' be in the oven. I done bin there, done that."

Roper raised an eyebrow. "What are you two talking about?"

"None o' yer bees wax. Dat's girl talk b'tween Maggie an' me." Lizzy stuck her nose in the air. "Well...you might have a *li'l* somethin' to do with it, boy." Her laughter bounced off the walls of Fox Run.

"Oh my, that Granny of ours, she beats all," Roper said.

"Yep, and we're blessed to have her." Maggie nodded.

"She's getting forgetful in her old age. I sometimes worry about her. The other day she left a pot of rabbit stew on the stove till it evaporated, burned the pan, and almost started a fire in the shack. We may want to keep her out of the kitchen here."

"We'll at least see that she has some oversight if she's in there. I don't want her to think we don't like her cooking. After Uncle Nick died, I hired a lady to watch over things when I'm not here. Name's Marcy, and she does an excellent job of taking care of Fox Run. I told her the other day I was going to hire someone to help her with all the chores around here—maybe just a housekeeper. I'll let Marcy do the cooking and be in charge of the kitchen and dining room. What do you think, Roper? Dad's still at the lodge most of the time, so he's not here to pitch in."

"Don't know. Got to learn more about Fox Run and Marcy before I pass an opinion on that." Roper retorted. "But you're right, just to be safe. We sure don't want Granny to burn this beautiful house down."

Chapter Thirty-One

*K*at grabbed the bottom of her nightgown and pulled it up between her legs.

"Dawson, wake up."

She punched him on the arm a couple times before he turned over, opened one eye, and looked at her. "Huh, what's wrong?"

"Turn on the light. I have a problem."

He fumbled for the table lamp switch and squinted when he finally turned the light on. "What's going on? It's three in the morning."

"I don't think Willow cares what time it is. My water broke. Please, get me a towel, hand me my robe, pick up my bag, and get ready to go to the hospital."

"What?"

"Must I say that all over again?"

"No, I got it. You need a towel for your water and a robe for your bag to go to the hospital in."

"Something like that."

"I'm going to take a quick shower, Kat, and run a razor over my face."

"You're going to *what*? I take it you're planning to deliver this baby right here. We need to...owwwwww." She panted through a contraction.

"Are you okay?"

"I never felt better. Please get a move on. We need to go *now*!"

He tried to put his pants on, managed to get both feet into one leg, and landed on his backside on the floor. She would have laughed if she hadn't been having another contraction.

"If you can figure out how to get dressed, will you please call Dad and Maggie? And call the doctor! I need to go to the bathroom."

Dawson helped her down the stairs and into the car, found his place in the driver's seat, and started the engine. At the end of Willow Walk Lane, he pulled onto the main thoroughfare.

"Did you get hold of Dad?"

"Yes, he said he'd call Maggie." The rear end of the car whipped back and forth as he fishtailed around a corner.

"Dawson, please slow down. You're going to get us killed."

"Sorry, honey, just trying to get you there in time."

"Did Dad say they'd come?"

"They'll probably beat us there."

"Probably. They both know how to put their pants on." A broken sob tore past her throat. She pressed her lips together and shook her head. "You better start praying, Daw. I'm getting too close for comfort, and your daughter isn't messing around."

The emergency room entrance was the sweetest sight she'd ever seen. Dawson stopped under the canopy, ran through the automatic door, and came out with a wheel chair. Willow was coming. Her wish for a short and normal labor seemed to be coming true.

Before he had a chance to call a nurse, several came running toward them, grabbed the wheelchair away from him, and rushed her toward the elevator. He followed alongside, holding her hand. She tried to talk, but all she could do was grunt.

"My wife's having a baby." Dawson stated the obvious.

I think they know that, Daw. You're not making any more sense than I am.

"How far apart are the contractions?"

"One...one...oh, hurry. One...after another." Kat forced out the words.

"Yeah, one after another." Dawson repeated.

They hustled out of the elevator. One of the nurses pointed to the waiting room across the hall. "Stay there until we examine her. Then we'll call you. Have you notified her doctor?"

"He's on his way. The baby's early."

The nurse stopped. "*How* early?"

"Four or five weeks," Kat panted.

"Get a neonatologist in here STAT," the nurse ordered as they passed the desk.

They checked her as soon as she was wheeled into the labor room.

"Oh, my. A three-minute job just like the last one," a nurse with long black eyelashes doused in makeup said in a stage whisper.

"What's...a three-minute job?" Tears sprung to Kat's eyes.

"Nothing to worry about, honey. It's just nurse talk. You'll be okay."

She'd never thought any different...until now.

"Your doctor's on his way." A cute little nurse patted her hand. "And we're on our way...to the delivery room.

"Doctor Morgan's on his way?" She gasped and panted as another contraction rocked her body. "You mean he isn't here yet?" Tears tumbled down her cheeks. "I can't have this baby without him, but I can't wait much longer." She began to sob.

"You aren't going to have to. I meant he's on his way to the delivery room, the same place we're going. He'll stop just long enough to scrub up, and then he'll be right there." She turned to another nurse. "Get her husband. He's going to delivery with her."

Dawson stood at her head and held her hand. "They're going to give you something for the pain, sweetheart." He watched the nurse prepare the shot.

"No! Don't let them do that, Daw! Having a baby is natural for a woman. I want to experience every minute of it. Please! Don't let them give me a shot or anything else."

"We're not going to give you something you don't want," the cute little nurse said.

Doctor Morgan walked into the room and examined her. "You're doing fine, Kat. You're fully dilated, and I see the head. Now give a big push."

"Push, honey. Push."

"I'm pushing as hard as I can, Daw."

"Good girl. She's coming now."

"Good girl. She's coming now," Dawson repeated. He wiped her brow with a cool, damp cloth.

"One or two more pushes and we'll be home free. You're doing great, Kat. And so is Willow. She's a rambunctious little tadpole."

"A few more pushes, honey, and we'll be home free. You're doing—"

"Stop, repeating...owwwwwwww! Oh, honey, I couldn't do this with... with...without you." Pain ripped through her.

"You're doing fine, Dawson," Dr. Morgan took a quick look at him. "Just hang in there, and don't pass out on us."

"I would never do that..." He tottered back and forth.

"One more hard push, Kat, and I think we can welcome your little girl into the world."

Kat pushed and screamed, pushed and screamed. She glanced up at Dawson's white face. The veins in his forehead looked ready to pop. He reeled, grabbed hold of the bed railing, and shook his head. He was still holding her hand, but his cold and clammy fingers squeezed way too tight. One of the nurses ran up behind him with a chair.

"I'm okay. I'm okay now. No problem."

"Ah...there we are."

She felt the head emerge and heard the lusty cry even before Willow's shoulders cleared. Then the doctor was holding the baby up for her to see.

"You can rest now, Kat. All is well. You can rest too, Dawson."

"Does she have all her fingers and toes?" Kat raised her head.

"Hmmm...let's see. One, two, three...eight, nine ten. She sure does. Exactly the right number of each." Dr. Morgan nodded.

"Can I hold her?" Kat stretched out her arms.

"In a minute or two. We need to weigh her first and clean her up a bit."

"Five pounds, three ounces," one of the nurse's said.

Dr. Morgan smiled. "Great size for a preemie. Let her mother hold her for a bit."

All the tears Dawson had held back erupted and cascaded down his cheeks. He kissed the top of Kat's head and touched Willow's cheek with his forefinger. "Welcome to the family, my precious little Willow."

The baby opened her eyes and stared at him. He changed positions. She followed him with her gaze. He thought his heart would explode with love. All the anxiety and fear he'd felt at the trauma of Joey's birth melted away in the trusting look in his little girl's eyes.

"This is the way it should be to have a baby, Kat. Thank you for allowing me to learn what it's supposed to be like, for giving me a beautiful daughter, for making our family complete. I have never felt so proud or so humbled. Seeing our baby's birth defies description. I'll never, ever forget this moment as long as I live."

Kat's face glowed with the radiance, the joy of having just given birth. "Thank *you*, Daw. She wouldn't be here if it weren't for you. You're the one who helped me through every minute of this."

Dawson bent down and kissed her.

"Sweetheart, I'm awfully tired now."

"Me too." The excitement of the show and Willow's birth caught up with him. He felt frazzled. "May I hold her before you take her away?" he asked.

"Just for a minute. We have a specialist waiting to check her out."

Dawson left to call the lodge while they wheeled Kat to a private room. The waiting room wasn't far from the delivery room; but when he got there, Maggie and Cannon jumped up to meet him.

"How's my daughter doing?" Cannon asked.

"Is the baby okay?" Maggie's worried expression became a wide smile when he told her mother and daughter couldn't be any better.

"But I'm worn out," he added.

"Will the baby be able to go home with you?" Cannon frowned.

"I don't know."

"Who does my grandbaby look like?"

"Like you and Jedediah, of course." Dawson grinned. "Actually, she's a whole lot prettier than the two of you. She looks like her mama and her Aunt Maggie." The tears welled up again. "Everything's fine. Kat's fine. Willow's fine. She looks like a baby doll. She's a few weeks early, but she weighs a little over five pounds. The doctor didn't seem to think she'd have any problems, and she's got great lungs if her loud cry is any indication. A specialist is checking her out as we speak, but she'll probably be going home with us in a couple of days."

"Let's go see her," Maggie suggested. "Is she in NIC-U?"

Dawson turned to look at her. "NIC-U? Oh, yeah, that's where Joey was."

"Neonatal Intensive Care Unit. Since she's a preemie, I suspect they'll keep her there, at least for twenty-four hours. It's just a precaution. They have more extensive monitoring equipment, and the babies are watched very closely."

"Does that mean we can't see her?"

"You can. So can we if you give us permission."

"Consider it given."

"Aha. She sure *does* look like her auntie, doesn't she?" Maggie beamed as she looked at the sleeping baby.

"I think she looks more like her maternal grandpa," Cannon said. "Whoever she looks like, though, it was worth the two-hour wait to see her and hear the specialist pronounce her healthy."

"Worth the wait, yes, but I don't think she looks like Granddad...or you. In fact, I see some of me in her. Take a good look at that nose."

Cannon laughed. "Truth be told, I think she looks like Willow." He hesitated. "Have you picked out a middle name yet?"

"Didn't Kat tell you?"

Cannon shook his head.

"She's Willow Suzanne, after her grandma."

Cannon's mouth dropped open. "I...I'm so sorry Suzanne isn't here to see her namesake. She would have loved her. She was so excited when she found out she was pregnant with Kat, but then her parents entered the picture..."

"You're right. Suzanne would have loved to see her." Dawson nodded and wrapped an arm around his father-in-law's shoulder.

Dawson stared down at the small hand that curled against his chest. A tremor of love shuddered through him. He felt the onset of tears, but pushed them back as they walked from the car to the mud room entrance.

Carla and Joey met them at the door. Joey tugged on his pant leg, and Carla kept pushing the blanket away from Willow's face. Finally, after each one greeted the baby, Dawson carried his sleeping daughter up the stairs and placed her in the bassinette beside their bed.

Kat followed him into the bedroom and looked down at her little girl. "I still can't believe she's here and she's okay and our family is so perfect."

He reached out and pulled her into his arms. "Katarina Kahill, you are the love of my life. When I was a kid running away from Cable and Polly Dee in Mexico, I never imagined I could one day have a real family or be this happy. Now look at me. I have the most beautiful, most wonderful wife in the world. My son, like his father and great-grandfather before him, will carry on the name and tradition of the Kahills of Willow Walk. And now my precious baby daughter has come to complete my family. I am so, so thankful for all of you."

Chapter Thirty-Two
Sixteen years later

Molly Anna and Joey sat on the front porch, shoulder to shoulder, hand in hand, gazing at the half-sun slipping behind the mountain.

She scowled and twisted her head around to look at him. "No, Joey, I don't want you to kiss me now. I told you, we're too little. And if you don't stop trying, I won't marry you."

"Molly Anna, I told cha! If you don't want me to kiss ya, I won't. But if I can't kiss ya, I won't marry ya. I'll just marry someone else that I can kiss."

She stuck her tongue out at him, grabbed him around the neck, and laid a kiss on him that he would never forget.

"Wow! You must've changed your mind." They both laughed.

"Yes, sixteen years is what changed my mind. Now I can't resist you. I've had lots of practice on how to keep you all to myself, and now I am master of it. Oh, I let you date a few times just so you'd have some girls to compare me to."

"I thought I was the one who let *you* date."

"Yeah, and you followed me everywhere I went. Doesn't matter anymore. We're getting married next week." She waggled a finger at him. "Don't you *dare* try to get out of it!"

"I wouldn't think of it." He grinned. "I've always loved you, even before I knew what love was."

"Me, too. Now stop talking and kiss me." Molly lifted her chin and stuck her lips out.

"Nope!" Joey's eyes widened until they were almost round.

"What do you mean... *no?*"

"If you try to kiss me, I won't marry you. I'll just find someone else to marry." Joey laughed so hard he almost fell off the porch swing.

Molly jumped up and ran down the steps, Joey chasing right behind. He grabbed her, and they both fell to the ground and rolled in the soft grass. Their lips met in a long, sweet kiss.

Joey pulled away and looked at her. "You know what, Molly O'Malley?

"What, Joey Kahill?"

"I think we're finally all growed up."

By quarter-till-the-hour, the guests had assembled around the chairs set up on the grounds of Willow Walk Lodge for the four o'clock wedding. A soft medley of Irish melodies played over outside speakers of the lodge's sound system. Inside, Molly paced back and forth in the room where she had dressed for the ceremony.

"Mom, I think Dad is going to be late for his only daughter's wedding."

"No, sweetheart, he'll be here shortly. He has a surprise for you." Bonny smiled.

"What is it?" Molly asked.

"You have to wait and see."

"Before he comes, I want to tell you something, Mom. I never knew my real mother because she died right after I was born. But I do know this—I could never have had a better, more loving mother than you. I know you were disappointed because you couldn't have children of your own, but you got a big instant family when you married Dad. You always say how blessed you are to have us. That's a two-way street, Bonny O'Malley. We are so blessed to have you. Thank you for being the very special person you are." She spun around when someone tapped her shoulder. "Daddy! I thought you were going to be..." Behind him, all seven of her brothers filed into the room. She screamed and began to cry as she hugged them. The two oldest from Ireland brought wives with them, and she squealed and hugged them, too. Clancy handed her a card.

> Molly, Our Sweet Lassie,
>
> Didn't know what to give you for a wedding gift, so we decided it would be bang on to bring your brothers home from our grand Emerald Isle. If you ever need a thing, I'll be right here close to you, our lassy. Don't forget to make your mom and me a grandma and grandpa fiercely soon. We love you... and Joey, too.
>
> Mom and Dad

"Oh, Daddy...Mom, you couldn't have gotten anything better than this. Thank you so, so much. This is going to be the most special wedding ever."

She hugged her brothers again. Bonny dabbed at her makeup and touched up her mascara and blush as the strains of Simon and Garfunkel's "Bridge Over Troubled Water" began. The O'Malleys and the Kahills took front row seats.

Maggie, Roper, and their three children—Elizabeth, Nicholas Cannon, and Katarina—sat with Kat, Dawson, and Cannon. The rest of the guests filled the two sections of white chairs that faced the platform where Joey, Molly's fourth oldest brother, and the minister waited. Willow, the maid of honor, stood opposite them. Pots of white daisies, yellow roses, and baby's breath lined the front of the platform and sat on either end of each row of chairs.

When the song ended, Molly stood at the back of the aisle that ran between the rows of chairs. She slipped her hand through her father's arm. Two trumpeters, one on either side of the platform, raised their herald trumpets. The familiar strains of Wagner's "Bridal Chorus" rang through the valley as Molly and Clancy began their slow walk toward her husband-to-be.

She blinked back the tears. *I'm in love with a wonderful man for the first time in my life and the last time in my life.* She glanced down at her wedding dress. *This is Kat's most beautiful design ever.* The pale blue silk shantung gown honored the ancient Irish tradition that blue represented purity. White Shetland lace covered its fitted bodice. A ring of English lavender and baby's breath sat on her head in place of a veil, and the same lavender and baby's breath were interspersed in her bouquet of white daisies and yellow roses. *I feel like a princess marrying a prince.* She stole a look at her father. His face glowed with more happiness and pride than she had ever seen. For the first time in many years, he had his whole family with him—and his daughter was marrying a man he loved as though he were his own son.

When she reached the front where they were to say their vows, Clancy kissed her cheek and placed her hand in Joey's. For some reason, the vision of a five-year-boy popped into her mind. She could still hear that little boy's words. *Molly Anna, I ain't never wearin' that yellow thing that ever'one calls a vest, under my tu…my tuxe…oh, never mind…under my suit. Ain't wearin' that yellow rose in my buttonhole neither. Flowers are for girls to wear, and I ain't never gonna look like no girl. Yuck.* She gazed at Joey and smiled so wide she thought the corners of her mouth would crack. He was wearing a yellow vest and a yellow rose boutonniere just as they had planned.

Joey couldn't take his eyes off Molly Anna. She looked so beautiful, no— more than beautiful. The gown his mother had designed made her look like a princess, and no princess was ever more stunning. He returned her smile and remembered the words of a little girl. *Oh, Joey, I just like you so much. I know you will always take care of me and do what I tell you to do. Well…most the time anyway. And…well…if you don't, Joey Kahill, I won't never let you kiss me.*

The little girl's words vanished, and they began their vows.

"Jedediah Joseph Kahill," Molly Anna said softly, "I love you from the grass on the ground past the clouds in the sky—just like I told you when we were too little to know what love meant. Now I know. And now I pledge to you that yours will be the name I cry aloud in the night and the eyes into which I smile in the morning. I promise to love and cherish you for the rest of my life. You are a man among men, the very best of men, a credit to your family, and a tribute to the memory of Granddad Jedediah. He would be very proud." She pressed her finger to her lips and blew him a butterfly kiss.

Joey's steady tone reflected the conviction of his words. "Molly Anna O'Malley, you are everything I could ever want in a woman. I promise to do my best to always make you happy, and most of all, I will love and cherish you above all others for the rest of my life. And I will follow the fine example set by my parents and great-grandparents. Granddad would most certainly have given us his blessing, for he loved you almost as much as he loved me. Thank you, Molly Anna, for accepting my proposal of marriage. I will cherish you with all my being till death do us part." He kissed his fingertips and blew her a butterfly kiss. She plucked it from the air and put it to her lips.

"By the laws of West Virginia, I pronounce you man and wife," the minister said. "You may kiss the bride."

They looked at each other and burst out laughing. "Now we have permission," Joey said.

A slight drizzle of rain began as the small orchestra behind the platform played the opening bars of Mendelssohn's "Wedding March" from *Midsummer Night's Dream*. The guests scrambled for the lodge and the refreshments that waited inside as Joey and Molly walked up the aisle to the resounding beat of the music, oblivious to everybody and everything except each other.

"Do we want a boy or a girl, Joey?"

"I think one or two of both. Okay with you?"

"Just fine. I'm counting on it."

"I love you, Molly Anna Kahill."

"And I love you Jedediah Joseph Kahill."

The guests had gone, and Joey and Molly would be leaving on their honeymoon in an hour. Kat kicked off her shoes and picked them up. She and Dawson walked through the soft grass toward the rope swing that hung from the large willow tree in the meadow behind the house, the one they had swung on countless times when they were children. Dawson had replaced the rope and the wooden seat for Joey and Molly Anna, and now it hung in wait for the next generation of Kahills.

Dusk gathered the light spilling out of the sky as she reached for his hand. "Our boy has taken the big step. It won't be long before Willow does the same thing. It's hard to believe she's already sixteen. Daw, why did they grow up so fast? It seems like yesterday that they were babies. I'm not ready to be an empty-nester."

"Let's not marry Willow off quite yet. She should be home a few more years, at least I hope so. I still remember that flying trip we made to the hospital just in time for her birth. Did I ever tell you that I prayed all the way we'd make it in time? No way did I want to deliver that baby. Speaking of babies, someday soon we may have grandbabies to spoil. The fun part about that is we get to enjoy the good times and give them back to their parents at our discretion."

"Ah, yes. I can only hope that Joey has at least one that's just like him." She giggled and then stopped to stare at the swing.

"Sit down in it, and I'll push you." Dawson's crooked grin peeled the years away, and he looked just like the fourteen-year-old boy who had pushed her in the swing so long ago.

"Are you serious?"

"Try me."

She dropped her shoes on the ground, sat down, and grabbed the ropes. "I'm ready." For several moments she swayed back and forth while he pushed. Then the swing gradually slowed to a stop. "Thank you, Daw. I needed that."

"We've come almost full circle, sweetheart. We'll soon be back to where we began—just you and me and Willow Walk."

"In a way, I like that. You and me and forever Willow Walk."

She picked up her shoes and looked up at him. Pressing her fingers to her lips, she threw him a butterfly kiss. He plucked it from the air, put it to his lips, and threw her one. She caught it and winked.

"I love you, Dawson Kahill."

"And I love you, Katarina Kahill. Let's go home."

Cable slapped his cap on his head. Shoving his hands in the pockets of his jeans, he spat on the ground and started down the long, dusty road that led to the small Mexican town.

Dawson forced himself to the rented shanty's kitchen window. He cleared a small circle of grime with his shirttail and watched his father walk away. Puffs of dust flew up with every footstep, hiding first Cable's ankles, then his legs, and finally his hips. Soon, all Dawson could see was dust.

Maybe his dad would be gone for days, maybe not. Who knew? Who cared? Not him. Tears surfaced, but he fought them back. He was thirteen, almost a man, and men didn't cry.

Besides, he had a bigger problem now—an almost-seventeen-year-old blond maniac. What she had in mind terrified him, but he understood. And he wanted no part of it.

Polly Dee stood up, grabbing the kitchen chair for support and knocking it over. She smelled like gin mixed with sweat; the odor made him sick. He'd felt that same awful queasiness ten months earlier when his dad dragged him away from his step-mama, Suzanne, and little sister, Kat. He thought then he'd rather have a tooth pulled; he felt the same way now.

I gotta get out of here. She's serious this time.

"Ya never liked me at all, did ya, honey? Or maybe ya just wanna' get to know lil' ol' Polly better. I can teach ya some grown-up stuff. And I bet you'll like me then. Ever'one does. You'll see. You'll be my little man."

"Get away from me, Polly. You're drunk and you're dirty. Dad'll be home soon." That was debatable. "You want him to see you like this?" Stupid question. Polly didn't give a hoot, and Dad didn't care.

"That's okay, sweetie. Come to Polly Dee." She crooked her finger, motioning him closer.

He couldn't move. He couldn't even breathe. *Oh, please, pass out. Anything. Just leave me alone.*

Polly staggered to the left. He charged to her right.

Faster than lightning, she dug her nails into his arm.

"Leave me alone, Polly! Get away." He planted both hands on her chest and pushed.

She tottered backward and fell. Her head bounced off the edge of the overturned chair. A broken rung sliced into her cheek and forehead. She groaned.

Sweaty blonde hair swung across her face and stuck there.

He opened his mouth to scream, but nothing came out. Tears rushed to his eyes.

Polly covered her face with both hands. Blood drizzled between her fingers and down her chin. She stopped moving.

His feet wouldn't obey his brain. After what seemed an eternity, he reached her motionless body.

"P-P-P-Polly?" he stuttered in a stifled voice. Then louder he said, "P-Polly?"

He bent down and nudged her arm. He did it again, harder. Her finger twitched. He thought he heard a murmur.

At least she's alive.

He ran out of the kitchen and returned. Then he did it again. Looking down at her, he knew he needed to get help. *Don't cry like a baby. Think like a man.* Stupid place—not even a telephone.

He grabbed Polly's liquor money from the coffee can and stuffed it in his pocket. Then he knelt by her side and touched her one more time. She wheezed and stirred. He'd find a pay phone and call for help.

"Run," he told himself aloud, "now, before it's too late."

Rushing out the open kitchen door, he leapt over the fallen screen and jumped down the steps. He bounced on his bike and peddled for the border.

From Book Two of the Kahill Family Saga
For the Love of Willow Walk

A siren blared.
Doors flew open.
The stretcher winged down hallways.
First left.
Then right.
The room was so cold.
It was too soon.

"Help me, please!" Kat's lips shaped the words. Her tongue forced them out.

In seconds, muffled sounds roared in her ears. *Disseminated intravascular what? Not in labor? Impossible!* Pain clamped like claws around her abdomen and stabbed into her back.

"Prep her for a C-section STAT!" Dr. Morgan's voice cut through the commotion.

No! She tried to speak. The words wouldn't come.
Voices faded.
Lights dimmed.
Nothing.

To purchase these great books, go to
www.amazon.com

Other places to order them:
http://tinyurl.com/2rh34t
www.willow-walk.webs.com

E-mail:
peewee2234488@yahoo.com

They are also available on Kindle.